THE UNDERCOVER BRIDESMAID

KIMBERLEY MONTPETIT

THE UNDERCOVER BRIDESMAID

Spellbound Books
Published in the United States of America

INTRODUCTION

~

In the world of fiction, first meetings are a critical piece in the structure of the story. But in real life, first meetings are rarely as interesting. However, Kimberley Montpetit and I met in an unusual way when I picked her up at the airport, sight unseen, and gave her a ride to the writer's retreat we were both attending. I can only imagine what Kimberley must've been thinking as she was sitting outside at the passenger pickup, with her luggage stacked around her, waiting for some person she'd never met.

Kimberley and I had an instant connection and became fast friends. I could tell from talking to her that she's a seasoned writer who really knows her craft. And then I read one of her books. Boy, oh, boy, can she write! She's since become one of my favorite authors. It gives me great pleasure to introduce *The Undercover Bridesmaid*, from the Dangerous Affections Series. Kimberley has a wonderful way of crafting a multi-faceted story that caught my attention from the get-go. It was the perfect combination of suspense and romance. I was drawn in from the first page and know you will be too. Pull up a comfy chair and clear your schedule, because you won't be able to put this one down until you're finished.

Happy reading!

Jennifer Youngblood

Author of *I Know You'll Find Me.*

FREE BOOK OFFER!

When you subscribe to Kimberley's Reader Newsletter, you'll receive the romantic novel, RISKING IT ALL FOR LOVE with lots of other goodies as a Welcome Gift!
   SUBSCRIBE AT THIS LINK:
   http://eepurl.com/NBXon

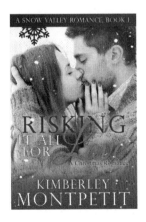

CHAPTER 1

*C*hloe Romano's office line rang while she was wolfing down a chocolate-frosted donut and pouring herself an ice-filled glass of Diet Coke.

The fizzing soda melting over the ice cubes was a sound made in heaven—especially when she was overbooked and underpaid. Which described most days.

Scratch that. *Every* day.

"Can we finish this conversation later, Mom?" she said, leaving the First Lady's office while her mother pored over the details of a fundraising party scheduled in a few weeks. The governor's mansion cook had brought brunch, including the homemade donuts. Mrs. Harvey knew Chloe's favorites were the pastries that boasted at least a thousand calories each. Which she should apply directly to her hips.

"Come back when you're finished, darling," Diana Romano said. "This paperwork for the Romanian orphanage has to be done by tomorrow."

Orphanages and adoptions—anything to do with children—were the First Lady's passion and life's work, and Chloe often pitched in to help with fundraisers or visits to the children's hospital.

In an attempt to grab the still-ringing telephone, she dashed across the floor to the tiny anteroom. It was originally a closet. Just big enough to hold a small desk and chair.

When Chloe was at the governor's mansion, she had her calls forwarded from her apartment to this office. She kept her cell phone line private, only giving out the number for clients under contract.

"Breakfast of champions," she murmured in ecstasy as she downed the last bite of chocolate.

Chloe managed not to fall into a sugar coma when she snatched up the landline and darted a quick glance at the caller ID, which read Mercedes Romano.

Mercedes Romano? Why in the world would *she* be calling? She hadn't spoken to her cousin since Grandpapa Tony's funeral almost a year ago.

The days of family reunions petered out when all the cousins reached adulthood and spread across the Eastern seaboard. Instead, they relied on the month of August for family reunions and indulging in their former teenage pastimes of sunbathing at Myrtle Beach while eating cherry snow cones and boy-watching.

Growing nostalgic for a real vacation, Chloe quickly said, "Undercover Bridesmaid, Chloe Romano speaking."

"Chloe, is that you?" Mercedes's voice came through ever-so-slightly British and cultured.

"The one and only." Chloe swallowed a gulp of her soda and grabbed for a napkin.

Even though her father was in his second term as the governor of South Carolina, Mercedes had a knack for making Chloe feel like she was wearing overalls and chewing on a wad of tobacco.

"This is Mercedes, your cousin," she said, as if putting on airs.

Chloe laughed. "You're the only person I know with perfect diction and a slight English accent, even though you're not British."

"I did an internship in London for my MBA," Mercedes retorted.

Chloe suppressed a smile. "Blame my despicable lack of memory. So, how are you? To what do I owe this unexpected phone call?"

"Is this new business of yours genuine? Do you really hire yourself out as a bridesmaid?"

"Sounds crazy, but yep, I actually do."

"People pay you money to walk down the aisle, carry a bouquet, and hold up the bride's train?"

"That's part of Package A," Chloe replied, wondering if Mercedes was trying to demean her job, or if she had some other motive. "But it's nowhere near as simplistic as you infer. Sometimes I have to hold the dress up for the bride to use the restroom five minutes before curtain call."

Mercedes let out a sudden laugh. "Spare me the gory details, but enlighten me on what else you do."

"Is your request purely curiosity?" Chloe asked. "Or is this out-of-the-blue call an invitation to hang out with you at the beach this weekend? Because I could definitely pencil you in for that."

Despite her cousin's businesslike tone, she gave a small snort. "Don't be so suspicious, but a day at the beach does sound heavenly. I've hardly slept for a week. My wedding is becoming downright evil to navigate."

Typing on her laptop, Chloe logged on to her website to catch up on the latest email from the various brides she was currently managing. She had a secure interface so they could send email to one another that nobody else could access—like overly curious mothers of the bride, fiancés, or snooping "best friends."

"I understand more than you know," Chloe empathized. "One week out, and most of my brides are ready to bag the whole thing and elope. Or bag the groom and go on a cruise by themselves."

Mercedes gave a light tinkling laugh. "You're so funny, Chloe. I'm honestly curious about your chosen career. After flunking out of your FBI training at Quantico—"

"—I did not flunk out," Chloe cut her off. "I graduated, became an official agent, and then resigned after a year. End of story. If you bring up *anything* about that—so help me I will wring your pretty little neck with my bare hands."

"Wow. Chloe. Okay. Back off, sweetie."

"I'm sure you know the entire story from your mother," Chloe added, a swell of emotion rising in her throat. The memories of her best friend Jenna dying in the FBI house raid often caught her off guard. Clenching her fist, she willed herself not to break down on the phone.

Mercedes went silent for a moment as if she knew she'd pushed Chloe's buttons. "Don't mention my mother. She's driving me up a wall."

Chloe perused her messages, trying to multitask. No bridal meltdowns today. "In what way?"

"Isn't it obvious? I'm supposed to get married in a week."

It was a good thing Mercedes couldn't see Chloe's face. She had completely forgotten that her cousin's wedding was coming up so soon. At the moment, she was swamped with five other brides and *their* wedding to-do lists.

Quickly checking her calendar, she saw that, yes indeed, she and her parents and older brother Carter had tickets to fly up to D.C. for the jolly event.

"So, um," she stuttered, trying to recover. "What's your mother doing that's especially aggravating? Actually," she amended, "don't tell me. I don't want to get involved."

"If you're a true bridesmaid for hire, you should know that mothers of the bride always drive their daughters insane. Or push them into getting sloshed on their wedding day so they can't walk down the aisle without teetering. I'd wager a bet you've seen that up close and personal if you hire yourself out."

Her cousin made her sound like she was a call girl. "That's true," Chloe admitted, thinking of Sarah Schultz's mother out in the Bay Area, who tried to micromanage every aspect of her daughter's wedding. So much that Sarah came *this close* to ordering her mother to stay away from the ceremony.

In an effort to take the pressure off of Sarah and help her have a good wedding day, Chloe concocted outrageous stories about accidentally forgetting Sarah's mother at home—or suggesting that a cousin kidnap her. The only downside was that Sarah laughed so hard she nearly split her side seams while dressing for the wedding rehearsal, but Chloe only had to whip out her sewing kit and mend the crisis.

"Are you the same as a wedding planner?" Mercedes asked, steering the conversation back to her original question.

"Nope, a wedding planner helps rent the church, organizes the caterers, flowers, invitations, and all the reception details. Think of me more as the bride's personal assistant."

"Sorry for all the questions. Can you do anything that the bride wants you to do?"

"In a nutshell—yes," Chloe replied. "You have a dress issue, I can help. You forgot your makeup bag, I can run errands. Your other bridesmaids are flakes, I can whip them into shape. You need help writing a speech for the reception to tell your new husband he's the man of your dreams, I have a degree in creative writing. I can do flowery sentiments or false promises."

Mercedes actually giggled at that, and Chloe stared at the receiver in shock. Her cousin's demeanor was usually prim and proper. She'd make a perfect senator's wife.

"Okay, it only happened once," Chloe admitted with a grin. "A speech filled with false declarations of love, that is."

"The girl actually went through with the wedding? To someone she didn't love?"

"Let's just say the bride had the wedding jitters so bad she almost backed out. But she went through with it and danced until two in the morning."

"Are they separated now?" Mercedes asked, assuming the worst.

"Not at all. They're about to have their first child next month."

"That is simply too peculiar, Chloe. These people—these brides—you work for do not sound ready for marriage."

"Weddings bring out the worst in people." Chloe twirled a pencil between her fingers, a thousand tasks from her to-do list running through her mind. "I know I have an unusual job, but what did you call about? Yes, I can confirm that my family will be in attendance at your wedding next week. Got our e-tickets all ready to go," she added brightly.

"Actually," Mercedes said, "I want to hire you, Chloe."

Chloe took a gulp of her Diet Coke, but the ice had melted, turning the drink watery and warm. "I'm sure you have a dozen best friends that are doing you the honor of being your bridesmaid."

"That's not exactly true," her cousin said slowly. "Since we're getting married at my parents' home instead of a big church or hall, I was only going to have three attendants. And they've all backed out."

Chloe stifled a gasp. Three bridesmaids had canceled on her? That was almost unheard of. "That's terrible. I'm so sorry."

"It's *not* what you're obviously thinking," Mercedes went on coolly.

"I'm—I'm not thinking anything," Chloe assured her.

"My old roommate from college just joined the Peace Corps and left for Africa this morning. Another childhood friend is about to give birth any day, and my younger sister has decided to boycott the wedding."

"That's a drastic measure. Why would Celine not see you married?"

Mercedes gave a dramatic sigh. "We had an argument last night. She hates the idea of spending money on a lavish wedding. She's into the whole concept of minimalism. Lives in a studio apartment in the basement of somebody's house, volunteers at the soup kitchen twice a week, and likes to grow her own vegetables. She even got rid of most of her shoes. She only owns one pair now."

"The horror," Chloe said drily, amusement spreading across her face. "So, Celine has rejected the idea of filthy lucre."

"In a manner of speaking," Mercedes sniffed.

Chloe had worked for enough brides to understand the underlying panic Mercedes was trying to hold at bay. Knowing her cousin, Mercedes was hiding the fact that her pride was hurt by her sister's rejection—although Chloe often had her doubts about a warm heart underneath Mercedes's ice-queen persona.

Her cousin needed a bridesmaid. Any bridesmaid, even one for hire, to save face in front of her guests.

"What are your rates—or is there a family plan? Hint, hint."

"I'm actually in the middle of other jobs. Most brides hire me months out from their wedding date." Chloe flipped through her calendar. Her next on-site wedding wasn't for two more weeks, although she'd lose a few days flying out early for Mercedes. She'd just have to work extra hours when she returned home, but she couldn't resist giving her cousin a hard time. "Hey, I was going to kick back with Granny Zaida and gorge off the buffet table, not stand in a receiving line. Boy, you're asking a lot, blood relative or not."

"Oh, goodness, Chloe, just name your price. Surely, it can't be that much. You'd probably faint at the bill from my wedding planner."

"Define what you want from me. Walk down the aisle in a hideous bridesmaid dress? Chat up lonely guests? Be the first on the dance floor and make a fool of myself? Gather all the single women for the bouquet throw? Run interference between you and your mother? Dance with drunk Uncle Stan?"

"Oh, that all sounds fantastic!"

The relief in Mercedes's voice threw Chloe for a loop. The girl was actually desperate, and a twinge of empathy rose in her throat. Mercedes Romano was one of the D.C. society elite's, and her wedding was probably going to be a major event.

"Hey, we don't have a drunk Uncle Stan!" Mercedes suddenly said.

"Oops, that was my last wedding." She laughed, and Mercedes seemed to relax a little.

"I'd also like you to help me write up something to say for my vows to Mark. I hadn't even thought of that part yet. The list keeps growing!"

"Don't panic, your wedding will be perfect. Okay, my rate for all that is normally fifteen hundred, but you don't have to pay me. We're family, after all."

"We'll discuss that more fully when you get here," Mercedes interrupted. "You don't charge sales tax, do you?"

"We won't talk about filthy lucre any longer and if your wedding is in a week, we need to get going. I need you to send me a bridesmaid dress pronto. You did order bridesmaid dresses, correct?"

"Of course. Text me your measurements, and I'll have one of the dresses altered. I have a size 6, 8, and 10. You're not a 12 or a 14 are you?"

Chloe bit her lips to keep the sarcastic retort from leaking out. "A size 8 will do nicely. With an alteration for length—I'm probably taller than your other friends."

"Oh, you must have lost weight since I saw your family Christmas picture."

Chloe squelched the annoyance rising up her throat. Mercedes could be so passive-aggressive.

"There's just one more thing," Mercedes said. "I have something else to tell you. Something you may not like."

CHAPTER 2

*C*hloe should have known better. Brides always used their chipper, happy voice before laying out a bombshell request. Like flying to the rainforest for a tree house wedding. Or wearing a hideous orange bridesmaid dress. Or flirting with a newly divorced brother-in-law.

Chloe worked with a bride who had pre-wedding jitters so bad she started an argument with her man just to have an excuse to break off the whole thing.

An hour later, they were hugging and kissing like nothing had ever happened. But only after Chloe had gone hoarse talking them both off the ledge.

"Well, " Mercedes began slowly, "the thing is, my father is sending an FBI detective to your parents' house today. He'll want to speak to you and your father."

The FBI? Chloe slammed her kneecap into the tiny desk and stuffed down a cry of pain. "What's going on, Mercedes?"

"Let's not speak over the phone about this. The line is probably not secure. I know about such things. My father, you know."

"Hmph," Chloe growled.

Uncle Max, the international real estate magnate with deals in

THE UNDERCOVER BRIDESMAID

every country, ran a tight ship. Whenever Chloe had met one of his employees, they were carbon copies of one another—tight-lipped without a sense of humor. Sounded like a few of the FBI agents she'd known when she was with the bureau.

"Do you personally know this detective? Is there a family connection? Besides, my parents are currently at the governor's mansion, not their house. I'm not at my apartment, either. It's been a morning of Mom's fundraisers."

"Dad says he sent him to the governor's mansion, but I have no idea who the detective is," Mercedes said. "We'll talk about this more when you get here. I assume you'll arrive a few days before the wedding?"

"I'm thinking about three days ahead of time, but I need to spend the *next* three days doing a bit of rearranging and hand-holding with my other clients."

"Well, I don't need you to hold my hand."

Chloe smiled at that. She knew her cousin better than Mercedes thought she did. "I also don't want to talk to an FBI agent. You should know that."

"Why would I know that?"

"Doesn't your mother ever speak to my mother? They're sisters-in-law."

"I'm not sure. . ."

Chloe's palms were suddenly clammy. Never again did she want to be in the same room with an FBI agent.

"Mercedes, I don't think this is going to work. I'll be at your wedding with my parents and brother next week, but I think it's best if you find someone else to stand in place of your AWOL bridesmaids."

"But you just promised, Chloe. I don't understand what the issue is. I thought it was all worked out."

"Until you mentioned the FBI. Are you in some kind of trouble? I don't want to get involved. I don't even want to know what it is! Please leave me out of it." Just talking about the possibility caused Chloe's heart to beat erratically. "Are you in trouble? I won't do anything illegal and go to jail for you."

"Nobody is going to jail, now stop it! Speak with the FBI guy —and then call me back. He's probably almost there."

"What do you mean, he's probably almost here? Do you have him on FaceTime or something? This is getting weird."

"I'm not sure how secure this line is—even if it is the governor's mansion."

"Great. Now I'm being listened to by the NSA. The FBI is going to unmask me and make my life miserable."

"Stop being so dramatic."

"Hey, that's *my* line," Chloe said, choking out a laugh.

A knock came at the open door to the anteroom. Her father, Albert Romano, poked his head inside. "Hey, honey, do you have a minute?"

Chloe placed a hand over the receiver. "Can it wait until tonight? I'm sort of in the middle of wedding stuff."

Her father gave her a sheepish smile. "Sorry, its pretty urgent."

Chloe spoke into the phone again. "Mercedes, I'll draft a list of tasks and we'll go over it in a couple of hours. The only reason I'm doing any of this is because you're family. And sometimes I love you."

She hung up and swiveled the desk chair around to face her father. "What's up?"

"Was that Mercedes?" he asked.

"Yep. Wedding bells are ringing."

Albert Romano let out a low whistle. "That's coming up fast. I almost forgot."

"Got your security ready to surround Uncle Max's castle, Dad?" Chloe teased.

"Are you doing something with your bridesmaid thing for her?" he went on, not answering her question.

Chloe gave her father a sweet smile. She was still trying to get her family to take her new profession seriously. "Yes, I'm doing a bridesmaid 'thing' with her. I am now her *official* bridesmaid. The cousin I was always jealous of as a kid because she was so poised and beautiful."

Maybe that's why Chloe had joined the FBI, she thought with sudden clarity. Her career was the polar opposite of her cousin's estate sale management company.

"Oh, honey," her mother said, rising from her desk. "You are just as beautiful and smart as Mercedes."

Chloe grimaced, wishing her mother wouldn't patronize her. "I forgot to ask Mercedes what her colors are. I hope they're not something hideous like lime green. I look best in red or deep blue."

"Oh, goodness, Chloe," Diana Romano said with a small laugh. "Mercedes has very good taste. I'm sure her wedding will be the talk of Washington this fall. How lovely that you're going to be her bridesmaid! I just hope I'll get to see you in white one day, before I'm too old to enjoy grandchildren."

Chloe chomped down on her lip to keep from saying something she'd regret. The fact that she was twenty-nine and not married was a sore point with her mother. "Mother, you're barely fifty-nine. There's plenty of time for grandchildren."

"Only if you have a serious relationship that might be crowned with an engagement party and a ring in the near future. The clock is ticking."

"Not many eligible bachelors in my line of work. Mostly married couples or drooling old uncles."

"Chloe," her mother chided. "You need to give men a chance."

"I vowed I would never go on another blind date. Or a date set up by Match.com."

"That severely limits your options—"

Her father raised his hands. "Okay, my beautiful girls. I have to get downtown soon, and Chloe and I have an important meeting at the moment."

An older gentleman stepped into the doorway. Mr. Smith, her

father's secretary—and the man who ran everything on schedule for the governor's mansion. "Mr. Romano, sir, your guest has arrived."

"That's our cue, Chloe," her father said, holding out his hand.

Chloe glanced at his palm with skepticism, attempting to brush her sticky fingers on a napkin. "Um, Dad, *I* don't have any guests scheduled."

"I'm afraid you do now, sweetheart."

"What's this about, Albert?" her mother asked, looking cool and crisp in her green and white pantsuit, despite the fact that they were having a heat wave these last days of September.

Most of the time, Chloe wasn't actually at the governor's house where her parents lived.

Usually, she worked from her own apartment, lying backwards on her mattress with her laptop, the television running old movies on the Turner Classic station or A&E.

So far, Chloe had never met a man who liked old movies, and that was a must for whomever she said yes to. Instead, they wanted to go to all the action flicks with actors like Jason Statham or Vin Diesel.

Those macho guys were very nice, but car chases all looked alike to Chloe, and how many times in a single movie could the bad guys blow up a building? Although she *could* appreciate Chris Pratt or Evans or Hemsworth. So many hunky Chris's to choose from these days.

But today's remakes were nothing like the witty banter between Humphrey Bogart and Katherine Hepburn.

While daydreaming about movies and nonexistent boyfriends, Chloe had lost the gist of the conversation. She glanced up to see her mother striding out of the office, clicking her heels on the parquet floor. "Is Mom okay?" she asked her father.

"I told her she couldn't be a part of our upcoming meeting."

Dad lifted Chloe to her feet. "Its time to stop stalling. I need to leave for the capitol, and I'm taking precious time away for this."

Chloe hurried after him. "You're being so mysterious."

"We have thirty minutes before tourists descend," the governor said briefly.

Mr. Smith opened a door that led to the carpeted library filled with antique furniture and shelves of ancient tomes.

"Hello, Agent Esposito," she heard her father say to a male figure standing at the window with his back to the room.

Chloe staggered against the doorjamb. Her stomach dropped clear to the basement with a queasy sensation. "No," she whispered, staring at the tall, well-built man who was gazing down at the mansion gardens below.

When the FBI agent turned toward them, the morning sun slanted across his face so that Chloe was blinded for a moment. But she was not blinded by who he was. Memories rushed at her so fast she felt as though she was being attacked by the past she had desperately tried to bury over a year ago.

A thousand emotions streamed through her body while she pressed a hand to her head. The room whirled so badly Chloe thought she might get sick.

Fight or flight were two options she'd been trained for as a rookie FBI agent at Quantico when confronted by a threatening situation. Assess, evaluate, calculate, and then employ the appropriate action or maneuvers.

Most of the time it meant the first option—confrontation, which often included fighting.

Chloe chose the second. She was so out of here.

CHAPTER 3

*S*pinning on her wobbly heels, Chloe tried to walk back through the door to escape, but unfortunately, Mr. Smith had already closed the door and the doorknob didn't seem to be working no matter how much she twisted the thing.

Yanking at the library door again, she let out a cry of frustration and her face burned with embarrassment.

Agent Esposito took a step away from the window. "Chloe, I'm not here to cause any trouble. I just—I've been given orders to talk to you about a case that has to do with your family."

"That makes zero sense." Her voice was hard and brittle while she fought the conflicting emotions that threatened to overwhelm her at seeing this man—her old team leader—after all this time.

"Chloe," her father said soothingly. "Sweetheart."

"Please, Daddy," she said, keeping her eyes focused on her father instead of Liam Esposito. "What is *he* doing here?"

"There's something important we need to discuss."

"There is *nothing* I will discuss with him."

"It's about Mercedes," her father added.

That took Chloe off guard. "I was just talking to Mercedes

five minutes ago. What could *he*—" She pointed, but wouldn't speak his name out loud. "Have to do with my cousin?"

"I think we'd better sit down," Governor Romano said. "Please, Agent Esposito." He gestured toward the grouping of sofas on the opposite side of the room.

Chloe remained standing by the bookcase, her arms folded across her chest. Agent Esposito was the one person she had never wanted to see again in her life.

Even now, watching him cross the room, his stride was confident and smooth, his slacks pressed to perfection, that dark, wavy hair perfectly cut. A pair of sunglasses dangled from his jacket pocket. If he was auditioning for the role of an FBI agent, he had the look perfected.

This encounter was all too convenient. But even if it had been a different agent, Chloe was done with slick FBI Agents. A year ago done.

"Thank you, sir, for allowing me to intrude on your busy day," Liam Esposito said politely to Governor Romano, glancing sideways at Chloe. "How are you, Chloe?" he asked tentatively. "I'd shake your hand properly, but it's a little chilly on your side of the room."

"Oh, please," Chloe snapped. "Don't pretend you have no idea how I feel about seeing you here in my parents' home—out of the blue after all this time."

Her father lifted a hand helplessly. "The agent can request an appointment any time he'd like. The governor's mansion *is* a public building after all," he added with a small smile.

Chloe knew her father was trying to lighten the tension, but she wanted to run out the door, yelling all the way to her own apartment where she'd be alone and safe in her private cocoon.

A lump of emotion filled her throat. "You know how I feel about—" She stopped.

"I'm afraid I'm the elephant in the room," the agent interjected. "I tried to get the assignment changed, Chloe, but they wanted someone who knew your family. To make it more real."

"What on earth are you talking about?" she demanded, speaking directly to him for the first time. "Make what more real —the moment I throw you out on your ear?"

Governor Romano said, "I think we all need to sit down and discuss the matter you came here to tell us, Agent."

Chloe grudgingly crossed the carpet, duly noting that her father's words were directed at her to act like a mature adult and hear the agent out.

She took a seat on the edge of a wing chair opposite the man she'd hated for the last year, and tried to swallow her emotions. "Okay. I'm listening. Spill it."

"What would the FBI want with Mercedes?" Governor Romano said. "Is she in danger?"

"Mercedes is getting married in a week. Your appearance makes no sense. *Agent*," Chloe added, enunciating his title as she gave Liam Esposito a glare.

Instantly, his dark brown eyes connected with hers. As if he'd been waiting a lifetime to sit across from her, just so he could gaze at her. Shivers ran down Chloe's neck and arms. Her hair stood on end as though she'd been jolted by a lightning bolt. She turned hot all over. Darn him anyway.

Chloe's eyes smoldered back at his so he'd know she wasn't going to be taken in by him ever again.

Liam had the grace to blush, but he was a professional detective, so Chloe might have just imagined that tint of red. She wanted to see him get on his knees and beg her forgiveness and weep all the same tears that she had suffered over the last year.

"The bureau is tracking a jewel thief," Agent Esposito said. "We've been honing in on a professional group after two years of trying to get a lead on them."

"What do they do?" Albert Romano asked.

"It's very simple. They switch out real diamonds with

fake ones."

"How do they gain access?" Chloe asked, hoping to move things along. "Do they break into millionaires' homes in the dead of night? Or rob jewelry stores at gunpoint?"

"None of the above."

Chloe's eyes darted away from Liam while she sat uncomfortably on her two-inch edge of chair. It was harder than she'd expected to be sitting in the same room with him. The man she had been falling in love with more than a year ago—and then banished from her life the night he left Jenna to die.

She hated herself for the magnetic pull that still came over her when she was in his presence, or smelled his distinctive cologne. The close proximity was both intoxicating and infuriating.

Chloe wanted to jump into her car and drive home where she could pound the pillows and hate Liam Esposito again. But she sat and gritted her teeth, because of her cousin. She suddenly felt like a protective mother bear to Mercedes.

"What happens when they get the forged piece created?" she finally asked in a tight voice.

"The thief steals the genuine piece of diamond jewelry and leaves the counterfeit in its place. They're so good at it that a jeweler might not know the difference without close examination."

"But how do they manage that if they're not cracking safes or holding jewel owners at gunpoint? Pull it off a princess's neck and then run?" Chloe lifted her lips in a sardonic smile.

"You're closer than you think," Liam said with a quick grin, catching her eye, which Chloe quickly cut off by crossing her legs and glancing at her father. "They manage to acquire invitations to a public affair where they know the jewels will be locked away in a safe and do the switch when the owner is unaware."

"Can they crack a high-security safe, too?"

Agent Esposito nodded. "These diamond thieves have often worked in the security or high-tech safe industry. Or they've run gemstone businesses. Either the retail or wholesale markets. They know the buyers and sellers. Sometimes they intercept during a shipment from overseas."

"I guess that's why it's difficult to catch them," Governor Romano said, shaking his head.

"The problem is that the owner of the jewels might be completely unaware that their diamonds or rubies have been swapped with fakes. Not until months or years later when they get the jewelry cleaned or repaired. By then it's too late to figure out when it happened or who stole them."

"Ingenious." Chloe resisted the urge to lick the sticky spot on her thumb from the donut that was driving her crazy.

Liam leaned forward, placing his elbows on his knees. When he glanced up at Chloe, they were now only a foot apart. She slid deeper into the armchair so she didn't get burned by his gaze.

"It can take months or longer to set up the sting," he said. "Time to get the jewelry made, to make the connections at an event. A gala, a ball, a presidential inauguration, a political fundraiser, the Oscars. You name it."

A lightbulb went on in Chloe's mind. "Or a wedding."

Liam gave her an admiring smile. "Bingo, Agent Romano. Your instincts are still there."

"Don't call me that. My time with the bureau is over. For good." Even so, Chloe tried not to smile at the compliment, forcing her expression to remain impassive. "I take it Mercedes is having some jewelry delivered."

"Yes. I did a little research of my own before I showed up here today, Chloe. You're a hired bridesmaid. An *undercover* brides-maid. Interesting career choice. Do you use an alias?"

"Yes. Not telling what it is, of course. I have experience with false names and identities in my current career." Chloe lifted an eyebrow. "*One* of the perks of my past training at Quantico."

"What's your backstory?"

"I'm never a relative—except in the case of Mercedes's

wedding, I will be exactly who I am. Chloe Romano, beloved first cousin."

Her father cleared his throat, obviously trying not to laugh. Chloe refrained from throwing back a beloved daughterly glare.

"Usually, I'm just a friend of the bride from sometime in their past job or college experience. I currently live in New Mexico on a ranch. Hard to find me there. Hard to find anyone in the wilds of New Mexico. People move there to disappear."

Liam nodded approvingly. "I like your backstory. What do you raise on your ranch?"

"Cattle, a few horses for round-ups. Of course."

A smile twitched at the corners of Liam's mouth. Chloe resisted the urge to wipe it off and yell at him at the same time. She'd been holding in a year's worth of telling this man off and threatening him to a duel.

"Do you ride?" Agent Esposito asked.

"Enough to fake it if I ever need to when I'm out on a job. Of course, weddings don't usually call for unanticipated horseback rides."

"What does this diamond heist stuff have to do with Mercedes?" Governor Romano glanced at his watch. "I have five minutes before my car comes around."

"Agent Esposito clearly thinks there's going to be an attempted jewelry heist at Mercedes's wedding next week," Chloe told him. "But what does this have to do with me?"

"I think you know perfectly well. Your cousin is getting married, you'll be there, and you were once trained as an agent."

"I barely got the diploma framed before I quit, as you well know," she added meaningfully. "I'm not an agent now."

"The bureau realizes that, and we can't force you to help us, but nobody else will have the kind of access you'll have to Mercedes Romano's jewelry. You'll be with her most of the time. You have your family's trust and confidence. A stranger in their midst will be much too suspicious."

"Are you saying that *she's* going to be the one wearing the jewelry that's going to be stolen?" Chloe asked.

"Precisely. And," he added, glancing up into Chloe's face, "you obviously have nerves of steel if you can fake your way through dozens of weddings pretending to be someone you're not."

She tried not to blush at the way he was looking at her. The emotion in his eyes was making her heart thud and her nerves shake. "All I do is put on a hideous bridesmaid dress, drink punch, and try not to catch the bouquet. In addition to making sure the bride doesn't have an emotional meltdown and nobody sabotages her special day."

"Is that all? I'll bet you're great at your job." Agent Esposito laughed, and the timbre of his deep chuckle was close to making Chloe melt into a puddle. She had to remember how callous he actually was deep down.

Chloe shrugged. "I'm not an expert at catching a jewel thief, Agent. I was never assigned to a case like that."

"You don't have to be. We just need to get some clues as to who is doing this. We need you to take pictures not only of the diamonds, but the guests, too. You'll also be inspecting the jewelry three or four times a day to make sure it's genuine and hasn't been swapped out."

"Where is Mercedes getting jewelry that's worth this kind of manpower? Uncle Max is wealthy, but he's no billionaire." Chloe noticed that her father's eyes flickered up to hers and then away. "What, Dad?"

"You don't need to know," he said vaguely.

Liam said, "Mr. Romano is renting a set of fine diamonds for his daughter's wedding from Davis Jewelry. Mercedes will wear them for the weekend and then return them afterward. They'll be delivered by special armed guards."

"Sounds like Hollywood stars who rent out jewels for the Oscars."

"Exactly. Mercedes will have a necklace, earrings, and, um, a tiara. I think that's how you pronounce the last word."

Chloe tried not to laugh at the uncomfortable look on Liam's face. "Your pronunciation is fine."

"Is Mercedes in any danger?" Albert Romano asked. "Potentially, this *could* be dangerous. What's the jewelry worth? Give me a ballpark number so we know what we're dealing with."

"A few dozen carats set in twenty-four-carat gold. Probably more than half a million dollars."

Chloe gave a low whistle and then realized that the governor's mansion probably had the first tour of the day already gathering in the foyer. "We need to get him out of here," she said to her father, jerking a thumb at the FBI agent. "He shouldn't be seen here—if anybody is watching, I mean."

Liam took a breath. "We'll need to go over details about this job."

"I'm not doing this job," Chloe said, shaking her head. "Find somebody else. I'll be busy helping Mercedes with her makeup and dancing with Uncle Stan, the family drunk."

"We do not have a family drunk named Uncle Stan," Governor Romano chided.

"Agent Esposito didn't have to know that," she chided right back. Her father gave a snort of laughter. "Besides, you'll have your own security detail, Dad. And since Mercedes's wedding is fairly high-profile, Uncle Max will be hiring security as well. You don't need me."

"I have to agree that this could be dangerous, not only for Mercedes, but Chloe, too," the governor said skeptically. "Despite Chloe's past training."

"These thieves don't carry weapons. They stake out the place. Lay low, play it cool. Find the perfect opportunity."

"They won't be trying to sneak into our bedrooms, will they?"

"Absolutely not. The diamonds will be in Max Romano's safe in his office," Liam assured her. "They'll be watching and waiting for a time when nobody is around. You're the perfect person,

Chloe. You have the best access to the bride, her bedroom, and the guests that come and go within the house. Especially if we get you set up several days ahead of time."

Chloe didn't tell him that she was already planning on flying up in three days' time. "I'm sorry, Agent Esposito, but I have no interest in helping the FBI. I have no obligation. No motivation. You can catch this gang of jewelry aficionados at their next gig."

There was disappointment in Agent Esposito's eyes. "That's what I figured you'd say."

"Then why come all the way out here to convince me? Maybe I would have considered it, if the FBI had sent someone else, but I certainly don't owe you any favors."

Agent Esposito nodded. "No, you don't. I know there's bad blood between us."

"Don't go there—you have no right—"

He cut her off, changing the subject back to the case at hand. "I thought you'd do it for your cousin. She needs your help. And I'm not just talking about a potential thief rummaging through her negligee drawer."

"What haven't you told us?"

Agent Esposito pursed his lips and then cleared his throat. "We suspect the jewelry thief may be Mark Westerfield."

It took a moment for the implication of the name to register with Chloe. She'd seen the name "Mark Westerfield" before, but couldn't place him. She'd certainly never met him.

Her father rose and took something off the library desk. He handed a gold-engraved wedding invitation to Chloe. "Look," he said softly.

Chloe glanced at the gold calligraphy on the printed wedding announcement that had arrived in the mail a month earlier.

The name of the FBI's suspect sank in while she gripped the invitation, almost crumpling the perfectly scalloped edges with her thumb.

"Mark Westerfield is Mercedes's fiancé."

CHAPTER 4

"This information changes everything," Governor Romano said, his brow furrowing. "No wonder my brother arranged all of this and asked for you, Chloe."

"How terrible for Mercedes," Chloe said, her heart sinking. She certainly didn't wish this nightmare on her. "You're saying that my cousin is about to marry a jewel thief?"

Suppressing all the curse words running through her mind, Chloe wished she could punch Agent Esposito in the jaw for being the one to pressure her into this. "Why did Uncle Max rent outrageously expensive jewelry for his daughter's wedding day, putting Mercedes at risk?"

A muscle in Agent Esposito's jaw flexed. "We were the ones who came to him with the information of who Mark Westerfield might be—after Max had already reserved the jewelry for his daughter."

"How in the world did Mercedes get mixed up with a jewel swindler?" Chloe said, speaking her thoughts out loud. "And fall in love with him? And want to marry him?"

"Those are questions we're hoping you can find the answers

to," Liam said. "Discover what Mercedes knows, if anything. Or if she's mixed up with this jewelry swap herself."

Chloe stuck her hands on her hips. "Okay, that's insulting to my cousin—even if I've been trained to consider all the options."

"It might be completely unintentional," Liam said, spreading his hands. "She may not even know she's being used as a pawn."

"I've never taken Mercedes for naiveté. She might look like a fashion model, but she's inherited shrewd business skills from her father."

"These types of crooks—jewel gangs—they're smooth operators. You'd be surprised who might be involved, even in unassuming and presumably innocent ways. Passing along information, dates, times, etc. These are white-collar criminals who prey on the rich and famous. That category fits your cousin perfectly."

Chloe shook her head. "How would a woman like Mercedes, who only circulates in the most influential and best circles, get mixed up with a low-life criminal?"

"Diamond thieves don't consider themselves criminals. Most have never served any time in prison. They don't start out robbing liquor stores or gas stations."

"How long has Mercedes been dating Mark Westerfield, Dad?" Chloe asked.

"Your mother would know more about that."

"Those are questions we'd like *you* to help the FBI answer, Chloe," Liam said, watching her carefully.

His eyes on her face made a flutter of nerves crawl up Chloe's spine. There was a peculiar feeling in her stomach, like swarms of butterflies migrating for the winter.

If any other agent had shown up asking her to do this job, she wouldn't be feeling so resentful and angry. Curse Liam Esposito. The haunting nightmares of the fateful day she'd last seen him were finally beginning to recede, and here he was, alive and in the flesh two feet away, bringing the anguish up all over again.

Didn't his director check their past histories in the database? Didn't they know that Liam Esposito had left her best friend, Jenna Fielding, to die?

Chloe shoved the sorrow deeper into her gut. "Why can't you send some other undercover agent to take pictures and sneak around the house?"

"It's harder to explain who they are in a wedding party where most guests know everyone else. Especially the family," Liam answered. "As you know perfectly well."

"What's that supposed to mean?" A throb of tension pulsed in Chloe's throat.

"I just meant that in your business, you know how weddings work. The family dynamics, guest lists, that sort of thing."

Was he making fun of her? He made it sound so trivial when, in fact, managing an emotional, high-strung bride—and they all were on their wedding day—took finesse, tact, and intuition. All skills she'd honed during her training at Quantico.

"I apologize again, but I've really got to leave." Governor Romano opened the door to the library where Mr. Smith was standing at attention in the hall. In the distance came the sound of chattering voices—the first morning tour. Thankfully, they were rounding the circular staircase to the rear parlor.

Chloe wondered if her mother was still in the vicinity, but most likely not once the tour group showed up, tickets in hand.

"Governor, your car awaits," Mr. Smith said.

"I'm leaving now, too," Agent Esposito said. "I apologize for taking up so much of your morning, sir."

"I'm just sorry to hear that this will be going on in the background at Mercedes's happy celebration. And distressed to hear who your suspect is."

Liam politely reached past Governor Romano to shut the door to the library while they finished their conversation. "This is between the three of us—and Max Romano, the bride's father. The fewer people who know, the better. We cannot raise any suspicions. Act as natural as possible in front of Mark Westerfield."

"We've never met him, so he won't know our natural state of being," Chloe said drily. "Does Uncle Max know your suspicions about the groom?"

"No, and we need to keep it that way. All he knows is that he wanted extra security with the diamonds on the premises. While you're both there next week, don't speak of this. Not behind closed doors or in whispers. That will merely alert the wrong people or make them nervous. The last thing we want is for anyone to get hurt."

"I do know how to act in these situations," Chloe said. "I haven't forgotten all my training."

Agent Esposito gave her a sheepish smile. "I never thought you did. Just a simple reminder."

"I can't carry a weapon," Chloe said. "I didn't renew my concealed carry license."

"I—we—don't want you carrying anyway. You have orders not to confront anyone, even if you think you've caught the thief."

"Does Mercedes know *anything* about this?" Chloe demanded.

"All Mercedes knows is that you'll be helping guard the diamonds, nothing more." Liam reached out to touch Chloe's arm, and she flinched at the heat of his skin on hers. "So, you'll do it, Chloe?"

He spoke her name so softly and gently, Chloe found herself trying to catch her breath. "It disturbs me to spy on my own cousin on her wedding day," she said in a chilly voice. "I don't like this one little bit."

"None of us do," Liam said while the governor gave his daughter a quick hug and disappeared with Mr. Smith to the rear exit of the mansion where his car awaited.

Chloe's heels clicked on the floor when she passed through

the front foyer to let Agent Esposito out—or kick him out, she wanted to think.

"You're doing this for your cousin," he said quietly. "Not the FBI. And certainly not for me."

His warm palm touched her arm, and Liam dipped his head in a gesture of compassion, dark brown eyes filled with a strange expression.

Chloe jerked backward and swung the door even wider. Humid morning air wafted across the wide veranda. A hint of freshly cut grass. She stepped onto the porch and shut the door behind her.

Speaking in a low voice, Chloe said, "Let's get one thing clear, Agent Esposito. You're the last person at the FBI I would agree to help on a case."

The FBI agent's shoulders slumped. The light seemed to go out of his eyes. "I'll never make that mistake again, Miss Romano, but for the next week we need to work together. I'll be supervising your training—" He broke off, clearly reluctant to mention any specifics. "A car will pick you up tomorrow morning at nine. Do you still live at the same address?"

"I should have given a bogus forwarding address," she said grimly.

Liam hid a smile when he turned to take the porch steps to his car. "We have ways of finding anybody we need to."

"Bite your tongue, Esposito," she warned, turning on her heel and slamming the front door behind her.

CHAPTER 5

*A*n hour later, back at her apartment, Chloe had prepared the paperwork for Mercedes. Actually, just a to-do list with potential tasks for her cousin to think about regarding the wedding. She signed, dated it, attached it to a secure email through her server, and hit Send.

Her stomach was in knots. What in the world had she just agreed to do? Being a spy at her cousin's wedding was insane. It could get someone hurt or killed. If that happened to her again, she'd never be able live with herself.

"Just admit me straight to the asylum," she muttered, her head in her hands, elbows on her desk. She wished her waistline could afford a second donut to distract her from what had happened that morning in her father's library.

Why couldn't she ever attend a wedding as a regular, boring guest, eat cake, drink champagne, and dance until midnight?

Quickly, she typed out a second, more personal message to Mercedes. ***Had the appointment Uncle Max set up. If I wasn't your cousin, I'd double my usual price.***

Check your secure Dropbox account for the wedding list. We'll discuss more tomorrow.

P.S. You have a lot of explaining to do!

CHAPTER 6

*A*s promised, a black sedan arrived promptly at nine the next morning. Liam was sitting in the rear seat when Chloe slid into the back. Her breath caught in her throat at the sight of him, and her pulse quickened. She hadn't expected to see him this morning.

A glass panel separated them from their driver. She was stuck with Agent Esposito for the duration of this trip, because the car was already pulling into traffic and headed for the freeway entrance.

"Good morning, Chloe," Liam greeted her.

The agent's dark brown hair fell over one eye, slightly damp as if he'd come straight from the shower. Chloe tried to shove the sensuous images out of her mind and reminded herself that she despised this man.

"I didn't expect you to be part of my training," she said with a curt nod.

"I'm not training you. Merely accompanying you to make the necessary introductions."

"It appears as though you're babysitting me."

"I'm the one with the security clearance."

"Ouch," Chloe said drily. "Way to rub it in."

"Hey, I'm not trying to do that at all," Liam said, glancing sideways at their driver. "I'm in charge of the case. Need to check all the boxes on my case report."

"Just like you did with our last job together? When you were team leader and Jenna died? I never did see *that* final report."

Liam winced at her harsh words. "That's because you turned in your badge," he told her quietly. "It was classified, and you no longer had access to it."

"If you recall, I spent that week with Jenna in the hospital." Chloe paused, placing a deliberate finger to her chin in a sarcastic gesture. "No, you weren't aware, since you never came to visit her—your own team member—while she lay fighting for her life."

A wave of emotion hit her unexpectedly, and Chloe had to bite at her lips to keep her watery eyes from spilling over. *This* was the reason she quit the FBI. She couldn't handle the devastating loss, especially after Liam's negligence. The man she had been falling in love with all during the previous year.

"Chloe, please," Liam pleaded. "Can we have this conversation somewhere private?"

Turning away to gaze out the window, Chloe fought for composure.

Liam continued, his voice low and rough. "Emotions always run high and charged during a raid, and that was one of the worst tragedies I've ever been part of."

Chloe let out a sharp laugh, angered by his woefully insufficient response. She whipped around to glare at him. "Jenna's death was more than just a 'tragedy.' It was catastrophic. Life-changing. Do you know how difficult it is to keep in touch with my best friend's mother and younger sister? Jenna was their life, their hero. Every time I see the pain of Jenna's death in their eyes, I want to jump off a cliff from the guilt."

Liam's eyes were fastened to hers, his gaze not leaving her face. She recognized a sudden sorrow welling up in his expression, the muscles of his own face twitching, but she wouldn't give in to any empathy for him.

"And despite the past horror," she added, "here I am, agreeing to do another job with you. I must be a glutton for punishment." Chloe wanted to spit a curse word at him, but swallowed it down and tried to regain what was left of her composure. "How much further is it? I'm toying with the idea of jumping out of the car."

Before Chloe could blink, Liam lunged across the seat and grasped her hand. "Don't say that. Don't ever say that again. If you ever purposely hurt yourself, I'll go insane, Chloe Romano."

A rush of warmth from his hand flooded over her and rushed up her arm, burning a hole in her chest. Slowly extricating her hand from his, she said, "Please don't touch me."

"I'm sorry," Liam said. He blew out a breath and leaned back against the seat to stare at the car's ceiling. A moment later, he looked forward again. "We're here."

The driver pulled up in front of a nondescript office, and Chloe gratefully exited the car, Liam following close behind.

Just before they reached the entrance doors, Chloe turned to him. "Why aren't you being trained in diamond detection? Why can't you do this job? Why me?"

A small smile crossed his full lips and Chloe forced herself to glance away. She had to ignore how much she used to want to kiss those lips a year ago. She and Liam had never once kissed each other despite spending time together in their off hours.

It was against the rules to fraternize with members of the same training teams—worse if a team leader got romantically involved with one of the newbie recruits.

"Like I mentioned yesterday, it would be so much more suspicious to both your family and the Westerfield family if I was lurking inside the house and seen going in and out of Max Romano's office where the safe is located. We want the potential

THE UNDERCOVER BRIDESMAID

thief to let down his guard. For him to think there isn't any risk to attempt a jewelry swap. You're the perfect person. No questions will be asked about a cousin as a bridesmaid. You can go anywhere, do anything without raising suspicion."

She nodded, trying her best not to look at him any longer so she could brush off the lingering effects of his alluring pull on her. "Right," she said briefly.

"And now, let me introduce you to Jim Greene, our gemstone expert. I have another appointment right now. I'll be in touch later."

If I deign to answer the phone when I see your number on my caller ID, Chloe thought while shaking hands with Mr. Greene and exchanging pleasantries. He was shorter than she was and unassuming with a shock of tousled black hair and coke-bottle glasses perched on his nose.

Within two minutes, Liam had disappeared, and she was sitting at a work table next to Mr. Greene while he showed her the tools of the trade.

"The most difficult aspect of diamond authentication that you do *not* have to worry about is determining a value—or price—for the jewelry. That's the part that can confound a new diamond trainee. Muddy the waters, so to speak. All you're going to do is verify that the stones you are inspecting are indeed diamonds —or fakes."

"Got it," Chloe said.

"This small bag of lights and magnifying tools is yours to take with you." He handed her a small black bag about the size of two open palms. "Go ahead and open it. We're going to go through each step."

"Will I have trouble taking the bag with me on the airplane?"

"None at all. They're benign tools for any gemstone seller or buyer. You have two different magnifying glasses, two different power lights, as well as a loupe."

Chloe noted that the light looked similar to a small flashlight.

"The lights will help you look straight through the entire stone to see the flaws and cut angles. The loupe is the most valuable tool you have in your arsenal. It will easily allow you to detect real diamonds from cubic zirconia, for instance."

Jim Greene helped Chloe fit the loupe to her eye and showed her how to hold it and do adjustments on the lenses while inspecting a stone.

On the opposite side of the loupe, which stuck out from her eye like a telescope, he snapped on the light. "This one is easiest to use since it allows you to use both hands to hold the stones and position the light directly into the diamond."

Chloe nodded. "That's helpful. How hard is it to tell if a stone is actually cubic zirconia?"

Mr. Greene smiled. "Not hard at all, actually, despite how well they're made. You'll be able to see the difference right away. Your biggest problem will be if someone is trying to pass off a stone called moissanite, which often fools diamond experts."

"How will I be able to determine the difference, then?"

"You are going to map out the diamonds when they first arrive from Davis Jewelers. As soon as they reach their destination at the safe, you'll inspect them and create your map. Meaning that you'll know exactly what each stone looks like, how many imperfections there are, and the difference in the internal angles and cuts of the stone."

"I've heard that a true diamond will sink to the bottom of a glass of water while fake stones float," Chloe said. "I did a little bit of reading last night in preparation for our meeting today."

"Good, good," Jim said approvingly. "Just like an experienced agent."

"I also read that a heated diamond will crack in a glass of cold water. But the diamonds I'll be inspecting will be set in twenty-four-carat gold. Of course, the gold will make them sink."

"You're correct. I actually have a brother-in-law who works for the Davis Jewelry company. They have stores all over the country and Europe. Alan sent me pictures of the jewelry and a map of each diamond."

Chloe raised her eyebrows, pleased that this job didn't seem as difficult as she'd feared. "That's convenient."

"Hey, we're FBI," Jim said with a quick grin. "We get our hands on all kinds of things. That's one reason I became a gemstone expert. Because of my brother-in-law. So, it's really not a coincidence. I was assigned to your training because of the case Agent Esposito is working."

"Makes sense. The bureau is always on top of things with the best people," she said tightly.

"You also have a special UV light in your packet. That will test the refractivity—the 'sparkle' and 'fire' the stones give off under the light. On individual stones, an amateur could use the fog test. After breathing on the stones, you can see how quickly the fog disappears. A real diamond disperses the fog immediately. Or, holding a diamond on top of a newspaper, you won't be able to read the words underneath."

"Why is that?"

Mr. Greene grinned. "Because diamonds refract light so spectacularly, you can't see through them at all. I forgot to mention that the UV light I gave you will make a real diamond look blue. Not so with fakes or cubic zirconia."

"There are a lot of methods for determining authenticity— more than I thought."

"Thankfully so, especially when we're talking about half a million dollars in stones."

"That kind of money makes me dizzy."

"It's actually not that much for renting a complete wedding set. I once saw a diamond necklace that was intricately set with forty carats, including a yellow diamond, which is very rare. That one piece alone was worth more than two hundred thousand dollars."

"Guess my uncle is a cheapskate," Chloe said, laughing.

"High-end jewelers rent out jewelry all the time, so a wedding set is not unusual."

"My father will have a security detail about the property, too. We should be fine during the wedding weekend."

"I'm sure that's helpful in making Davis Jewelry feel more secure. And don't forget, jewelers insure their stones well."

The next two hours were spent practicing Chloe's ability to spot genuine diamonds from imitations. It didn't really take very long to spot the differences under the special loupe light.

Jim had an array of gemstones for her to experiment on, as well going over the tiny details in mapping out the stones she'd inspect the following weekend.

"There are definitely different angles between a real diamond and a cubic zirconia," Chloe mused. "I didn't realize that the imperfections can be anywhere within a stone."

"Exactly. That's why you will map out the jewelry, making notes and creating sketches on the actual diamonds so that if there is ever anything out of place, you'll spot it immediately. Here's my business card and private number. Please call if you have any questions during your assignment," he said.

Chloe pocketed the card and then wrapped the tools in soft cloths to return to the bag. She glanced at her phone and was shocked to see that over four hours had gone by with only a brief break. "I had no idea it was so late. I'm sorry for taking up so much of your time."

"That's what I'm here for. You caught on quickly, and you were identifying the stones faster and faster."

"That's good to know. Thank you so much, Jim."

After bidding him goodbye, Chloe exited the building to the parking lot. The same car was waiting to return her to her apartment. She glanced about, wondering if Liam was going to accompany her, but he was nowhere to be seen.

Of course, she didn't need a chaperone or a chauffeur, but it bothered her that a twinge of disappointment ran through her at not seeing him again. Perhaps their encounters yesterday and today were the only ones they'd have during this operation. That was that. She'd never see Liam again. So why did her throat grow thick with an ache she couldn't define?

Shaking her head, Chloe forced herself to banish the sentimental thoughts from her mind.

CHAPTER 7

*T*hree days later, it was pouring rain under a blanket of heavy black clouds when Chloe landed at Ronald Reagan Washington National airport.

Thankfully, she was prepared with an umbrella, but her hair had an antagonistic relationship with the extra humidity. Using that expensive straightener before she left home had been a waste of time.

Just before landing, she had spotted the FBI Quantico complex from the airplane window where she had spent those many months training to become an agent. Seeing it now after all this time brought a wash of bittersweet emotions.

Would she ever be able to resolve the memories she and Jenna had created there? Including the memories with Liam Esposito?

Unfortunately, the second she walked off the plane and over the jet bridge, curls were frizzing around her neckline. By the time Chloe retrieved her luggage, she looked like a dandelion.

The Washington D.C. airport was packed with tourists and politicians. Congress was in session every day this month, and yet the autumn season was still as hot as Hades.

Thank goodness her parents weren't arriving until Friday

afternoon, just in time for the rehearsal dinner. Diana Romano had one of her adoption center fundraisers tomorrow, and Dad was always doing governor "things." Endless meetings, fighting with the state legislators, fundraising for his next campaign, cutting ribbons for new businesses and schools.

Lugging an oversized suitcase in each hand, Chloe was startled to read her name written in black marker on a placard at the bottom of the escalator. A young woman who looked like she was barely out of high school was holding it, smiling brightly, her hair in a perky ponytail the color of the red maple leaves turning color on the nearby hills.

She'd assumed Mercedes would meet her, and Chloe had a moment of disappointment. She and her cousin had a thousand details to go over about her wedding. Not the least of which was her FBI "assignment."

"I'm Chloe Romano," she said to the girl, a question in her voice while she pointed a finger at her name on the placard.

"Oh, Miss Romano, my name is Katey Higgins. I recognized you right away from the picture Miss Romano showed me. I'm her assistant, and I'm very pleased to meet you."

Chloe blinked. "Her assistant? She doesn't hold office yet, does she?"

"Not yet, but one never knows, does one?"

Chloe suppressed a laugh at the girl's choice of words. She was perfect for Mercedes. "No, one does not," she replied, holding back a smile. She didn't want Katey to think she was laughing at her. "What do you assist her with?"

"Well, a hundred years ago, young women like Mercedes Romano had personal maids. Think of me as a modern-day personal maid."

"So, you help her get dressed, tighten her corset, button up her boots?" Chloe was joking, but it appeared as though Katey was taking her question seriously.

"Mostly I help her with her estate sale business. I keep her books, make hundreds of phone calls, pay bills, run her personal errands, pick up dry cleaning. That sort of thing. Sometimes I'm needed to help her dress for elegant evening events. I can create a fabulous chignon and ringlets."

"Sounds full-time," Chloe said facetiously.

"Oh, it is," Katey said earnestly. "Miss Romano leads an exciting life. To work for her while she's getting married is thrilling."

"In more ways than one," Chloe agreed.

"Miss Romano, the baggage area is down this escalator. Please follow me." Katey picked up one of Chloe's bags and jumped onto the moving stairs.

Chloe kept pace. "It's going to be difficult to call both me and Mercedes Miss Romano, so why don't you just call me Chloe. After all, I'm just the bridesmaid."

"There is no such thing as just a bridesmaid, Miss—I mean, Chloe." Katey swallowed as if it was difficult to get her first name out. "A good bridesmaid is worth her weight in gold."

"Did Mercedes tell you that?"

Katey blushed. "She was *so* distraught after losing her other bridesmaids. You are a true lifesaver."

Chloe smiled at the young woman's exuberance. "She's got a talent for twisting arms. How long have you worked for her?"

"I started over the summer." Just before they reached the luggage carousels for United Airlines, she leaned in conspiratorially. "Is Chloe your real name? Miss Mercedes told me you do this for a living. That you're an *undercover bridesmaid.*"

"You must have misunderstood. I'm just Chloe Romano. Mercedes's actual blood-by-birth cousin."

"Oh, I was hoping to hear some good gossipy stories."

"I've been in a lot of weddings for friends. You know the saying, 'Always a bridesmaid, never a bride'?"

"That doesn't describe you. You're *so* pretty, Miss Romano—I mean, Chloe!"

"Unfortunately, I'm in need of a shower. I thought the hot humid summer would have already ended up here. This is so much further north than Charleston."

"The weather is playing tricks on us this October. Miss Romano hoped it would be cooling off. Especially since the reception is going to be in her parents' backyard."

"At least it will be evening, right? No bright, hot sun for glare in the pictures."

"Exactly!" Katey exclaimed when the automatic doors shut behind them as they exited the baggage claim area.

A car was already waiting for them at the curb.

Thirty minutes later they'd left the hustle and bustle of historic and political D.C. with its tourists and the Smithsonian.

When they drove through McLean, Virginia, the neighborhoods of stately homes sitting on large wooded lots brought back a rush of childhood memories to Chloe's mind.

The homes were palatial, and Chloe had forgotten just how posh and impressive this area was.

"It's been a long time," Chloe murmured when they arrived at the Romano mansion. She only saw her extended family at the beach during family reunions so it had been at least five years since she'd been at her uncle's house.

Last year, everybody had traveled to Boca Raton, Florida, for her grandfather's funeral, where he and Granny Zaida had retired a decade earlier.

The car purred as the driver pulled through an impressive set of stone gates and drove up the long drive, circling around to the wide veranda and front doors. A moment later, he cut the engine and smoothly exited the driver's door to unload the luggage.

Sliding out of the back seat, Chloe leaned back against the car door to stare up at the massive white house with green-shuttered windows, bay windows, and cupolas.

"When we were kids, my brother and I, along with Mercedes and her sister, Celine, played tag and hide-and-go-seek among

43

the gardens and shrubbery around the back. I think the house sits on five acres."

"Your childhood sounds idyllic," Katey said.

Chloe gave her a faint smile. They did have moments that were idyllic, but both she and her cousin had shared a lot of stress, too. Mercedes rarely saw her father, who was often away on international business, and her own father was constantly in campaign mode from the time he first ran for mayor when she was a young teen.

Her parents often warned Chloe to watch her back and be aware of what she said and to whom, because they were constantly quoted out of context and had to choose their staff carefully for loyalty.

"Where did you grow up, Katey?" she asked now, wondering if she was up to the week's task. First in the role of bridesmaid for a demanding Mercedes—and second as a spy for the FBI.

What made her agree to this? she wondered for the hundredth time. It was insane.

What if Mercedes's fiancé actually *was* part of a jewelry theft gang who manufactured copies to pull off a heist? She could be here for weeks cleaning up the emotional mess.

"I grew up in Hollywood, actually," Katey replied, pulling Chloe out of her reverie. "My mother's an actress who does commercials. Playdates with her were watching hair and makeup people transform my mom into a star—that and shopping along Rodeo Drive."

"Washington isn't so different, then? Everyone here is playacting, too." Chloe gave a wry grin, and Katey laughed.

"East Coast, West Coast—totally different, let me tell you! I want to do something more with my life. My dream is to become a congressional aide. Be part of the democratic process. Watch history being made. That's what brought me to Washington."

"Really?" Chloe wouldn't have guessed that at all.

"Miss Romano said she'd introduce me around. She knows a lot of politicians."

"That's probably true. A congressional aide is ambitious. Do you have to get a college degree for that?" Chloe asked, wondering how long Katey had been out of high school.

"That helps immensely. Unless you're an offspring of a politician, of course. I have a B.A. in political science."

Chloe had newfound respect for the young woman. She must be older than she looked. "Impressive. But such a long way from the hills of Hollywood. Do you get homesick?"

Katey shrugged. "Only for the ocean. Trips to San Diego with my friends. My mom. When she's home. Filming is very demanding."

Chloe suppressed a smile, realizing that she played a role as an actress every time she got on a plane as a hired bridesmaid with her alias and New Mexico desert cover story.

When their driver carted her luggage up the brick steps to the house, long-forgotten memories continued to assault her senses. The smell of jasmine growing along the side yard. The creeping ivy. The towering woods surrounding the property.

"We built a tree house one year," she said now. "The cousins, I mean. I wonder if it's still in the back acre." Chloe had a sudden memory of Mercedes, Celine, and herself with a picnic hamper up inside the huge limbs of a big oak, chewing pink bubble gum and competing for the biggest bubble before the sticky gum popped all over their faces.

When the front door swung open, Mercedes stood before them in a white, sleeveless dress and heels, her hair dark lustrous, and one hand on her hip in a striking pose. Who was the Hollywood starlet in Washington, Chloe thought with amusement?

"Chloe, darling!" Mercedes cried, pulling her inside. "You're doing something different with your hair. I don't think our humidity is doing you any favors."

"It's nice to see you, too, Mercedes," Chloe said with a small grimace.

"Katey will work wonders on us both. She's a whiz with a curling iron and makeup kit."

"She must get her talents from her mother." The early morning flight suddenly hit Chloe, and she wavered on her feet.

Katey gestured toward the wide, curving stairs leading to the second floor. "Your bags are already in the guest room next to Miss Romano, Chloe. I'm sure you two have a lot to talk about. I'll bring up some food and tea."

After the young woman ran off to the kitchen, Mercedes led the way up the wide, graceful staircase. "She's adorable, isn't she? I found her through a temp agency a few months ago."

"We always think Valley Girls are just airheads," Chloe said. "But she's impressive, actually. The house looks fantastic. It's the same, but different, too."

"Mother has such a brain for interior decorating. The floors and wainscoting are all new, including the two-tone paint."

Reaching out a hand, Chloe ran her fingertips over the smooth mahogany wainscoting, made from the same stunning wood grain as the staircase banisters.

"Peek into the kitchen when the cook goes home tonight. Completely remodeled two years ago. All black and white and stainless steel with granite counters ten feet long. Gorgeous picture windows galore and French doors that lead straight to the grounds behind the house."

"Makes me want to race in and out of the rooms and sing as loud as we can," Chloe said. "Remember when we did that as kids, back when your parents had just bought this place, and we came to visit? The rooms were mostly empty, and the sixteen-foot ceilings echoed gloriously."

"Oh, yes, I do remember," Mercedes said, her lips curving upward at the childhood memory. "Such ancient history now."

"And now you're getting married," Chloe said, giving

Mercedes a hug. Surprisingly, her cousin didn't pull away and didn't just air-kiss. Perhaps she was developing a heart after all these years. "Right here at home."

"Such a quaint idea to get married at home, isn't it? I spent months looking at halls and in the end decided that Mother did such a spectacular job with the landscaping last year that we should have the ceremony and reception right here."

"Honestly, it sounds lovely," Chloe agreed. "I love more personal weddings."

"Just wait until you see the fountains and the multi-level flower beds. The first crew begins setting up tomorrow. Bowers and tables and gazebos. It's going to take them two days and five truckloads." Mercedes gave a quick wink and a laugh. "Now that it's all happening, maybe renting a hall would have been easier."

"It's going to be beautiful," Chloe assured her. "If I know you and your mother, it will be *the* wedding of the year."

"You're so sweet, Chloe. Thank goodness for my wedding planner. She knew exactly what I wanted. I found a picture of the perfect backyard wedding, and we're replicating it almost exactly."

"On Pinterest?" Chloe asked with a grin.

Mercedes smiled faintly. "Something like that. Before I forget, Mark and I have the final meeting with our minister first thing in the morning, so sleep in, and we'll go over the dresses and hairdos after that."

"Sounds good." Chloe paused. "We need to talk. Sooner rather than later."

Mercedes lifted an eyebrow. "Oh, Chloe, more wedding lists? I think I'm going to lose my mind."

At the landing, Mercedes turned left, passing closed doors, the carpet plush under Chloe's feet. The interior of the mansion was pristine and brand-new. When they came to another turn in the hallway, the wall disappeared and a railing opened up, over-looking a breathtaking view of the open great room. High ceilings and French furniture in golds and blues decorated the room in stunning décor.

"This is absolutely gorgeous. I love it," Chloe said.

A door slammed below and Mercedes cocked her head. "Probably Mother. We'll meet up with her later for dinner. Meanwhile, here's your room, two doors down from mine."

She opened the bedroom door with a flourish into a bright, cheery room painted lemon yellow with windows that over-looked a rose garden two stories below.

The canopy bed was the main feature of the room, with graceful, gauzy curtains and a high mattress that looked extremely inviting after the crack-of-dawn flight.

"I adore canopy beds," Chloe said, resisting the urge to sprawl all over the thick duvet.

"It's en-suite, and you even have your own private balcony," Mercedes went on, pointing to the walk-in bathroom with gleaming tile on the far side of the room and a pair of French doors that opened to the balcony. "But no nude sunbathing, darling," she said, putting on her slight British accent. "We do have neighbors this high up, unfortunately, and there will be oodles of men setting up all over the grounds for the next few days."

"Have you ever known me to sunbathe? Let alone naked?"

"That's true. You always were a tiny bit prudish. No bikinis. No miniskirts. And you have such a fantastic figure, Chloe." Mercedes eyed her up and down. "I don't know why you hide it. Or *how* you manage to keep looking so fabulous. I'm intensely jealous, you know. And I'm the bride."

"I promise I don't upstage any of my brides. It's written into the contract," Chloe added with a grin.

"Do you run fifteen miles a day or something hideous like that?"

"Only four. Guess I get it from my FBI training, and it just stuck. Mom hired a healthy cook last year, too. Mrs. Harvey prepares super-healthy meals at the request of Mom and never makes sugary desserts, except for donuts, which are my kryptonite."

"You actually eat donuts? My envy just rose to a ten. If I merely breathe the smell of a donut, I gain a pound." Mercedes glanced around the guest room and headed for the door. "Let Katey know if you need anything. I'll let you unpack and get settled, and then we'll discuss the wedding itinerary."

"Um, Mercedes." Chloe wasn't letting her get away without answering her questions first. "We need to talk. Like, now."

Her cousin heaved a sigh. "There's no time to have a sisterly kind of chat. My to-do list is a mile high."

Chloe sidled toward the bedroom door to prevent her from darting away. "You're not leaving this room until we talk about why an FBI agent showed up at my house three days ago."

CHAPTER 8

"*H*onestly, Chloe, I hardly know a thing about that."

Grabbing Mercedes's hand, she dragged her cousin to the bed and made her sit knee-to-knee on the thick duvet. "You sicced an FBI agent on me—like a dog."

"But was he devastatingly handsome?" Mercedes's eyes twinkled.

Chloe tried not to blush. What she really wanted to know was how much her cousin knew about a planned diamond heist—and the man she was planning on marrying Saturday night.

Agent Esposito said that Mercedes knew nothing about Mark Westerfield's potential involvement. That Uncle Max had only told his daughter that Chloe would be assisting in keeping the diamonds safe while they were under the Romano roof.

She wouldn't be marrying him if she knew the FBI suspected her future husband. Would she? It was a sobering thought, and Chloe had to make sure, although she couldn't come right out and ask her point-blank.

Mercedes glanced up at Chloe under long lashes. "I know all about how you're going to be guarding the wedding diamonds. Daddy told me that since you were an FBI agent you would be perfect, and nobody would suspect that you have dual roles as guard and bridesmaid both."

"Right. Yes. Did Uncle Max say anything else?"

"No. Like what?" Mercedes's expression was so innocent and disarming, Chloe was sure her cousin knew nothing about her fiancé's potential involvement.

"Nothing. I got trained in the diamonds, so we're all set. All good."

Mercedes twisted her finger around her engagement ring. "When I heard that Daddy was going to have you be my guard—well, the diamond jewelry's guard—I told my father to request that agent you used to know. To be the one to talk to you and Uncle Albert. The one you trained with at Quantico, although I've never known his name. And you never came to visit me here in Virginia while you were training. But I forgive you. I figured you were a little busy."

Chloe gave a small laugh. "That's an understatement." She blinked back the sudden emotion biting at her eyes. Talking about Quantico did that, including the memories of Jenna, her best friend since kindergarten.

Jenna's father had been a police officer and used to regale them with stories about life on the streets. She and her best friend had played softball on their high school team and ran cross-country in the fall. They had signed up for the FBI rookie program together. Aced the tests.

That first month of training was the best. Challenging both physically and mentally, but forging she and Jenna's friendship stronger than it had ever been. They always had each other's backs. Until it was too late.

"I heard rumors that you had feelings for that FBI agent," Mercedes said now.

Chloe let out a snort. "Are we talking about the same man? I can hardly stand the sight of him. You know about Jenna, don't you?"

"I do," Mercedes said, her eyes holding Chloe's with sympathy. "Daddy and Mother told me all about it."

Chloe tried not to cringe. Nobody knew the real details of the worst night of her life.

"I also know that the heart knows who its true love is," Mercedes said quietly. "Even when hate clouds the heart's vision."

"You've been watching too many rom-coms," Chloe said.

"I'm not sure you know this, but I talked to Jenna when she answered your phone one night while you were here at Quantico. I think you were in the shower or something. Anyway, I heard that dating another FBI agent was forbidden. And wasn't he your team leader?"

Chloe pressed her lips together. "We did *not* date! Oh my gosh, you have this all twisted."

"Jenna said all the women thought he was the dreamiest FBI agent they'd ever laid eyes on. I do believe there was some jealousy within the ranks of the other female rookies."

"This is not a game, Mercedes. Please, I don't want to talk about it."

Her request fell on deaf ears. That's how it was with her cousin. When she got an idea into her head, there was no correcting it. "It's time you faced this guy. You need to clear the air."

"My best friend in all the world is dead, Mercedes. And at least part of the fault lies with him. I never wanted to see him again, let alone talk to him or get blackmailed into working with him."

Mercedes's features lit up. "So he *is* the one that came to your house and gave you the assignment to guard my crown jewels?"

Chloe sucked in a breath, holding herself still. "Yes, Mercedes. He is. End of story."

"Crown jewels—don't you love that?" her cousin continued dreamily. "I feel like a Duchess of England. Kate and William are so gorgeous together. I love keeping up with them online and their precious babies."

"I think you have royal family envy, dear cousin."

Mercedes laughed, twisting her long hair into a knot on top of her head. "Anyway, you're here to guard the jewels, right? Seems straightforward, and I trust my guests implicitly. Besides, nobody is going to walk up and yank them off my body."

"You hope," Chloe muttered while she rose to unzip her suitcases and hang up her clothes in the walk-in closet.

Wearing the diamonds all day wasn't exactly true. She'd read the details ahead of flying here. Memorized them and then burned the brief back at the governor's mansion where there was security. She'd even stirred the ashes in the library fireplace to make sure there was nothing left.

Davis Jewelry would send an armored car to deliver the jewelry to the Romano residence on Friday before the wedding rehearsal dinner. They would be stored in Uncle Max's safe in his office. Sunday morning, the armored car and accompanying guards would whisk them away again.

The entire charade reeked of vanity and flaunting how rich Uncle Max was. As if they were D.C.'s royalty. On one hand, it was amusing, but on the other hand, it smacked of just plain showing off. Mercedes would be wearing so many diamonds she'd probably tip over from the weight.

Perhaps renting out wedding jewelry gave prominent jewelers a chance to show off their wares—while also bringing publicity to both the store and the Romano family.

Chloe was under instructions to inspect the jewels at least twice each day and keep Mercedes in her sight during the rehearsal dinner and on the evening of the actual wedding—just in case someone did try to steal them right off of Mercedes at gunpoint. The probability of that was highly unlikely with so many guests and the governor's security on the premises, but you never knew how desperate somebody might be.

Her role as bridesmaid was the best position to be in for the job. Chloe often said that "multitask" was her middle name.

"Before I forget," Mercedes added, "my dressmaker is coming tomorrow afternoon to do a final fitting. You're getting your own fitting done, too."

"I meant to ask you about that. My bridesmaid dress didn't arrive at my apartment."

"The dressmaker made alterations according to the measurements you sent us. There wasn't time to ship it off. What if FedEx lost it?"

"It's probably for the best," Chloe agreed. "I didn't have to worry about stuffing it into a suitcase."

Mercedes flopped backward on the queen-sized bed, the fluffy sunshine-yellow duvet sinking into an outline around her figure. "I can't wait for you to meet Mark! He's a dream. You'll love him."

"How did you two meet? I haven't heard the story."

"Let's just say it was love at first sight."

"That's rare," Chloe said with a smile.

"It was at the wedding of one of my old college roommates. Yes, I met him at a wedding of all places. And, get this. I caught the bridal bouquet that day."

"No way! I guess it was meant to be."

"The bouquet was this obnoxious thing two feet in diameter filled with every color flower of the rainbow. Sally was dressed like a flower child from the sixties. They got married up in the mountains, and there was dancing under the moon. With music on an iPod. I've never eaten a potluck meal before. It was quaint. Very different and so unorthodox but quite fun in the end. Especially when Mark kissed me during the last dance."

Chloe raised her eyebrows. "Ooh la la, he moves fast."

Mercedes lowered her voice, her eyes softening like a woman in love. "He showed up at my next three estate sales and flirted outrageously, finally convincing me to go out to dinner. Oh, there were fireworks, Chloe. I knew at that moment that I was going to marry him."

"How lovely and romantic." A vision of her own fireworks with Liam at Quantico training crossed Chloe's mind, but she shoved it aside, stuck the memory in a box, locked it, filled it with weight, and then let it sink to the bottom of the ocean.

Liam Esposito turned out to be the worst human being on the planet when the drug raid went south and bedlam ensued, including the bomb that went off to trap and kill the FBI officers.

"Don't doubt yourself so much, Chloe," Mercedes said now. The words were unexpected, and Chloe mentally staggered backward. "I can tell what you're thinking, but love and hate are close. Too close sometimes. Your first instincts were probably right."

"Don't play matchmaker, okay? It's done and over, and I can hardly bear the sight of the man. In fact, there was nothing there to begin with."

Chloe was lying, of course, not only to Mercedes, but to herself. She'd been denying the attraction for so long now, what was the point of admitting it? The fact didn't change anything. It certainly couldn't bring Jenna back.

"You two didn't date a couple of years ago?"

"No!" Chloe wanted to explode. "We were part of a team—which means hands off—until we weren't any longer. Our mothers talk too much."

Mercedes laughed. "You're so funny and endearing, Chloe. I'll get out of your way and let you unpack. We have three glorious days ahead of us."

"Glorious for you," Chloe said darkly, but she smiled. "Actually, I'm very happy for you, Mercedes."

"The next few days could change your life, too," Mercedes said with a wink. "Your groomsman is Brett Sorenson, Mark's cousin. Best man officially. You'll adore him, we all do. He's movie-star handsome, terribly sweet, and best of all, he loves strong women. Like you."

"I'm a professional bridesmaid, for heaven's sake. Nothing more girly than that."

"You used to be FBI. I'll bet that's a turn-on for lots of men."

"Not necessarily. A couple of times I told a date I went through FBI training and never heard from them again. Strong women can also be threatening."

Mercedes waved a hand. "Only for the insecure ones. I'm getting married and beyond happy, so I'm dying to match you up with the love of your life. I have this great feeling about you and Brett. This could be *your* weekend."

"I'm only here to help you." Chloe paused, lowering her voice and checking that the bedroom door was firmly closed. "By the way, does Katey know that I'm also here to keep an eye on the diamonds?"

"Not a thing. The only people who know are you, me, and our fathers."

"We need to keep it that way."

Mercedes nodded just as her cell phone rang. "Its Mark!" she squealed, sliding off the bed. Within two seconds she'd disappeared out the door, and Chloe could hear her chattering while she went down the hall.

Chloe was positive she had never seen Mercedes squeal over a member of the male species. She and Mark must be meant to be.

The only problem was that Mark Westerfield was the FBI's number one suspect in a heist they were 99% positive was going to happen this weekend.

It was also now apparent that Mercedes had no idea about Chloe's full mission—or the suspicions on the man she was going to marry on Saturday.

Chloe intended to keep it that way, but she was mighty curious about Mercedes's fiancé. The most eligible bachelor in Washington and one of the richest. Why would a guy like that need to steal jewels?

These were unnecessary questions, and Chloe knew it. All

sorts of people committed crimes that made no sense. Was Mark Westerfield a thrill-seeker, or was he hiding a personal financial meltdown and the Romanos renting the wedding jewelry gave him an idea for a method to stay solvent? He had access, that was for sure.

But did the man have the motive, too?

While Chloe unpacked her clothes, placing dresses and sweaters on hangers and sliding lingerie into the bureau drawers, she was still annoyed that Mercedes was trying to throw men at her like Brett Sorenson—and Liam Esposito.

Which reminded her. As if she needed reminding. Chloe pulled out her phone and sent a text to Liam, informing him that she had arrived and was on the premises of the Romano mansion.

Good, Liam texted back. **Call me later.**

Chloe: **Why? I only need to inform you when the diamonds arrive tomorrow.**

Liam: **I want to hear your voice.**

Chloe: **Believe me, you're better off not. Especially if you want to keep your eardrums intact.**

Liam: **I always loved a good spar with you. Remember that time we partnered on the boxing mat and you caught me unawares and took me down to my knees?**

Chloe: **Go wash your mouth out with soap. Or your mind.**

Liam: **I'm not insinuating anything. I'm a gentleman.**

Chloe: **Tell that to Jenna when you forgot her in the exploding house.**

There was no response for several long moments as Chloe fumed a little while she finished unpacking. When her cell phone rang, she picked it up reluctantly, but curious as to how Liam would respond.

"Wow, Chloe," he said in a low voice. "You may not believe it, but that night haunts me. It will forever. You've never given me a chance to tell you the truth about what happened. I kept waiting to hear from you after you turned in your resignation letter."

"Why would I contact you? I know what I saw. There is no forgiveness, which means there's nothing to talk about."

"That's not fair." Liam paused, and his voice was rough when he spoke again. "I know what we felt for each other, despite the rules and protocol. We both danced around the subject every single day while we worked together. Talked about it without talking about it. I'll never forget our night under the stars."

"Please don't, Liam." Chloe quickly closed the call and tossed her phone across the bed and stared at it, trying not to break down. She needed her wits and a clear head this weekend. Her emotions went crazy whenever Liam was around.

Clenching her fists and gritting her teeth, Chloe finally turned on the shower to dress for dinner. She'd been up since five a.m. lugging suitcases through a hot airport terminal.

Unfortunately, she feared that she'd never be able to get Liam Esposito out of her mind. He was like a thorn tearing at her heart. Why did the man she'd been convinced was her soul mate turn out to be exactly the opposite of the man she'd always dreamed of?

CHAPTER 9

*D*inner was lovely, and it gave Chloe a chance to meet all the players in this strange wedding game.

Aunt Aurelia still smelled like the jasmine she grew around the house. A memory that surprised Chloe when her aunt embraced her.

"Oh, Chloe, we're so pleased you're going to be Mercedes's bridesmaid. The perfect choice! It was so difficult to think about having twelve attendants when the perfect one was staring us in the face."

"I know! I was just staring at y'all all the way from South Carolina!" Chloe said, amused.

Aunt Aurelia laughed at herself, and her laughter was a sound Chloe had always loved. She made every family reunion enjoyable with stories of her escapades living abroad before she met Uncle Max at a hostel in Spain when they were both broke and used to go skinny-dipping at midnight in the Mediterranean.

"It works out perfectly," Aurelia went on. "Especially when Mark's brother Gary is already married to Debi. They have twin daughters, too, you know. Their single cousin is the perfect candidate for best man. You two will make a nice pair walking down the aisle together."

Aunt Aurelia lifted both eyebrows at Chloe, the hint as big as Mount Everest.

"As long as he's devastatingly handsome and clever," Chloe joked.

"He is," her aunt said, taking the comment seriously. "You will have a difficult time not succumbing to his charms."

Across the dinner table, Mercedes caught Chloe's eye. "Wouldn't it be amazing if we also became sisters-in-law by marrying two brothers? No, not sisters-in-law—cousins-in-law. Oh, you know what I mean!"

Aunt Aurelia clapped her hands in delight. "What a perfect idea. Do fall in love, Chloe. We need another wedding in the family. Don't put it off too long. The years are whizzing past much too quickly."

Chloe took a sip from her water goblet. The chicken cordon bleu was suddenly very dry. She patted her mouth with her napkin while Mr. Vincent, the man Uncle Max employed as butler/server, began whisking away the dinner plates to serve a strawberry and peach trifle loaded with whipped cream on fine china plates.

Uncle Max cleared his throat from the end of the table. He was a distinguished man, older brother to Chloe's father, broad-shouldered and trim with an impressive mustache that was the same salt-and-pepper color as his hair. "Let Chloe enjoy her dinner, please."

Chloe smiled at him and he winked in return. She'd always liked Uncle Max. He was easygoing and always welcoming, despite his frequent scarcity due to work travel.

"Mark's nieces will be the flower girls," Aunt Aurelia went on. "Beautiful children, they'll look so lovely in the photos. Oh, that reminds me. Will you please check with the wedding planner about the photographer, Chloe? I think we need her to arrive a little sooner tomorrow for the rehearsal dinner. She could take family group pictures."

Chloe whipped out the small notebook she kept tucked into the pocket of her skirt and jotted a note.

"Dinner was splendid," Uncle Max said to Mr. Vincent after eating every morsel of his dessert and leaving the plate practically spotless. "I'm going to have to walk two hours to burn up all these calories. When I look around the dining room, I get nostalgic thinking that this is the last meal we will have as a family before you are married, Mercedes."

"I was just thinking the same thing, Daddy."

"Oh, Max, you sentimental old thing," Aurelia told him, patting his hand. "Tomorrow's rehearsal dinner will be with the new in-laws, and it will never be like this again."

"Families that grow bigger with each new generation stay alive with love," Chloe told her aunt. "You're gaining a son."

"You're so wise, sweetheart," Aunt Aurelia said, smiling through watery eyes.

A sick feeling swept through Chloe. She hoped this jewelry stakeout and her undercover job would end up for naught. She hated to think that Mark Westerfield was really up to his eyeballs in a scheme to steal his bride's jewelry.

"Did Celine change her mind about attending the wedding?" Chloe asked. "I hope so."

"Actually, she did," Mercedes answered. "She called late last night. She said that despite her protests over our family's brazen display of wealth, she couldn't miss her own sister's wedding. She arrives sometime later tonight."

"I don't think I've seen her in years. She was in India, wasn't she, when Grandpa Tony passed away? And she missed the last couple of family vacations. I'm not sure I'd even recognize her," Chloe joked.

"You wouldn't," her aunt replied in a sideways hush. "My youngest daughter is an anomaly. I don't understand her. She went to school clear across the country at Berkeley and hasn't been the same since. She's a ..." Chloe's aunt paused and glanced about the dining room with its gold-papered walls and flower-filled alabaster urns. "An activist protestor."

"What Mother means is that my sister is an environmentalist and likes to march for lots of causes. She saves the whales, hugs trees, spends weeks in remote jungles to help orphan children learn how to read, and organizes rallies to protect impoverished children."

"She and my mother have similar passions," Chloe said. "She's very active in adoption programs and helping with the Catholic orphanage charities. Last week it was the Presbyterians who are doing a joint project with several churches, including the Baptists and Mormons. She's really quite something. Manages to bring people from all sorts of backgrounds to rally together for the sake of children who need foster parents."

"Aunt Diana and Celine will have a lot to talk about," Mercedes said. "We'll have to seat them next to each other at the rehearsal dinner."

"Seat me next to who?" a voice said from the doorway. Celine Romano sauntered into the dining room and glanced around. "Did you save me any food, Mom?"

"Of course, darling. Mr. Vincent, will you bring a fresh plate for Celine?" Aurelia asked the man who was hovering near the door.

There were moments Chloe thought she was living with royalty. It was disconcerting, despite the fact that her own father had a secretary assistant in Mr. Smith and a full-time staff as governor. But that was temporary, he only had two years left of the second term. After that, her parents would return to "civilian" life in their old house across town.

"Did your flight get in early, Celine?" her mother asked, rising to embrace her youngest daughter.

"Yes, I caught a cab. Thanks for the travel dough, Dad."

Uncle Max rose from the end of the table, giving Celine a quick kiss and holding her by the shoulders for a moment to gaze into her face. "I didn't want you missing your sister's wedding because you're unemployed or some such."

Celine winced and gave Chloe a grimace from across the room.

"I must attend to some phone calls before the night is over," he added. "I will see you beautiful ladies in the morning."

He winked around the room before swinging through the outer door back to the foyer. His footsteps on the black marble floor faded quickly.

Chloe jumped out of her chair to hug Celine. "It's great to see you. Gosh, it's been a long time."

"So I heard." Celine's eyes were filled with mischief.

"You've been eavesdropping, haven't you?" her mother accused. "You have never outgrown that naughty habit, my girl."

Celine flounced around the room in shorts and a T-shirt, plopping herself down at an empty plate. She filled a water goblet and drank it down in three gulps. "But it's the only way to learn such interesting things. I think the last time I hugged a tree was when we built that tree house."

"I was merely speaking in metaphors," Aunt Aurelia said.

"Is the tree house still there?" Chloe asked.

Celine gave a sigh. "A couple of holes where the wood rotted away, but we'll have to check it out tomorrow when its daylight. If you can spare five minutes away from the wedding of the century."

"Oh, stop it," Mercedes told her. "It's my *wedding*. I want it to be perfect, and special. Something I'll remember for the rest of my life."

"And you will," Aunt Aurelia reassured her.

"It's going to be a lovely day," Chloe added. "No nerves, no jitters, no worries. We're under control. You just focus on getting enough rest so you don't have bags under your eyes—and loving on Mark."

"That's the easy part," Mercedes said slyly. "Speaking of dark circles under the eyes, I have a professional coming to the house to do facials tomorrow, Chloe. Cucumbers and everything."

"Alrighty." Chloe clicked her ballpoint pen and made a quick note. The schedule for Friday was heating up. She tried to remember when her parents' flight came in, but couldn't recall. She sent a quick text message to her mother under the tablecloth.

Five minutes later, Celine had wolfed down her dinner, but only ate the salad and veggies. "Vegetarian," she told Chloe.

Chloe smiled. "I figured. You look wonderful, Celine. Very fit and healthy. I want to know more about your overseas adventures and humanitarian projects."

"We can grab a hammer and some nails and do some repairs while catching up in the tree house," Celine replied. "Perhaps after the wedding is over."

"We can figure it out after Saturday night. I left my return ticket open-ended. Sunday should be quiet, and we can all catch up on our sleep before flying back home."

But only if the more than half million dollar diamonds made it safely back to the bank.

"In forty-eight hours, I'll be Mrs. Mark Westerfield," Mercedes said. "I want to show you my wedding dress, Celine and Chloe. Come upstairs."

Mr. Vincent entered the room just as they were all rising from the table. "Excuse me, ma'am," he said to Mrs. Romano. "Mr. Mark Westerfield has just arrived. I put him in the front drawing room."

"He's here," squealed Mercedes, then quickly composed herself. "You could have just brought him into the dining room, Mr. Vincent. There's piles of fruit trifle left, and I know how much he loves it."

The butler smiled. "I'll have Mrs. Benson fix him a dish to take home."

"Perfect." Mercedes grabbed Chloe's hand and tugged her out of the room.

This Mercedes was unlike the lifelong Mercedes that Chloe had always known. The proper, cultured girl who liked to put on airs, pretend she was a princess, and speak in accents when they were growing up, was excited and in love. It was nice to see, but the sight only made Chloe's stomach ache. *Please be wrong, Liam Esposito,* she thought. *Darn you, anyway! I banished you from my life once already.*

Eager to meet the mysterious Mark Westerfield, Chloe allowed herself to be yanked from the dining room. They crossed the foyer and walked down a short hallway to a sitting room decorated in white couches and silver trimmings.

Chloe hoped she didn't have grass stains on her sandals. Surreptitiously, she lifted a foot to check, trailing behind her cousins.

Celine gave a knowing grin and spoke under her breath. "It's all a little much sometimes, right?"

Mercedes was already in her fiancé's arms when Chloe entered the drawing room. He was much taller than his bride, bending down to embrace her and nearly lifting her off her toes.

When they parted, Mercedes was beaming and began introductions while Chloe tried not to stare too hard.

Mark Westerfield was in his early thirties, dark blond hair in a styled and shaggy cut brushing along his ears. Not too long, not too short, but perfectly coiffed. Did the man have a personal stylist? The thought made Chloe smile, and she immediately stepped forward to shake his hand so he wouldn't think she was laughing at a secret joke.

The one accessory Mark wore that threw Chloe off was a pair of black-rimmed glasses. She hadn't expected that. He hadn't worn them in the engagement pictures tucked into the envelope with the embossed wedding announcement. The spectacles gave him a brilliant and studious air.

Mark Westerfield also spoke with a slight Boston accent, but he didn't elongate his vowels as much as she would have expected. Perhaps he'd gone across the country for his university studies.

"Very pleased to meet you, Chloe," he said easily before giving Celine a quick brotherly hug.

"Congratulations on your upcoming marriage," Chloe replied. "Be good to my cousin. I don't have too many of them."

"I don't have too many relatives either, but I've told Mercedes we should have a big brood of offspring."

"Even Prince William and Kate have three children. I think that's lovely," Mercedes added.

Chloe had to bite her lip to keep from laughing. Her cousin was a royal wannabe, and it came out in so many funny ways.

Behind her, Celine let out a small, weary sigh. "You should travel the world sometime."

"Oh, we have," Mercedes said. "Mark has been all over with his IT company."

Celine shook her head. "I mean travel in places where there aren't five-star hotels. Backpack through villages. Float down the Amazon. Walk the streets of Bangladesh. Visit the poor in Nepal."

"I'm sorry, but that sounds—difficult. How often do you get a shower?"

"Once a week," Celine said, grinning. "But you're wrong, sis. The world is breathtakingly beautiful and achingly hard for millions of people. And yet, I find that most poor people and tribal people in Africa are quite happy and content and live their lives with purpose. And yes, lots of children and elders. Families with dozens of members. You never get lonely."

"Some people say that living so close to D.C. is like living in a bubble. Perhaps they're right," Mercedes conceded. "I'm just not sure I could last a week without washing my hair."

Mark gazed down at his bride with affection while Celine lounged across one of the pristine couches, kicking off her shoes and stuffing them under the furniture.

Chloe sat across from the bride and groom, and the four of them chatted about their university experiences. Turned out Mark had gone to Yale, magna cum laude, with a master's in computer science as well as an MBA. Good grief, he must have spent the last decade in school.

His father was turning his burgeoning tech company over to Mark, who was on the board and would soon run it as CEO when his father retired in a few years.

"Both our degrees will come in handy," Mercedes said. "The tech side and the management side."

"I planned it that way deliberately," Mark said, but not in a bragging manner. More of a matter-of-fact tone.

"Where are you two going to live?" Chloe asked.

Mark sat up, placing an arm around his fiancée. "This past spring, I purchased a home in Newton, outside of Boston."

Chloe nodded, aware of the affluent neighborhood. Business must be good. "Will you miss Virginia?"

"I'm going to hate all the extra snowstorms up north," Mercedes said. "Especially moving right as winter is beginning. I told Mark we must have snow plowers on staff. But he's promised me a honeymoon in Italy. We'll have our own villa for three weeks."

Celine yawned. "See what I mean, Chloe? You two need to get out more. Rich Boston neighborhoods, villas in Italy. Doesn't it get dull, the same old, same old?"

Mark lifted his eyebrows, glancing between Mercedes and Celine. It was obvious he didn't know how to take his future sister-in-law, but didn't want to insult her, either.

A man of high privilege, education and fortune. A man who wanted to make nice with his in-laws, too. Mercedes had chosen the perfect husband.

But was he everything he appeared to be? There had to be a motivation for the FBI to be watching him. A reason he was their prime suspect. Whether she liked it or not, the next two days would unfold, and Mark Westerfield's true colors would be revealed.

The possibilities made her sick. It took all of Chloe's mental strength to sit on the couch and make small talk—and not run screaming from the room.

CHAPTER 10

*F*riday morning started off with a bang. Chloe's alarm went off at seven a.m., and then she had to rouse Mercedes from the dead.

"Go away," her cousin groaned, tugging the pillow over her head. "I need my beauty sleep."

"You've got beauty on a silver platter, Miss Bride of the Year."

Mercedes rolled over, bleary-eyed. "I need a power drink with a few shots of caffeine."

"I'll have the maid bring it up to you," Chloe joked. "Oh, that's right. The maid is me this weekend. Your very own professional bridesmaid."

"Ooh, I like having a personal maid AKA bridesmaid that I can boss around."

"For the next two days, my wish is your command. But we have a massive to-do list, woman."

"All I want to do is dream about Mark. Tomorrow is my wedding night! The two of us alone at last." Mercedes sighed, sinking back into the downy four-inch-thick duvet with luxurious satin sheets and outrageous thread counts.

"I'll let you keep those dreamy thoughts all to yourself," Chloe warned.

"Party pooper."

"Into the shower with both of us. I'll meet you downstairs for breakfast in thirty."

Chloe ran lightly down the hall back to her own bathroom with its cool green tiles and towel warmer in the corner.

Butterflies swarmed her stomach. She could only imagine how the pre-wedding nerves were settling over Mercedes.

She beat Mercedes downstairs, but the breakfast nook was empty and quiet. Since it had just passed eight o'clock, she imagined Uncle Max was long gone to work, but the women of the house were all sleeping or showering. Or staring at their cell phones while lying in bed.

Chloe wondered what Celine did in the morning. She wished she'd had enough time for a run herself, but it was better not to leave the premises or Mercedes alone until she was safely off to the honeymoon hotel tomorrow night, rained on by guests throwing rice or blowing soap bubbles.

An array of breakfast provisions had recently been brought out because the food was still hot, and it looked fantastic. Eggs, bacon, crisp waffles, syrup, butter, homemade jam, scones, juices, ice water, and herbal teas. There was even a mixture of sausages and hash browns that looked tempting.

"Our very own breakfast buffet," Chloe murmured, thinking of the Easter Sunday breakfast buffet at the Hilton she'd gone to with her family as a teen.

Mercedes arrived about fifteen minutes later, just as Chloe jumped up at the sudden sound of truck engines coming up the driveway. She peered through the curtains.

"It's the wedding planner and a truck load of décor," Mercedes said, taking a peek before sitting down with a bowl of yogurt and berries.

"Yogurt is not going to sustain you until dinner. Who knows

if we'll have time for lunch," Chloe told her. "Get some nourishment or you'll be fainting by three o'clock."

"I wanted to drop two more pounds before tomorrow night so my stomach is flat on my wedding night."

"It's flat enough. I think Mark would rather have a coherent bride than a fainting waif."

Mercedes assumed an innocent expression. "Don't men like shrinking violets they can carry across the threshold?"

"I predict Mark could pick you up with his pinkies if he wanted to. He's at least eight inches taller than you. I don't know when the man has time to lift weights—unless he's naturally blessed."

"He's naturally blessed," Mercedes said dreamily. "But he also takes time for the gym at lunchtime. There's a workout room in his office building."

"The perks of being a millionaire must be nice. I say that with all due respect, of course. Hey, where's Celine and Aunt Aurelia?"

"Mom had an early morning hair appointment, and I'm sure Celine is out in the back meadows eating grass for breakfast. She's so thin it's disgusting."

"I'm right here," Celine said, pushing through the swinging doors to the breakfast nook. "And yes, the grass is very sweet and tasty this morning. You should try it sometime." Celine poured herself a cup of hot water and dunked a raspberry tea bag into it. "I get up with the sunrise. Backpacking in the wilds of India will do that to you. I find the culture and the Hindu religion fascinating, too."

"Celine likes to study religions," Mercedes put in, making a face.

"I'll let that comment go," Celine retorted, speaking directly to Chloe and ignoring her older sister. "I also inspected the tree house back along the Potomac. With a few nails and a couple of fresh planks, somebody could rendezvous there."

"Perhaps a quick walk after breakfast when we check in with the wedding planner and her team."

Celine made a face. "I have to brave the shopping mall to find something decent to wear tonight for the rehearsal dinner. Mom says I need to burn my T-shirts and at least get a skirt."

"Mothers can be such hard-noses," Chloe joked sympathetically.

"Do you think Target will have anything good?"

"Celine Romano," Mercedes said, squaring her shoulders. "If you wear something from Target to my wedding, I will never speak to you again!"

"Is that a promise?" Celine said with a wink to Chloe.

"Ergh!" Mercedes shoved her chair back. "You're impossible!" She thrust the drapes aside and stared down at the side yard.

"Come on, Mercedes, laugh at yourself once in a while," her sister told her. "You take everything too seriously."

"It's my wedding. I can be as serious and uptight as I want to be."

Celine glanced at Chloe, who shrugged. "The bride is allowed to be moody and irritable. It's her weekend, and the rest of the family and wedding party must bow to her wishes."

Celine set down her spoon. "I'll catch you later."

"Please don't bring one of your backpacking friends as your date to my wedding, Celine." Mercedes pleaded. "Please? Try to be normal for once."

"Big sister, you're the one that needs to figure out what normal is, not me."

When Celine left, the room went absolutely still.

Mercedes twisted her fingers together. "Our first wedding weekend fight. There's bound to be at least one, right, Chloe?"

From her vast year of experience, Chloe knew it was only the beginning, but she just nodded. "The rest of the day is going to be fantastic and tomorrow the highlight of your life. Take me outside and introduce me to the wedding planner. We're going to have a blast today. Pinky promise."

The morning was warming when Mercedes led Chloe out a side door to where a train of five trucks had pulled up one behind the other, emblazoned with logos of various rental companies.

More than a dozen men in jeans and work T-shirts were systematically unloading the trucks while an anorexic-looking woman barked orders, clipboard in hand.

"Yoohoo, Suze!" Mercedes called out, running down the side yard.

The woman shaded her eyes when the morning sun slanted along the roofline, hitting her square in the face. "Mercedes! I thought you'd still be in bed. It's the weekend for the bride to luxuriate and relax and think happy thoughts."

"My bridesmaid said otherwise. We have a busy schedule today."

"Your bridesmaid?" Suze pivoted toward Chloe. "Since when did you get yourself a bridesmaid? I thought you and Mark had decided to focus on the two of you and let my magnificent decorating be the weekend's focus. You will be dazzled beyond belief by the time we get done with this place."

Chloe glanced around the corner of the house, already bedazzled by the flower gardens, columns, and fountains shooting water. "How could it get any better?" she said out loud.

A mistake. Suze overheard her. "Get any better?" the woman asked. "You're about to witness the wonder of Suze Perry's miracles. Mercedes Romano's wedding will be talked about long into the next decade, perhaps century."

Chloe studied her curiously. The wedding planner didn't look to be much more than thirty-five, but expensive clothes and a few doses of Botox could often be deceiving—especially in Washington D.C. "You're very—confident."

Suze pinched the bridge of her thin nose and pointed a long, red fingernail to a passing man carrying pieces of a gazebo. "Confidence has nothing to do with it. I'm called the Wedding Miracle Worker. Mercedes knew exactly who to hire."

"She's very wise," Chloe said, trying not to get into an argument.

"Innate talent. This is my calling. My purpose. My art. Unbelievers will become converts by six p.m. tonight. Mark my words."

"I can't wait to see this place transformed," Chloe said, attempting to smile at the fierce woman.

"Suze," Mercedes interrupted. "This is my cousin, Chloe."

"Oh. Your cousin is your bridesmaid."

"Celine refused, as you know. Chloe hails from South Carolina. Her father—my uncle Albert—is South Carolina's governor," Mercedes explained.

"Oh," Suze repeated, putting a different tone on the word every time she said it. Appraising Chloe, the wedding planner's eyes ran up and down the length of Chloe's stylishly ripped jeans and flouncy red blouse. "How fascinating."

Chloe hoped she'd risen in the estimation of the miracle worker Suze Perry who was literally spilling over with self-confidence.

"Before you start bossing everyone around again, Suze," Mercedes said with a tinkling laugh—a feat the bride could get away with, but if Chloe had said that, Suze would throw metaphoric daggers at her. "Show us where you plan to set up everything. I'd love to get Chloe's opinion, too. She's so experienced with weddings."

Chloe wanted to clamp a hand over her cousin's mouth. What she did for a living as a professional bridesmaid was not to be spoken of to any outsiders while working a job.

Suze's eyes latched onto Chloe's face. "You mean, always a bridesmaid, never a bride?"

Chloe laughed weakly. "Something like that." Despite the put-down, she'd dodged that bullet. She linked an arm through Mercedes's elbow. "Let's stroll through the backyard and watch for a bit, shall we?"

Due to the unusually warm autumn season, the rosebushes were still blooming. Flower beds spilled over with every color along the stone paths that surrounded the pond and waterfall.

"Who designed the new landscaping?" Chloe asked.

"That's my father." Mercedes's answer was surprising. "I think he has this secret wish to be a gardener, but has to content himself with overseeing two employees who create the magic he imagines. When he has more than a couple of hours at home, he's out here directing the work."

Not three minutes had passed before Suze hurried up behind them, her heels ringing on the stone walkway. "Let me show you where everything is going and if you absolutely hate something, we can discuss it."

Chloe bit back a grin as her cousin was tugged away from her, and the wedding planner took over. "The slope of lawn is where we'll set up the chairs in rows of five, leaving an aisle for the bride to walk up. I've decided we should have the wedding party face the house, since we can't get a view of the river from here, unfortunately."

The woman spoke as if it was a personal affront that the Romano mansion didn't have a better view of the Potomac to enhance the wedding.

"The backdrop of the house is so pretty back here, though," Chloe spoke up. She didn't want to argue, but the words spilled before she could stop them. "You can see the waterfall flowing into the swimming pool and the rose gardens at the same time. And look, there are already hanging lights in the trees."

Suze cleared her throat. "That's what I was about to say. We plan on hanging more lights in the trees and standing lamps along the pathways so nobody trips when dusk comes. The lights in the trees will look just like shooting stars, Mercedes."

She marched Mercedes—Chloe trailing behind—to the far side of the lawns. "We'll set up a dancing floor here. Superb quality, your guests will dance all night long, and you'll be kicking them out at dawn."

Mercedes gave a laugh. "I'll leave the kicking out to Chloe and Katey. I'll be long gone to my honeymoon suite with Mark."

Suze gave her a knowing smile but didn't miss a beat of her narrative. "The band will locate here on the wide pathway next to the dance floor. A perfect spot, if I do say so, because the food tables will be on the other side. If your guests want to chat and linger, the music won't be too intruding."

"What do you mean, food *tables?*" Mercedes asked, her voice tinged with panic. "What about the *catered* dinner?"

"Of course we're having dinner catered, my Mercedes. Sergio's chefs will arrive at three to begin cooking. But remember that we thought it would be charming to have dessert tables scattered about the garden so your guests could partake of desserts and snacks until midnight. The tables will have chocolate fountains, sponge cakes, and heart-shaped melons chunks. Strawberries and Italian ices. Waiters will float about the reception with trays of mini cheesecakes, wine, champagne, and hand-dipped chocolates. I guarantee that your guests will go home happy. I predict they'll gush about the Mercedes Romano and Mark Westerfield wedding to their grandchildren."

"It sounds incredible," Chloe said. "And you're making me hungry. Is it lunchtime yet?"

With a satisfied smile, Suze said, "Guests at *this* wedding will gain five pounds by the time they call a taxi to go home."

"We're not going to have drunk guests on the lawn, are we?" Mercedes asked, horrified at the thought. "Chloe, you need to make sure we do not have any inebriated guests making a spectacle of themselves."

"That would be a good job for Katey and the best man," Chloe suggested.

"Oh, right," Mercedes said, winking at Chloe. "Because of the you-know-what."

"What are you two talking about?" Suze demanded, frown lines crossing her forehead.

"She's my special bridesmaid," Mercedes replied quickly. "I have special tasks only for her."

"You two are being very mysterious." Suze did not look happy at being left out of any intimate secrets, even if it didn't concern her.

"Are you doing anything with the swimming pool?" Chloe asked, gazing at the shimmering blue water down the sloping hill. It was rimmed with stone and had a waterfall that looked tempting to stand under, as if the pool was on a tropical island.

"That goes without saying," Suze said huffily. "We're adding floating flowers and lights around the perimeter since it's such a focal point. Mercedes will walk up the length of the pool before entering the aisle between the guests. It's going to be spectacular."

"What if the evening turns colder than we expect?" Chloe asked.

Mercedes nodded. "Since it's early October, that was one of my worries, but we're setting up heaters around the reception and dancing area so guests don't get chilled."

"Sounds perfect," Chloe told her. "I think Suze is right. It's going to be the wedding of the decade. Everything is simply beautiful."

A look of satisfaction crossed Suze's face. "Of course it is. Mercedes was wise to hire me."

Chloe gulped down a laugh. She found Suze Perry more amusing than annoying, although she was pretty sure the woman would be exasperating to work for.

The wedding planner led the way around the water fountain and strode back to her clipboard of shipping manifests, checking off each item as they came off the trucks.

Watching the activity of at least fifteen men unloading high-end rentals, silk curtains, china, and real silver platters, Chloe's mind couldn't help adding up the high-ticket items in her head. The ten grand she'd contemplated threatening Mercedes with last week on the phone for her undercover bridesmaid services were a drop in the wedding budget bucket.

The wedding jewelry was scheduled to be delivered this afternoon. A niggle of anxiety swept through her, thinking of her first round of diamond inspection coming up in a few hours. That was the easy part, actually, now that Chloe had been trained in all the various methods of how to spot a fake.

But how did Chloe learn the truth about Mark Westerfield, let alone catch him in the act of criminal activity? The chances of that were almost zero.

Mark appeared perfectly harmless with his professor glasses and disarming smile, although appearances could be deceiving. In addition, Agent Esposito had explicitly told Chloe not to confront the thief—if the thief actually showed his face.

So how were they supposed to apprehend them and prove a theft?

The apprehension of the unknown caused Chloe to sweat. Was there something Liam hadn't told her yet? Her training at Quantico had prepared her for the endgame of a mission, not just the scheme's setup.

CHAPTER 11

*A*fter a quick lunch from the dining room sideboard, the dressmaker arrived for Mercedes's final fitting. The wedding dress was created from a spectacular satin with scalloped lace and ornate beading that dripped all the way down the three-foot train.

"Not too long, but not too short," Chloe told her cousin when she tried it on. "The gown is even more gorgeous when you're wearing it."

The dressmaker was a quiet woman with a tape measure, her lips pursed with an array of straight pins that Chloe hoped she didn't accidentally swallow. "A few small tucks—I always make it larger—so much easier to take in than to take out."

Chloe was next, trying on the floor-length bridesmaid dress in a burgundy chiffon that fell with an elegantly sophisticated drape. "Thank you for not putting me in yellow or orange," she told Mercedes.

"I would have gone on strike," the dressmaker said drily.

Mercedes glanced at Chloe, trying not to giggle. "The red color will match the changing maple leaves around the backyard —although I actually didn't plan it. I just now thought of it."

"You're a little taller than I thought," the dressmaker mumbled as she pinched and poked at Chloe. "But I think I can take the length down another half an inch." She turned to Mercedes. "The dresses will be fixed, pressed, and delivered later this evening. Call me if you have any trouble with them tomorrow when you dress for the ceremony."

After the woman left, Mercedes gave Chloe a list. "Can you please run these errands? I'm out of my favorite nail color and I'm not loving any of my lipsticks. Plus, get me two extra pairs of pantyhose in case I run one of them. Lord & Taylor is the store that carries my favorite brand."

"Pantyhose?" Chloe was surprised.

Mercedes made a face. "I don't usually wear them, but I want the tummy tucker style. Banish the tummy pooch! Our photographs must look perfect—and that starts with a perfect bride."

"There's always Spanx," Chloe said with a wink.

Mercedes groaned. "I can never get the blasted thing on, and then my thighs ache afterward. I want to be able to walk after my wedding is over," she added demurely. "We'll be on an airplane to the beaches of Italy Sunday afternoon."

"Swim a lap in the ocean for me," Chloe told her.

"I'm not sure I'll be thinking about anybody but Mark on Sunday."

Chloe reached out and smoothed the worry wrinkles across Mercedes's brow. "It was a joke. You shouldn't be thinking about anybody but your new husband."

Her cousin gave her a weak smile. "I'm trying not to freak out, but I feel it coming on."

"You're allowed, and I'll talk you off the ledge," Chloe promised. "Okay. Keys to a vehicle? Taxi?"

"What?" Mercedes looked confused.

"I need transportation to get to the mall and various department stores. Unless you have a chauffeur hiding somewhere around here. Or do you want to send Katey, although I haven't seen her today."

"Oh, right. Errands. I'm losing my mind already. Katey is at my office finalizing some paperwork for the estate sale I finished two weeks ago."

"That makes sense."

"I had no idea how difficult it is to put on a wedding while working full-time. Weekends are my busiest days. I swear I'd lose my arm if it wasn't attached," Mercedes added. She rummaged through a couple of handbags and pulled out a set of car keys. "My car is in the right side of the garage. The two-seater Mercedes-Benz convertible. Try not to run it over a curb."

"Aye, aye," Chloe said with a salute. "I passed my driver's test with flying colors."

Mercedes glanced at the wall clock and nearly had a heart attack. "Is it almost 1:30 already? We still have our facials to do before dressing for the rehearsal dinner at six."

Chloe took her cousin by the shoulders and gazed into her face. "*You* lie down and take a rest. The next two evenings are going to be late. You don't want to be exhausted for tomorrow."

"I'm too nervous to nap!"

Chloe took Mercedes by the hand and led her to her bed. She pulled off her shoes and forced her down on the pillow. "I'm drawing the blinds. Just close your eyes. Even if you don't actually sleep, you'll feel better when you get up in an hour. Think happy thoughts. Think about the lingerie you're going to wear for Mark tomorrow night."

"I'll have to lie on my back so I don't get wrinkles on my face from the pillow."

"That's the least of your worries. Pillow wrinkles are gone within two hours. Trust me, I've timed it before."

"You know so many interesting tidbits about weddings, Chloe."

"*Mais oui.* It's what I do for a living."

"At first I wasn't sure if I believed you, but I do now."

While Chloe ran downstairs to the garages, she glanced at the list Mercedes had scribbled down. Could she get back in an hour, especially with Friday afternoon traffic?

She ended up multitasking, making the phone call to the photographer while she maneuvered the sports car through McLean's streets. Yes, the photographer assured her, she would be at the rehearsal dinner early. Mercedes's assistant, Katey, had already called her twice that week.

Chloe rolled the luxury car into a parking space before dashing into Lord & Taylor. The beauty department was out of stock on the lip color her cousin wanted, but she hurriedly tried half a dozen others that looked close and made a wild guess. Mercedes would probably yell at her, but at this point she didn't have a choice. Pantyhose were next. Then she paid for her purchases with the credit card Mercedes had given her, scrawling a fake signature on the dotted line.

Thank-you gifts for Katey, Suze the wedding planner, and the photographer were next. This was the most time-consuming, and Chloe was gnashing her teeth by the end of it. Small baskets of fine candies and a jeweled box were tucked inside tissue and flowers. She also picked up some embossed stationary for the thank-you notes, which she would draft and Mercedes would sign sometime Saturday morning.

Chloe had already printed Saturday's schedule with copies to hand out to the wedding party. The only problem was that it kept changing slightly, so she was redoing her phone calendar and sending alerts out to Mercedes and Mark.

It was almost three by the time Chloe returned, hauling in the shopping bags from the car and running up the wide, curving staircase to her own bedroom.

Organizing the items, she wrote out the thank-you notes and left them to be signed by her cousin. Then she woke Mercedes, who had actually fallen asleep. Which was good and not so good. Her cousin was a bear to wake up and a bit groggy.

The doorbell rang, and Chloe left Mercedes to splash cold water on her face while she ran out into the hall to peek over the railing. Wedding gifts had been arriving from all over the world via FedEx for two days now, and Katey was responsible for organizing those.

A constant flurry of text messages was beginning to give Chloe her own headache. Last-minute questions and answers from Suze Perry about a florist emergency—a shortage of tiny roses for the boutonnières—and the dinner rehearsal chef at Sergio's.

Mercedes had changed her mind about the wedding dinner appetizers three times now. Final answer: a plate of all three appetizers for her guests. It was only a few hundred more dollars, so why not make her guests happy?

The sound of another vehicle came through the front door, which Katey had opened. No more trucks were scheduled to arrive from Suze Perry to decorate for the backyard reception, so the sound made Chloe curious. She ran down the stairs, wondering if it was a UPS van.

Katey turned when Chloe reached the bottom of the stairs. "It's the armored car with the wedding jewelry!" she said in thrilled tones.

An undercurrent of reverence was included, which made Chloe smile.

Katey laughed at herself. "Sorry to be such a goofball over it."

"Hey, it's not every day a girl gets to see jewels like these." Even so, Chloe's stomach jumped while she put on a pleasant face to mask her own nervousness.

Now her real work began. Over half-a-million dollars in diamonds were on the premises. It was her responsibility to keep them safe and not give herself away. Butterflies rose up her stomach, and her palms began to sweat, but first she ran upstairs to retrieve her wallet and diamond tools, which she stuffed into her purse so Katey wouldn't see them and ask questions.

By the time she raced downstairs again, two uniformed men from Davis Jewelers had already stepped out of a black SUV with opaque windows and what was most likely bulletproof glass. Chloe could see that there was a third man at the wheel who remained with the vehicle.

All three were checking the area around the house with solemn expressions. Taking in the surroundings for any potential trouble. Chloe recognized their mannerisms from working with the Secret Service a few times during her short tenure at the Federal Bureau of Investigation.

"Will you tell Mr. Romano that we've arrived?" the first one said, stepping forward when Chloe came down the porch steps.

"I'm Chloe Romano, and I'll be escorting you inside the house," she told him.

"Correct. I'm Mr. Davis's nephew, Roger Davis. You are our point of contact. May I see I.D.?"

"Perfect," Chloe said, avoiding eye contact with Katey, who was gawking as the two guards opened the back end of the SUV. The first man took out a plain black bag, which Chloe assumed held the wedding jewelry.

The second Davis Jewelry escort examined her photo I.D. "Thank you, Ms. Romano," he said, handing her driver's license back after jotting down the information listed on it in a notebook with the store logo imprinted on it.

Satisfied, the two men nodded to Chloe, who swept her arm toward the front door. "This way, gentlemen."

"I'll go upstairs and get Mercedes," Katey said while Chloe turned to lead the guards through the front drawing room. A second opening with pocket doors led to her uncle's library.

Beyond the library with its leather edition books and wood-paneled fireplace was Uncle Max's office, which Chloe unlocked with the key she'd been given by her uncle. Behind one of the cabinets was the wall safe.

"May I see the jewelry first, please?" Chloe asked, shutting the office door and locking it. "I want to verify the contents. I assume you have a manifest for me to sign?"

"Of course." Roger Davis opened the black suede bag and pulled out two inlaid wooden jewelry boxes while the other guard stood at the door. Snapping open the lids revealed the necklace and tiara in one of the boxes and the earrings in the other.

Under the overhead chandelier, the diamond-encrusted jewelry sparkled like a thousand stars, shimmering with such radiance Chloe blinked as if suddenly blinded.

The jewelry boasted dozens of stones, most between two and five carats, with rubies inlaid at intervals, Mercedes's birthstone and favorite color. The red would perfectly match the lip color Chloe had purchased earlier that afternoon. Her cousin would be a starlight miracle tomorrow for her wedding.

"Magnificent," Chloe whispered. "They're stunning."

Roger Davis smiled. "One of my favorite collections as well. We're proud to be a part of Mercedes Romano's nuptials. My father and I hope she'll be pleased."

"This is going to knock her socks off," Chloe joked. "Or the bobby pins from her ringlets. There wasn't any mention of payment in my instructions. Is that something I need to talk to my uncle about?"

"It's already taken care of. Prepaid and insured, of course."

"That's what I assumed." She stared again at the jewels, tempted to reach out and touch the dazzling light, but refrained from getting fingerprints or her skin's oils on the precious stones.

Instead, Chloe spun the numbers on the combination lock on the safe. After she swung the door open, Mr. Davis stepped forward to place the boxes on the second interior shelf.

Chloe shut the steel door and spun the numbers on the lock to secure it. "I've noted that the safe has a high precision combination lock and therefore not as easily broken into."

"Mr. Romano informed us of that when he rented the jewelry. You have your tools for inspecting the gemstones?"

"Yes, everything is set. I even have my phone set to an alarm so I don't get too distracted by wedding cake."

Mr. Davis gave a chuckle, and he and his employee reversed their path to return to the SUV in the driveway.

Chloe waved the black vehicle off, standing on the bottom porch step to watch as they pulled out of the Romano property. When she re-entered the house, Mercedes was already heading for Max Romano's office.

"What are you doing?" Chloe teased.

"I'm going to look at the diamonds, what else?" Mercedes said, jumping up and down on her toes like a girl on Christmas morning.

"Only if I open the safe," Chloe replied.

"What do we have here?" Uncle Max said, coming through the back entrance of the house where he had parked his car in the garage. "You girls are giggling like you're back in high school."

"The jewelry arrived, Uncle Max," Chloe told him. "Your daughter wants to take a peek."

"Let's all take a peek, shall we?" Uncle Max led the way and moved the cabinet to unlock the safe and open the two boxes of diamonds.

Mercedes gasped at the sparkling beauty of a hundred twinkling diamond stones arrayed in twenty-four-carat gold. The pieces were designed in a teardrop formation with scalloped edges that would match her wedding gown.

"Oh, Daddy, they're even more gorgeous than I imagined. You are the best!" She threw her arms around his neck. "I'm going to wear the earrings tonight and the whole set all day tomorrow, of course."

"Of course you will, my darling girl," Max Romano told her. "I think it's time for everyone to get dressed now. I hear we're having a dinner outside to practice walking up and down the aisle."

"Don't wear your high heels, Uncle Max," Chloe joked. "You'll sink into the grass. That's a talent only us women can pull off."

He chuckled. "Chloe, your parents just pulled up in the drive. Mr. Vincent is helping Albert unload the luggage. Mother is with them as well. They timed their flights to coordinate the rental car and travel out here together."

"Mother" was Uncle Max's reference to his own mother, Granny Zaida. Chloe was looking forward to seeing her grandmother. It had been awhile since she'd gone down to Boca Raton for a weekend visit.

"Everything go well with Davis Jewelry?" her uncle asked, lowering his voice.

"Perfect. We're on target for a painless wedding."

"Painless?" he asked. "Ask me that again after I get my daughter's American Express bill."

Chloe laughed at her uncle's comment, but the urgency in her stomach grew. It was time to inspect the diamonds before she met up with her parents and Granny Zaida, despite the fact that they had just arrived from the airport.

She quickly returned to Uncle Max's office, locked the door behind her, and pulled the shades at the window.

Jim Greene had given her a diagram for the three jewelry pieces from his contact at Davis Jewelry, which was going to make creating her final map of the stones so much faster.

Indeed, after spending an hour, Chloe had all of her own personal notes filled out with the details of size and imperfections of each diamond alongside the ones that had come from Jim Greene. Now she could compare the stones against the diagram each time she examined them over the next thirty-six hours.

CHAPTER 12

When Chloe left the office, she rushed across the marble foyer to the drawing room, where her family had gathered and were talking a mile a minute.

She kissed her mother and father and then enveloped her grandmother in a giant hug.

"Who are you, young lady?" Zaida Romano said, holding her at arm's length.

"Aw, Granny."

"It's been so long your face is slipping from my memory bank," her grandmother teased, giving her two big kisses on either side of her face. "You look skinny, my girlie. Don't you ever eat?"

"Donuts every morning for breakfast. Scout's Honor."

"I can attest to that," Diana Romano said, looking pointedly at her daughter. "Cellulite is the bane of sugar. Mark my words, sweetheart."

"Yes, Mom," Chloe said dutifully.

Granny Zaida leaned close, her pure white bouffant brushing softly against Chloe's face. "When you get to be my age, you can eat all the donuts you want. Breakfast, lunch, and dinner."

"I'll remember that. By the way, Granny, you look fabulous. I love your new dress. *C'est très chic* with all those swirly patterns and your red-hot pumps."

Granny Zaida placed a palm to her head and posed like a model showing off. Her son Albert laughed and began lugging suitcases up the stairs, followed by Mr. Vincent. "You can see the rest of my new wardrobe if you ever decided to come back to Florida. You're too busy playing at being a bridesmaid every weekend of your life. How will you ever find a man to date, let alone marry?"

"Ssh!" Chloe hushed her. "My profession is our little secret."

Her grandmother pursed her lips. "I hear you're even sending a bill to your own cousin."

"I am not! Mercedes and I have a special contract together."

"I'll bet you do," Granny said knowingly, although Chloe was 99.9% sure her grandmother knew nothing about her FBI assignment.

Chloe kept telling herself that nothing was going to happen. Inspect the diamonds every few hours, take pictures of Mark Westerfield, and then send her report to Agent Esposito—by certified snail mail, so she'd never have to see the man again.

"When's dinner?" Granny Zaida asked as she headed upstairs to change for the dress rehearsal.

"At 6:00. About two hours."

"I'm going to lie down. Come up in an hour and help me fix my flat hair. We need to have a chat." Granny Zaida gave her granddaughter a particular "look" that Chloe knew well.

"Okey-dokey," Chloe said, attempting a chipper tone but worried that Mercedes would come charging down the stairs any second for the facial that was interrupted by the arrival of the jewelers and now her family. At least her cousin's pillow wrinkles were fading.

The house was filling with people who would be biding their time to sneak around the house with crime on their minds. It was

89

hard knowing that Chloe had to maintain a professional sense of suspicion even with her own family, but the Westerfields were arriving shortly, and she hadn't met any of them except the groom.

First Mercedes and the facial, then Granny—and then get dressed.

"Where have you been, Chloe?" Mercedes demanded when she reached her cousin's suite. "We only have ninety minutes for my facial and dressing."

"Let's dig in, because I've been summoned to Granny's room in an hour."

Mercedes laughed. "Lucky you. Get ready for the third degree."

Chloe put on some soothing music for Mercedes to relax. "A little Pandora's classical stations, including the theme songs from *Pride & Prejudice,* are good for getting into a romantic wedding mood," she told the fidgety bride.

"My nerves are shot," Mercedes complained, scratching at her neck where the mask she'd applied was now drying out. "What if I twist my ankle coming up the grass? What if I stumble and fall flat on my face? What if my dress falls apart? What if I—"

Chloe laid a soothing hand on her arm. "You are going to be the most beautiful and poised bride in the history of weddings. Mark's jaw will drop when you show up at the end of that aisle tomorrow. He's going to think you are the hottest, most gorgeous woman he has ever laid eyes on. He'll sweep you off your feet all over again. That's how your wedding day is going to go down, girl."

"I love your cozy Southern accent, Chloe," Mercedes murmured, her lips barely moving as the purple-colored mask stiffened up.

"Okay, Katey, time to get this hardening face mask off," Chloe said firmly.

She grabbed a couple of warm washcloths and laid them over

Mercedes's cheeks and neck to soften up the mask. Katey rinsed them out and soaked Mercedes's skin a few more times until it was all gone, leaving her skin fresh and glowing.

"I'll be back to see how your dressing is going," Chloe told the bride, turning the doorknob to race down the hall to her grandmother's room. "Don't let her out of your sight, Katey. I don't want any runaway brides."

"You underestimate my love for Mark," Mercedes said, sticking out her tongue while she sank into the chair at her dressing table.

Chloe laughed. "My sophisticated cousin is reverting back to her teen years when we used to argue over which guy on the beach was the hottest—or which Navy Seal running sprints on the sand was the most built."

"I always had the best taste," Mercedes shot back.

Chloe made her way down the hall while unbidden memories scrolled across her eyes like a movie. Memories of Liam Esposito in shorts, working out in the weight room at Quantico. Running miles along the beach, his chiseled chest muscles rippling with each stride.

That man made her crazy. In a thousand different ways.

Her grandmother had already showered and was wearing a white slip. She leaned in close to the dressing mirror, attempting to powder her wrinkles into oblivion. "Do you think I look old?" She frowned.

"What a question. How am I supposed to answer that?"

"I look pretty good for seventy-three, don't you think?"

"You don't look a day past sixty-seven."

"I should swat your behind for that impudent comment."

Chloe giggled. She adored her grandmother. They'd always had fun teasing each other.

"Come sit next to me on that stool while I attempt some makeup."

"Do you want some help?"

Granny Zaida shook her head. "When you get to be this age, it's mostly some foundation, powder, and lipstick. Brows. Don't forget the eyebrows, or you'll look as if you belong in a coffin. Eyeshadow and eyeliner just get lost in my eyelid folds."

"Here." Chloe reached down to retrieve a stray eyebrow pencil. "Can I help you get into your dress and zip you up?"

"Yes, darling, thank you. Now tell me. Who are you dating these days?"

"After training with a bunch of FBI guys, I got turned off by smelly, hairy men."

"That is not true. Give me a hairy, musky man any day."

"Granny!" Chloe said, swatting at her arm. "You are so bad."

"I'll telephone and tell you about my ancient neighbor who picks me up for a ride on his golf cart for a round of nine? He flirts like the devil!"

Chloe laughed again. "Call me any time. Except weekends. I work nearly every single one of them."

Her grandmother picked up a lipstick, twisting the tube up and down thoughtfully. "You should be having fun on your weekends. Meeting men, going out to dinner and concerts."

Chloe clasped her hands together tightly, lifting her eyes as they watched each other in the mirror.

Granny Zaida swiveled around on the dressing table stool. "What is it, my darling girl? I promise I won't tell your mother."

"Pinky promise?"

Her grandmother held up her pinky, and they clasped fingers.

"It's really not anything much," Chloe finally said in a quiet voice. "Ever since Jenna died in the house raid, going out and having fun just feels wrong. I force myself to meet my friends, especially Shelly—you remember Shelly Kelman, she's in New York now with a big fashion designer."

"Of course I remember. I'm not senile yet. Well, good for her in New York, living her dream job."

"We don't see each other too often, but sometimes she comes to Atlanta for a show. Or Charleston, and we try to meet up. But men—they don't fit my schedule. And I just don't seem to have the heart for it. He has to be *really* hot," Chloe joked, trying to lighten the somber mood that had come over the bedroom.

"If he's hot, then you'd better go out with him, or you'll be in hot water with me." Granny Zaida paused. "Your grieving process has taken a long time, darling. Longer than it should at your tender age. Do you want my opinion?"

"What if I say no?" Chloe smiled faintly, not sure if she could take a grim conversation right before the wedding rehearsal dinner.

"If you do, I'll hog-tie you to your chair."

Chloe gave a laugh, fiddling with the combs and brushes strewn across the dressing table.

Her grandmother twisted in her chair and grasped both of Chloe's hands. "I suspect there are issues surrounding Jenna's death that you haven't resolved yet."

"I have issues now?" Chloe responded, but she wasn't fooling anyone. She still had a hard time talking about Jenna. Her dearest friend from childhood, gone. So quickly, so suddenly, and in such a horrible tragedy. "You know I hate that phrase? *Jenna's death.* She was only twenty-eight, Granny. She had her whole life ahead of her. She was good at what we were learning. She was quick and sharp during training—and she adored it."

"I know, darling," her grandmother said gently, eyes shimmering with tears of her own.

"We were so excited about being placed in Baltimore on our first assignment together. It was going so well. We were only nine months out from our training when the world turned upside down."

"It was a total disaster, your father tells me," Granny Zaida said soberly, watching Chloe with a sharp keenness.

"We'd been working a case concerning a drug house and a high profile gang." Chloe let out a ragged breath. "Working tips, getting closer to the players. We finally got the green light to clear the house and arrest everyone. Confiscate the crack and heroin worth a couple hundred grand."

"How did the accident happen, sweetheart?"

"Somehow they got wind of the raid. They were waiting for us. Shots fired, men down. It was chaotic. We were clearing out of there, more local officers arriving on scene—and suddenly the kitchen exploded. They'd set a bomb, hoping to kill us all. If it had gone off sooner—" Chloe choked on the words. "I wouldn't be here either, Granny. Or the rest of my team. Jenna was heading to the hallway when it went off in the kitchen. She was knocked back inside and suffered third-degree burns."

"Good Lord in heaven, have mercy," Granny Zaida whispered, making the sign of the cross.

"She was in the intensive burn unit and fought hard to live, but her injuries were too much. The whole world was dark and numb for so many weeks. Months. When my leave was up and I was supposed to return to work after Jenna's funeral, I resigned. Then I got myself the silliest profession," Chloe said, her eyes swimming with the tears she was determined not to shed. "The one that takes my mind off the past."

Granny Zaida wrapped her arms around Chloe, holding her tight and hard. "I wish I could put a hundred Band-Aids on your broken heart, darling."

"They'd only fall off, I'm afraid. And even if they stopped the bleeding, how do you erase the scars?"

"You don't," Granny said firmly, brushing at the wisps of hair falling across Chloe's face. "You'll learn that scars never go away completely. You just learn to live with them. You keep *on* living despite them. Keep on loving, too. Closing off your heart to future friendships—or love—is worse than the scars. Believe me,

I know from personal experience. I miss your grandpa more than I can express."

Chloe couldn't speak. She nodded shakily, pressing a finger to her lips to stop their trembling.

"Are you still in touch with your old team leader or anyone else from your group?"

Chloe didn't know whether to be fully transparent or not. At the moment, she couldn't talk about Liam at all. "No, I haven't contacted any of them."

Which wasn't a total lie. Agent Esposito had come to her, not the other way around.

Swiping at her face with a quick brush of her hand, Chloe said, "We need to get a move on, Granny. Look at the time."

"Yes, I need to let you get dressed now, dear girl. But if you ever need a shoulder to cry on, I have a pretty empathetic pair, even if they wobble once in a while."

Chloe kissed her grandmother on the cheek. "I do love you, Granny. Thank you."

"Go help Mercedes, and I'll see you in about thirty minutes. I hope there's good food. I'm starving. They didn't feed us on the plane."

"Lunches on airplanes are a thing that went out with pantyhose—except for Mercedes's pair."

Granny Zaida let out a giggle. "Whatever does that mean?"

"Your adorable granddaughter will be secretly wearing pantyhose to keep her tummy smooth and flat."

"My old-fashioned girdle is forty years strong and still keeps it all tucked in."

"I'll pass the tip along." Chloe gave her grandmother a quick kiss and then closed the bedroom door behind her, leaning against it for a moment to center herself.

Talking about Jenna was rough, and something she had avoided for a year. Chloe's eyes swam with unshed tears. Tears that would have to wait. The next thirty hours were all wedding, wedding, wedding. She had to focus on Mercedes and her mission.

Fingers crossed that the diamonds stayed safe and this entire FBI operation was a huge, fat mistake.

An hour later, all the Romano women were dressed in evening attire, hair curled and spritzed, perfume behind the ears, and Chloe was opening the safe with Mercedes dancing on her toes.

Chloe forced her cousin to sit at her father's office desk while she turned the numbers on the combination. Taking out the first box, she opened it while her uncle stood at the door like a guard.

When Mercedes saw the diamonds sparkling like shooting stars under the light of the chandelier, she practically hyperventilated in awe. "Is it okay to touch them?"

Chloe laughed. "Either you put them on or I will." Holding up a mirror, she watched her cousin reverently clip the earrings onto her earlobes.

"I can't believe I'm wearing thousands of dollars of diamonds on each ear."

"You look like Greta Garbo," Chloe told her. "She's one of my favorite old movie stars."

"With my dark hair, I'll pretend I'm Sophia Loren," Mercedes said, holding up a hand to cover her delighted giggles.

Chloe nodded. "Perfect choice."

Uncle Max kissed the top of his daughter's head and put an arm around her. "You look beautiful. Tomorrow you're going to be a vision of loveliness."

"Thank you, Daddy, for making my dreams come true!"

Mercedes tucked her hand in the crook of her father's elbow, and Chloe watched them depart for the backyard while she secured the safe and the office. Glancing out the window that overlooked the back patio, she could see that four tables of ten seats had been set up for the rehearsal dinner.

Earlier, Chloe had briefly met Mark Westerfield's parents, including his older brother, Gary, and his wife Debi, as well as his cousin Brett Sorenson, who would be Mark's best man—and her escort to walk down the aisle.

Brett Sorenson could have been a movie star with his rugged cowboy looks and easygoing smile. She hadn't met such a charming, friendly man like Brett in a long time. Maybe Granny Zaida was right and she should get out more.

It turned out the man lived in Savannah and ran a shipping company—only a hundred and fifty miles from Columbia, South Carolina.

Chloe headed across the open foyer, hoping she could sit next to Brett and chat—casually, she warned herself. After all, she couldn't act like she hadn't had a date in six months. No quiet desperation on her face. Or laughing at his jokes too much.

Putting on her metaphoric undercover bridesmaid hat, she pushed through the front door to take the side path that led straight to the back gardens, locking the front doors so nobody could walk right into the house while they were all in the backyard eating dinner.

It was probably a good idea to do a quick scout around. With the house empty now, the diamonds seemed exceptionally vulnerable—especially if there was someone watching and waiting in the shadows.

Slipping the key into her shoe, Chloe glanced up at the dark sky, where ten thousand stars sparkled across the heavens. A half-moon shone down, silver light falling across the front driveway.

When she glanced along the road, dark trees formed hulking figures. Knowing what to look for, Chloe spotted two officers strolling about the front of the property. Her father's security detail. It was comforting to see them there. Perhaps she could relax and enjoy herself, after all.

The faint sound of conversation, music, and laughter floated on the air as she stepped off the driveway to take the side path.

But suddenly, from out of the darkness, a hand grabbed her arm and Chloe let out a shriek, her heart leaping into her throat.

Spinning around, she stared straight into the eyes of Liam Esposito.

CHAPTER 13

"What in the world are you doing here?" Chloe demanded, shaking off his hand and ignoring the shooting sizzle that ran straight up her neck. "How dare you show up. I'm working a job, remember?"

"How could I forget? I sent you here."

"It *is* my cousin's wedding," she hissed at him. "I'd be here anyway, although I don't appreciate getting strong-armed into this. I'm *not* FBI anymore. Or did you forget that little tidbit? Wait a minute, how did you know where the Romano home was? Isn't that classified information?"

"Oh, Chloe," he said with an amused smile. "Classified is my middle name."

"Go away, Liam," Chloe growled. "You're going to blow my cover for your little FBI 'job.'" She added air quotes with her fingers to make her point, then stared down at his attire. "Why are you wearing evening clothes?"

"All agents wear suits and ties. It's our uniform."

"You know what I'm referring to. That's a top-of-the-line suit, not off the rack. And your black shoes are way too shiny. I can see my face in them."

"You have such a pretty face to reflect back at me."

Chloe slugged his upper arm. "Stop that. I swear my next punch will be to your jaw to send you to the hospital. Remember my right hook?"

Liam chuckled. "I do indeed. I haven't forgotten our sparring days at the gym."

"Personally, I try hard to forget."

"Chloe, come on," Liam said, his voice turning soft. "Give me a chance to talk to you. You've shut me out ever since Jenna—"

"I said *don't*," Chloe warned, swinging her arm up again. Her voice suddenly cracked with emotion when Liam grasped her hand in his and pulled her closer. She swallowed hard as his breath warmed her chilly face.

Their faces were inches apart, and Liam's dark brown eyes stared into Chloe's face before grazing along her profile and mouth, making Chloe squirm, her entire body turning hot. She never dreamed she'd be this close to this man ever again.

"Don't shout anymore, or you'll blow both our covers."

"*What* are you talking about?" Chloe spluttered. "You shouldn't be here. How will I explain who you are?"

"I'm your date for the weekend. Your plus-one. Is that the correct term?"

"My date? Are you serious? I have a date—I walk down the aisle with Mark Westerfield's best man; his cousin, Brett."

"Ah, I see. It's you and the cousin now."

"Oh, please. Your innuendo is ridiculous. I barely met the man two hours ago."

"A lot can happen in two hours," Liam said, his eyes narrowing when he stared along the perimeter of the property.

"Believe me, I know what can happen in less than two hours. I was there. I watched Jenna die—and how you let her."

Chloe's voice broke. She bit down on her lips so hard she tasted blood. She hadn't said the words before now. All the agony that had been eating away at her rose up like a ghostly apparition.

Except her ghosts were much too real. And one was standing right in front of her.

She stalked back toward the front door to collect herself. It was cocktail hour, and she probably wouldn't be missed for a few more minutes. Except that she was getting cold and hungry, and there were heaters surrounding the rehearsal dinner ensemble.

Fighting the tears that pinched at the corners of her eyes, Chloe gulped a breath of air and gripped the porch railing to steady herself.

"Chloe," Liam insisted. "You have it all wrong. I wish you'd talk to me."

"I know what I saw," she said stubbornly, but that day had been a blur of intense fighting, gunshots blasting, and then the horrifying explosion.

She didn't trust her memory as much as she used to, but she *saw* Liam run away from the house. The opposite direction from where Jenna had gone down. There was no mistaking it.

"We used to be friends," Liam said softly. "Hey, you're shaking."

Chloe trembled at the touch of his hand on her arm. During their time at Quantico, she and Liam had actually met for occasional meals. They had taken long walks, talking for hours about everything under the sun—before their director told the team it was against the rules to fraternize. They had jobs to do. Emotions only confused and distracted everyone.

The director had been right. Because ever since the raid, Chloe's feelings for Liam had turned to hatred, despite the hours she'd previously spent dreaming about what his lips would feel like on hers.

She shook her head, banishing the old emotions and attraction once again. "I hate being so close to Quantico. The memories are eating me up inside. I have times where I just feel so hollow."

"You don't have to grieve alone, Chloe."

"Nobody else understands," she said, taking the porch stairs to the front doorway with its beveled glass and inlaid oak panels.

She halted at the door, blocked by Liam. He touched her shoulder with his warm hand, and a firestorm of thrills crackled through her body. "Chloe, you don't know the whole story. What really happened that night, but I do. And when you're ready to talk, I'll be here."

"Don't hold your breath. Meanwhile, I need to go fix my smeared makeup."

Chloe sensed Liam's demeanor go on sudden alert, noting the distant security guards dropping into a crouch when the neighbor's dogs began barking at a single car passing along the road before disappearing.

He bent his head toward her ear, and Chloe closed her eyes at his nearness, willing herself not to swoon into his arms. "The stones arrive okay?"

She nodded, barely able to breathe at his nearness. "They're in the safe. Mercedes is wearing the earrings tonight."

"Huh," Liam grunted. "Not sure it's a good idea to be advertising the jewelry until at least tomorrow."

"Tonight is just family. Tomorrow is going to be even crazier. A hundred people are expected, maybe more."

"'Just family' is not comforting. You do recall who our prime suspect is?"

"Mark is independently wealthy, and he seems like a really nice man. I know, I know, appearances are deceiving. Con men are good at sweet-talking and entrapping. But what could possibly be his motive?"

"That's what we need to figure out. Maybe it's all a false alarm. Perhaps the diamonds will remain intact. I assume they still are."

"It's only been a few hours, but I'm doing another quick inspection now—and again later. As long as I'm going back into the house for a few minutes." Chloe turned to face Liam under the porch lamps. "Do not go to the party in the back gardens without me."

"I plan on being your watch guard in the front hall."

"Suit yourself." Chloe twisted the house key and pushed through the front door, but Liam spoke again.

"By the way, where is the Westerfield family staying this weekend?"

"Right here. The Romano mansion has eight guest rooms, although my parents are at the Hilton at Tyson's Corner because my father needs security."

Liam whistled softly. "That's interesting, especially with Mercedes flaunting those gemstones tonight. That means everybody has access."

"What are you going to do—set up a sleeping bag in the foyer?"

Liam's perfect white teeth glittered under the light. "It's tempting."

"Don't entertain the temptation. I'll kick you out myself."

Chloe left him sitting in a chair in the shadows of the foyer and walked upstairs to her suite. Leaning over the bathroom counter, she fixed the black smudges under her eyes, blew her nose, and grabbed the diamond tool kit from underneath her underwear in the bureau.

Chloe's stomach was in her throat as she descended the stairs and headed through the drawing room to the office again. In less than a minute, Chloe was clicking through the combination numbers.

Her heart pounded inside her skull. The quiet house caused her own movements to sound louder than normal.

Fleetingly, she wished Liam were standing beside her to calm her nerves, but when had Agent Esposito ever been adept at that? He'd caused her more agitation than anyone ever had in her life.

The safe clicked open, and Chloe brought out the box which held the necklace and tiara, laying them out on the desk. She snapped on the table lamp and took out the special UV light as well as the powerful loupe magnifier.

Perching on the edge of the swivel chair, Chloe picked up the bracelet, letting the piece dangle from her fingers while she shone the UV on the diamonds, the loupe eyepiece secured around her forehead.

The light refracted with a thousand glittering sparkles all over the ceiling. The edges were sharp and exact. The stones possessed a particular blue color, indicating their authenticity. Just as they had late that afternoon.

After finishing her inspection, Chloe compared the necklace and tiara to the diagram she had created earlier, including snapping a couple dozen pictures of the stones and the chart with her phone.

When she rose, she realized that thirty minutes had passed. She hadn't inspected each stone for more than a minute or so, but they matched perfectly with the size and identifying flaws she'd jotted down in her notes. After this weekend, she'd have the diamonds memorized.

Quickly, she stuffed the jewelry boxes back into the safe, spun the numbers on the dial, and moved the filing cabinet back over the wall to cover it up.

Slipping out the office door, she returned her tools, and forced herself to take deep, cleansing breaths so she wouldn't appear as if she'd been running.

At the bottom of the stairs, Liam held out an arm. "I'm your plus-one, remember?"

"I'm going to get the third degree from everybody about who you are."

"Tell them I'm an old friend from high school in South Carolina. We used to hang out at the pool halls with our high school gang. Call me Stan Crowley."

Chloe rolled her eyes. "Are you serious? Pool halls? An alias?"

"If anybody in that wedding party is waiting for an opportune time to snatch those diamonds, you can bet they're going to be looking into who I am. Especially since I'm a stranger showing up tonight."

"You could have warned me, and I would have put you on the guest list."

"We'd have only had an argument."

He was correct on that point.

Chloe allowed Liam to lead her down the porch and to the side yard while she gathered her nerves.

That was another reason she'd dropped out of the FBI. She didn't have the steely bravado the job took, but it was nothing compared to what had happened to Jenna, the star of their recruitment group.

When they reached the party, Chloe quickly dropped Liam's arm. "If we're buddies from high school, it doesn't make sense that I'd be hanging on to your arm."

"Touché," Liam said, disappointment in his voice.

"Oh, stop it with the puppy-dog eyes."

"I miss bantering with you, Chloe. I miss *you*," he added under his breath.

Before Chloe could punch him in the arm again, he was accepting a drink from one of the waiters. Ice water. She took a glass of water as well, and the family descended thirty seconds later, swallowing her up.

"Where have you been, darling?" Granny Zaida asked.

"Bathroom run," Chloe whispered. Which wasn't a complete lie.

Her grandmother cocked her head. "Who's your young man?"

Chloe turned to Liam, who was already chatting with her parents like they were old friends. Dad was a pro at this himself. He didn't even flinch when he saw Agent Esposito appear out of the dusk and into the lights of the party.

"Granny, I'd like to introduce Stan Crowley, an old friend from high school."

Her grandmother held Liam's hand in hers and gazed up. "You're a tall drink of water, aren't you, Stan? An old friend? Why haven't I heard of you before?"

"I live up in this area now, so Chloe and I don't see each other very often. Last time was our ten-year high school reunion. And that was almost two years ago now."

"Hm," Granny Zaida said again. For some reason, Liam wasn't fooling her.

Her grandmother pulled Chloe close and whispered, "Thought you hadn't had a date in a year. Where'd you find this hunk?"

"He's Stan. You know, Stan Crowley."

"If you say so." Her grandmother clinked glasses with both of them and went off to find Celine, who was standing on the outskirts of the gathering, arms folded over her chest as if she was freezing.

The heater and fire pits were glowing, and it was toasty warm —as long as you stayed close. The evening had a tinge of chill to the air, but wasn't actually cold. Even so, Granny Zaida, Aunt Aurelia, and her mother were wearing shawls.

The entire yard had been decorated by Suze and her team in the nick of time. The gazebo and swimming pool were a spectacular sight of flowers and shimmering lights, glowing more vibrant as the sun disappeared behind the trees along the curve of the Potomac River.

The dinner tables were laid with fine china and crystal goblets. Idly, Chloe wondered who was assigned to wash dishes. Suze Perry's jurisdiction, not hers, thank goodness.

Mercedes sidled up to Chloe. "Where'd you find that hot man of yours? He's delicious and has such a tall, commanding presence. I thought you said you didn't have a boyfriend."

"I don't. That's Stan. From high school. Back home." Chloe's answers were short and sweet. The less said, the better, she had learned as a professional bridesmaid. At least here she didn't have to answer to her bridesmaid alias, Sadie Chapman.

"Well, grab him, honey. I would in a heartbeat if I wasn't in love with Mark."

Just then, Katey spoke up from behind them. It was obvious she'd been listening in. "If he's not taken, I'll claim him."

Chloe was suddenly possessive, and the realization was perplexing. She wasn't going to hand Liam over to every woman there. "Believe me, you don't want him. Boring. Shoe salesman."

Katey arched an eyebrow. "With those looks, I'll bet he sells a lot of shoes."

Chloe observed that the Romano family and the Westerfields were hovering on opposite sides of the yard. When the groom's family and the bride's family didn't know each other very well, that was typical wedding behavior.

Mercedes grabbed Chloe's hand. "You must get to know Mark's family better. You met earlier, but that was so brief."

She waved a hand across the pool at the Westerfield clan, and Chloe followed—anything not to be in such close proximity to Liam. His presence was unnerving.

"Chloe, this is Mark's brother, Gary, and his wife, Debi," Mercedes said.

Chloe smiled and nodded. "We met briefly when they all arrived at the house earlier. You have beautiful girls," Chloe added, gazing at the shy twin daughters hanging tightly to their mother's hands. "I love their matching dresses."

"Anna and Amy love to dress up," Debi said. "They're so excited about the wedding tomorrow."

"The twins are going to be my flower girls," Mercedes said. "They get to practice during rehearsal with the basket of rose petals. It should be somewhere around here."

"Sitting on the table where the guest book will go tomorrow," Chloe said, her response so automatic from her experience as a paid bridesmaid that she almost laughed out loud.

"You're a lifesaver, Chloe," her cousin told her. "You always have an answer."

"That's what a bridesmaid is for. To do all the behind-the-scenes work and let the bride enjoy her day."

Mercedes winked just as Chloe's brother, Carter, and her sister-in-law, Julia, walked over.

"You're here! I didn't see you earlier," Chloe said, giving them each a big hug.

"Our plane was late, so we just arrived fifteen minutes ago," Julia explained. "The taxi driver knew just how to get here, though."

"It's a long way from St. Louis," Chloe said sympathetically. "Especially when you're about to have the baby. I'll bet you're exhausted."

"Two planes and our connection was delayed. Hence, the late entrance," Carter said. They had moved to St. Louis for his new job as an accountant with a tech company since Carter had a minor in computer software, too.

"As soon as we eat, we'll probably say good night," Julia said, nodding. "Isn't that right, my little missy?" she said, speaking to her protruding belly.

Carter smoothed a hand over his wife's abdomen and then put a protective arm around her. "Six more weeks."

"Do you have a name picked out yet?"

"We're still debating between Megan and Bailey."

"Both are adorable," Chloe said. "You'd better call us as soon as you go into labor."

"I promise," Julia said. "If you promise to babysit sometime."

"When she's old enough to be out of diapers," Chloe said wryly. "And now, excuse me—duty calls. As in, let me check on my bride."

It was just an excuse to walk off her nerves. Besides, Liam kept watching her from wherever he was standing. She couldn't quite catch her breath, and it took all of her self-control not to repeatedly glare at him.

Aunt Aurelia and Uncle Max stood near the guest book table, which was currently empty except for the basket of flower petals. Aurelia Romano picked up a small bell, which she rang while Uncle Max raised a hand to get everyone's attention.

"My wife Aurelia and I would like to welcome everyone to our home on this lovely evening. We're so happy to see our two families meet at last to celebrate Mercedes and Mark as they take their vows and begin their life together. We'll rehearse the ceremony after dinner. At the moment, choose any seat you'd like, and enjoy the meal."

Gazing at the families milling around, the hired waiters already serving salads and beverages, Chloe had a moment of panic. So many people to keep track of and to watch. The FBI suspected someone here was planning to steal more than half a million dollars in jewels. It was preposterous. Insane.

She tried to count how many people actually knew where the jewels were located in the house. Her uncle, her cousin, Liam, her father, and herself. None of them had any motive to steal a cache of diamonds. How did someone liquidate diamonds, anyway? She supposed the only way to do so was by taking apart each stone and selling them to a fence who would find a buyer masquerading as a distributor.

Nobody could get into that safe. But did Chloe really know that? If it was true that Mark had means and motive, Sunday was going to be a horrible, ugly day for Mercedes when Mark disappeared, the police were called, and her cousin demanded an annulment. The idea of it made her stomach turn sour.

Chloe had no idea if the groom was the potential thief, but if he was, what could she do about it—and was there any chance of salvaging her cousin's marriage?

Probably not. If there was a plan afoot, it was already in motion, which made Chloe want to bang her head against a wall.

Having Liam here was both comforting and exasperating. The man had a knack for distracting her, which often left her unable to do her job very well.

CHAPTER 14

A few minutes later, Chloe found herself seated by Brett Sorenson, the groom's cousin whom she'd been eyeing from afar. She was still thinking about that interesting jump in her stomach when they shook hands.

Was he attracted to her? Did he have a girlfriend? She had surreptitiously glanced at his ring finger and found that it was bare.

"Hello, Chloe," Brett said, his deep voice running like smooth, hot liquid down her neck. "I've been hoping to get to know you better."

"How's your room in the house? Everything satisfactory?"

"I'm actually staying at the Hilton in town."

"You are? There's plenty of room here. Besides, you're family."

"I didn't want to intrude. You have a lot of true-blue blood family here, and with the wedding on-site, I thought it best to lessen the crazy. Besides, the hotel is only five minutes away."

"That's very thoughtful, but totally unnecessary. What if I need someone to lift heavy things?"

Brett laughed. "You have a lot of capable brothers and hired reception hands. Plus, I spied that you brought along a date your-self, but I think I kicked him out of his seat."

"Nope, I'm right here," Liam said, sitting down across the table.

Chloe gave her old partner a tight smile, hoping it didn't look like a grimace in front of everyone else. Really? Why did Liam have to sit only a foot away so she couldn't flirt with Brett? The first available man she'd met in ages.

Brett's blond hair was streaked by the sun. Like a transplant straight from California. What was it about west coast men that were ruggedly handsome with easygoing personalities?

Chloe had long ago determined that she could live in California and be very happy there. Santa Barbara for a summer cottage. San Francisco so she could ride the cable cars while the wind blew through her hair. All she needed to do was make a million dollars. Or maybe two or three. California was expensive, just like D.C.

Liam gave her a strange look, quirking his eyebrows up. Chloe wondered if she was speaking her thoughts out loud. Her face felt hot, and she was glad that the dark evening could hide the red that was probably racing up her neck.

"Brett, meet Stan Crowley," she said tightly, getting the awkward introductions over with as fast as possible. "Stan, Brett Sorenson. Did I hear you say earlier that you live in Savannah, Brett?" Chloe asked, lifting a bite of her cranberry salad with vinaigrette dressing to her lips and trying to chew. The worry gnawing at her stomach was making her lose her appetite. "How long have you lived there?"

"About two years. A transplant from D.C. I grew up on the same block as Mark and Gary."

"I'll bet you were a bunch of wild boys terrorizing your mothers."

From the next table, Mrs. Westerfield leaned over. "You are absolutely right, Chloe. I could never keep enough cookies in the freezer when they were home all summer constructing forts, riding bikes, and shooting off firecrackers."

Brett sipped at his drink. "You make us sound like heathens."

"If the name fits, wear it proudly," his aunt said with a smile, returning to her meal.

Soft music was playing in the background, and Chloe saw that Suze Perry had arranged for a DJ to entertain them with a variety of love songs from the last decade with a little Neil Diamond and Frank Sinatra thrown in for the older generations, although he was taking requests, too.

"Savannah is one of my favorite cities. Do you just love living there?" Chloe asked Brett.

"It's so completely different from the Beltway. Like a breath of fresh air—even though it's got an old history. I'm kind of a history buff, especially about the antebellum and Civil War Era. I guess you could say I'm boring because I spend at least one weekend a month touring old houses and monuments."

"That's not boring at all. When you live in the South, a person can't help being surrounded by the past. I grew up with a mother who took me to the old plantations all throughout Mississippi and Louisiana on long weekends."

Liam didn't speak, just shoveled his salad into his mouth and watched while she and Brett chatted. She wanted to yell at him to go away and find somebody else to bother. But she couldn't, since he was her "date."

"Have you stayed on the historic squares of Savannah?" Brett asked.

"A few times. I adore the Bonaventure Cemetery, too. It's so spooky and mysterious."

"I always feel like I've stepped back in time when I wander around there," Brett agreed.

"I often tell myself to stay on the lookout for wandering ghosts. Isn't that silly?"

Brett gave her a warm smile, which sent Chloe's heart

skyrocketing. Or was that the ice water she was gulping down? "Not silly at all. You must be a mind reader. We're two of a kind."

"Accused and convicted," Chloe said. "Earlier today, somebody mentioned that you're in the shipping business."

"My father's company relocated me there. Savannah is a smaller port than, say, Charleston, but busy. We send all kinds of goods overseas. Mostly wood products and steel. I feel like a goofy kid drooling when the naval ships come in. And the container ships are massive. Jaw-dropping, in fact. You should visit again and spend a day at the port ship-watching."

Chloe wondered if that was an official invitation to go visit *him*, too. She'd wait and see how the weekend turned out.

Meanwhile, the main course was served and eaten, with dessert a light lemon cheesecake. By the time Chloe was finished, she'd only eaten about half of every course and felt weighed down by the weekend. Brett was a lifesaver, distracting her from the FBI job at least for a little while. Their chatting grew friendlier over the hour.

Meanwhile, Liam had a severe look on his face. Pursed lips. Jaw twitching. Eating everything in sight as though he'd been fasting for a week.

Chloe didn't care what Liam thought about her friendly conversation with Brett, but underneath, the whole evening bothered her. *Why* it bothered her didn't make a bit of sense.

She had a history with Agent Esposito that was unforgivable. He should never have shown up here tonight. She was handling the assignment, there was no sign of a thief, the wedding was going off without a hitch, and even if there was a master locksmith on the premises, it would take a few hours to decode the combination to Uncle Max's safe.

The FBI were paranoid for no reason, or Agent Esposito was up to some shenanigans of his own.

"Time for rehearsal," Suze Perry said, clapping her hands for attention. "If you're not in the wedding party proper, please take a seat on the folding chairs on either side of the aisle and play the part of the audience. Mr. Westerfield, will you please stand in place of the minister?"

The groom's father nodded while chairs were pushed back. The chatter increased as everyone moved from the dinner tables to the wedding ceremony location. The waitstaff went into action, removing the dessert plates.

When Mercedes walked past Chloe, she had a pale expression on her face. "Are you all right?" she asked her cousin.

"I want to scream a little, Chloe," she admitted. "Its like we're all play-acting, but I know it's real. In less than twenty-four hours, I'll be Mrs. Mark Westerfield. For real. Forever. Am I ready for this?"

"That's good," Chloe assured her. "The man of your dreams will be all yours for the rest of your life tomorrow evening."

"I'm shaking with nerves."

"We'll jump on the bed and yell when we get back to the house."

Mercedes gave a weak smile. "The walls probably aren't soundproof."

"Do you have a trampoline in the vicinity?"

She mustered a half-smile. "Daddy put that away years ago."

Chloe took Mercedes's cold, clammy hands in her own and rubbed them. "Deep breaths. It's going to be fine. Spectacular and wonderful and dreamy."

"It *is* beautiful, isn't it?"

"Groom up here at the top next to the minister," Suze called out, moving like a cannonball around the yard to line everyone up in their places. "Bride, bridesmaid, best man, flower children, Mr. Romano—all down the slope to await the music."

The DJ put on the romantic background music that would play while guests arrived and took their seats. When everyone was ready to practice walking up the aisle, the music changed to Pachelbel's Canon.

"Tomorrow it will be performed live by a string quartet," Chloe whispered to Brett as she took his arm to walk up the aisle. "That will be beautiful."

Aunt Aurelia shoved a small handful of flowers into her hands and another one from the vases off the dinner tables into her daughter's hands to practice walking with them. Tomorrow, the real bouquets would be delivered, along with centerpieces, boutonnières, and fresh water lilies for the pool.

Brett looked down at Chloe and smiled. She swore her heart fluttered. Some days she was desperately lonely—especially after Jenna's tragic death—and wished she could find the right guy, and other days she was so desperately busy, she didn't think she had time for a man in her life at all.

A trip to Savannah could be interesting, though.

"Bridesmaid and best man!" Suze yelled out. "What are you doing? Did you hear the music? It's time to *walk*!"

"Oh! That's us," Chloe said, startled away from her daydreaming.

Brett placed a hand on top of hers and tucked her fingers into the crook of his arm. They began to walk in time to the music up the grassy aisle toward the canopy dais where Mr. Westerfield was standing.

He wore a stiff smile on his face as if unsure what he was supposed to do. Or worried that Suze was going to ask him to recite the wedding vows without notes or a Bible in hand.

The idea made Chloe smile, and Suze yelled, "No grinning. Pleasant smiles. And take your hand off the bridesmaid's, Mr. Best Man. It's too intimate. Let her take your arm while you crook it just so, your free arm at your side. Like this." Suze demonstrated, and the watching family members tittered with laughter.

"Hey, it's my first wedding," Brett said.

"Hopefully not your last," Mark called out, hooting at his cousin.

"Enough with the male testosterone," Suze said, her voice so stern the entire company went silent. "Mr. DJ, please increase the music's volume. With a rustling audience and birds chirping in the trees tomorrow, we may not be able to enjoy the ambience of it all. Let alone get our steps in sync."

The DJ waggled a button on his system, checking the speakers. Pachelbel soared forth again, and before she knew it, Chloe and Brett were at the dais. He clenched his arm just before breaking her grip, and Chloe could feel his biceps flexing.

Wow, it had been a long time since she'd felt a man's muscles. She wanted more of that, but Brett was already turning to stand by Mark while she went to the other side of the "minister"—Mr. Westerfield.

"Flower children!" Suze snapped with a gasp of remembrance. "Where are they?"

"Asleep, I'm afraid," Debi Westerfield said, and then lifted her shoulders in a shrug. "Nope, waking up now." She took her two daughters by the hand and scurried them around the chairs to the end of the aisle.

Placing a basket of rose petals in each of their hands, their mother tried to demonstrate what they were supposed to do, but the twins just giggled and began throwing the petals like confetti into the air.

Suze tapped her foot. "Mrs. Mommy, please show the flower girls the proper etiquette."

Debi Westerfield bit her lips and escorted Amy and Anna up the aisle while demonstrating how to nicely toss their petals along the bridal path, which allowed them to flutter softly to the lawn.

"Practice that tomorrow morning, please," Suze said. "Now for the bride and her father! Hold your hand lightly on his arm, Mercedes. Head up, back straight, smile as you walk down the aisle. You're headed for the groom, and you should look enchanted and in love."

"That's not hard to do," someone in the audience called out. Chloe swore it was Granny Zaida and bit at her lip to keep from laughing.

She watched Mercedes walk slowly up the aisle on Uncle Max's arm and sighed at how beautiful her cousin was in her evening gown and the diamond earrings swaying against her neck, dark hair flowing over her shoulders in perfect waves.

Tomorrow, Mercedes was going to sparkle and shine brighter than all those carats of diamonds around her neck.

All of a sudden, Mercedes let out a cry and stopped. "My feet are stuck!"

Chloe raced forward. "Are you okay? What's going on?" She kneeled down on the grass and lifted Mercedes's hem. Sure enough, her spiked heels had sunk into the grass and wouldn't lift up again. "Try to yank once more," she told her.

Mercedes tugged at her foot, but they weren't budging. Then, all at once, one foot shot up and then the other—just as the first one sank again.

"It's much too soft for these shoes, I'm afraid, Mercedes."

"But I adore my new shoes," her cousin said with a whimper. "How did you manage not to get stuck?"

Chloe glanced at her feet tucked under her. "Wedge heels. Not stilettos."

"My legs look better in stilettos," Mercedes said.

"Nobody will see your legs in your long dress," Chloe tried to assure her.

"But they'll see my shoes, especially during the dancing."

"You've got to use other shoes or else go barefoot."

"Trade me," Mercedes said. "I'll use yours. At least for now. We wear the same size."

"We do?"

Mercedes turned a slight shade of pink, but didn't answer.

"Okay, I'll wear your shoes tonight." After all, she was the professional bridesmaid, here to serve the bride for her once-in-a-lifetime day.

Bending over, she took off her wedged dress shoes, stuffed the hidden key that had slipped into the toe of the shoe down her bra, and then handed the pair over to her cousin. When Mercedes slipped them on, Chloe noted, "How about that? They fit perfectly."

"I told you they would."

"Okay, but that was pretty random."

Looking contrite, Mercedes admitted, "At our last family reunion, I sort of borrowed your shoes a couple of times."

A giggle rose up Chloe's throat. "Oh, Mercedes, I think I like you more all the time. And now I'll try not to fall over in your stilettos."

Suze clapped her hands. "Music from the top. Let's do this all over again. Everyone back to your places."

The second time went much more smoothly. Chloe held lightly on to Brett's arm, enjoying the texture of his suit coat and the feel of his hard muscles while he crooked his arm just so as per instructions.

She smiled when the twin girls tossed their rose petals, their chubby cheeks grinning from ear to ear, and then Mercedes was radiant once more when her father walked her up the aisle.

"I think we have the music timed correctly now," Suze declared after three trial runs. "The last run-through was perfect. Does anyone have any questions about when you come in or how fast to walk?"

Everybody was silent, eager to move on with the evening.

"The bridal party will wait down the hill by the river at exactly five minutes before the hour so as not to spoil the surprise of all the lovely gowns and suits and, of course, the magnificent wedding dress." Suze assumed a professional air. "We're also going to have a string quartet playing, and they'll be seated on the same side of the yard, which will help hide the view of the bridal party getting into position."

It seemed a little overkill, but Chloe just tried to enjoy the cool grass blades between her toes after so many hours running around like a maniac.

A few of the males, Liam included, began to saunter toward the dessert table, where leftover cheesecake had been laid out. The DJ was back to playing love ballads.

"I'm taking the girls up to bed now," Debi announced to no one in particular. "It's been a long day." Her husband, Gary, was already carrying one of them to the back door of the house, fast asleep on his shoulder.

Granny Zaida wobbled to her feet. "What time is it? I've lost track. I don't use a cane yet, but this is one time I wish I had one to lean on."

"Granny, I'll help you," Celine said. Chloe heard her cousin add, "I am so done with this and we still have all day tomorrow. Who knew weddings were such a production? If I ever get married, I'm eloping to Vegas."

"Your granddad and I got married before the judge more than fifty years ago. That was back during the war when young people didn't want to wait or plan a big wedding. Or wait until their love never returned from Vietnam."

"Oh, Granny," Celine murmured. "That's depressing."

"Fact of life, my dear. Goodness, these old bones are creaking up a storm tonight. Can you make sure I have my Bengay unpacked? I'm sure I brought it."

"Families, huh?" said a male voice in Chloe's ear. She turned to see Brett, who was eavesdropping on all the various little conversations.

"Families are adorable," Chloe replied, suddenly nostalgic. This was the first family wedding she'd ever been a bridesmaid for. "I see a lot of quirky families in my line of—while I've been a bridesmaid."

Brett gave a laugh. "How many times have you been a bridesmaid?"

"Oh, about seventeen—I mean seven. Feels like seventeen," she added quickly.

"You're joking."

She shook her head. "Nope."

"You sure have a lot of friends."

Chloe laughed, too. "I guess I do."

"Should I call you the maid of honor if I'm the best man?"

"Call me anything you'd like," Chloe said, feeling reckless. "What would you like, Best Man?"

From the corner of her eye she caught Liam watching. The scowl on his face took her aback. She had no idea Liam was the jealous type. He was so self-assured and confident. So utterly self-contained.

"Dance with me," Brett suggested, catching her hand to bring her close. Chloe's breath caught. "I like a good ballad and two-step, and the DJ hasn't closed up shop yet."

"The family's busy eating leftovers."

It was true. Mark and Mercedes, Aunt Aurelia and Uncle Max, Mark's parents, the Westerfields, Carter and Julia, as well as her own parents were sitting around one of the tables closest to the house, yacking away while sipping wine. Eating chips and salsa. She could see Celine and Granny Zaida making their way up the patio steps to the back door. Interior house lights glowed softly. It was a cozy, intimate sight, as if all was right in the world.

Chloe turned to Brett, raising a flirtatious eyebrow. She felt daring, ready to throw her hat in the ring. "You're lucky, Best Man. After all these weddings I've attended, I've become a pretty good dancer."

"I took lessons once a long time ago. Briefly. But it gets me by so I don't step on a girl's toes or drop my partner."

"Not dropping your partner is good. Very good."

Brett Sorenson pulled her in tighter, pressing her hand

against his chest and resting his cheek against hers in a romantic dance pose. They swayed to the music while moving along the stone pavings of the wide patio, circling sofas and patio chairs.

While Brett hummed to the music, Chloe closed her eyes, enjoying the moment—and tried to block out Liam. She wished he'd give up and go back to his hotel.

Slitting her eyes, she saw that he'd finally sat down next to her brother Carter with a plate of snacks. At last he'd stopped staring at her. Every single instance their eyes locked together, Chloe swore she was going to stop breathing. He'd cursed her somehow.

She wished she could put a magic spell on her brain to erase him from her memories. She wanted to stop feeling confused, excited, resentful, and allured by the man she wanted to continue hating.

Brett twirled her under his arm and Chloe threw her head back, enjoying the languid feeling of her body, her hand knitted tight with Brett's while they whirled around the patio.

Just when Chloe thought Brett would pull her back in close to murmur sweet nothings into her ear, the lights of the entire Romano mansion and grounds suddenly shut off.

The yard was a blaze of lights one moment, pitch black the next. Even the moon had disappeared behind a bank of clouds.

Thrown off balance by the unexpected darkness, Chloe tried to hold on to Brett, but a female voice shrieked in fright, startling her further.

Chloe's fingers slipped through Brett's, and instantly she was stumbling backward on the edge of the patio, falling—and falling —despite her toes trying to grip the wobbly stiletto high heels against the rough brick walkway, but nothing worked. She was going down.

She was going to crack her head on the sidewalk. She was going to get a concussion.

Chloe's arms flailed through empty air in horror, her legs

sliding out from under her—and unable to see a single thing in the pitch black darkness of the surrounding world. Now she was the one screaming.

An instant later, she fell backwards into the swimming pool with the biggest splash she'd made since her last cannonball at eleven years old.

CHAPTER 15

*T*he echoing sound of the splash was muffled in her own ears, because Chloe dropped to the bottom of the swimming pool. Like a stone.

Falling in the deep end of the swimming pool while it was pitch black was terrifying. She didn't know which direction was up or down. She hadn't taken any extra breath before she fell since she hadn't realized they'd been dancing so close to the swimming pool. She'd been expecting to fall on the pavings or the lawn, or crash into the chairs

Chloe's hands clawed at her dress which was floating upward, sticking to her face, and even getting sucked into her mouth. The evening gown was so heavy, her panic level soared. When her backside hit the bottom of the pool, Chloe pulled her arms down to try to push herself back toward the surface.

Where were the freaking house lights? Why hadn't the power come back on?

Her throat burned. Her nose was on fire. She was out of air. Strange dots floated in front of her eyes. She was drowning right in front of a backyard full of her own family. Where was everybody?

Suddenly she heard splashes. At last, someone was coming to help her claw her way through the yards of material that was impeding her ability to kick to the top of the pool. All air was gone, but she tried not to panic.

The surface of the pool should have been only five or six feet above, but she kept kicking her feet and flailing her arms, and getting nowhere.

Great waves of dense, heavy water moved around her. Someone was coming. Maybe several someones, but she couldn't hear anything that she could discern specifically. It was like she'd gone deaf.

A hand reached out to hers and she clawed at it in desperation. Just as quickly, the hand pushed her back down and she hit the bottom again, her toes grazing off the slippery decorative pool tile. Chloe cursed and took in a mouthful of water. What were they doing? Rescuing her or trying to drown her?

Chloe could feel herself passing out, her eyes bulging, her throat constricting.

The feeling of going unconscious had happened once during her FBI training when she was in a headlock practicing fighting moves. It was the most unpleasant experience of her life. That suffocating panicky feeling. Powerless to remain conscious.

For what felt like an eternity of silence and darkness, Chloe couldn't move or swim. As though she'd lost all control of her own body. Weighted down by her dress, lack of air, and most of all lack of any strength.

Just before unconsciousness hit, strong arms were suddenly yanking her upward, pushing her higher, and her face finally broke the pool's surface. She heard herself choking, as if her windpipe had been cut off from the oxygen surrounding her.

"I've got you," a male voice said, but her ears were so plugged with water she couldn't tell who it was. "I've got you."

Was it Brett? He would have been the closest to rescue her. Chloe closed her eyes. They were burning horribly, and she couldn't see properly. She pressed her face against Brett's chest, so grateful for air. For life.

Those biceps she'd been admiring carried her up the pool steps and then gently laid her on the patio. "Get towels!" he shouted. "Get an ambulance!"

Chloe tried to speak, but nothing came out. She tried to open her eyes, but she couldn't. It was the strangest thing. She could hear her mother crying, her brother speaking urgently into a phone. Commotion everywhere in the backyard.

It was so dark. So very dark. Chloe just wanted to go to sleep. She didn't even feel cold any longer, although she should have been freezing lying flat on her back on an October night in a waterlogged evening dress.

All of a sudden, someone started to kiss her, placing soft, warm lips around hers. No, they weren't kissing her. The person was *breathing* into her mouth. Then they were rolling her onto her side and pounding her back. That *hurt*.

Water dribbled out of her mouth. Oh, dear Lord in heaven, she was going to vomit. Everything hurt. Her chest, her stomach, her throat, even her eyes burned as if they were on fire.

Chloe's eyes fluttered. She wanted to see the light. She wanted to see Brett and thank him for saving her. She wanted to hug her mother. She wanted to tell her father how much she loved him. She didn't want to die.

When Chloe finally became coherent, the lights were back on in the yard. The silhouettes of a dozen people surrounded her. "Mom?" she croaked.

"Oh, darling, you're alive!" her mother murmured, kissing her forehead, smoothing slimy strands of her hair away from her face. "We thought—oh, Chloe, when we saw you at the bottom of the pool, my heart split into pieces."

"I hurt," Chloe managed to say past her raw throat. Who knew that a benign substance like water could hurt so badly?

The strong-armed male who had carried her out of the pool

and let her choke all over him bent closer, taking her pulse, examining her neck. His head blocked out the bright beam of a flashlight. Maybe the house lights weren't back on like she had first assumed.

Wait, the man who was looking down at her was Liam Esposito. Liam? No, it had to be Brett. She'd been dancing with him.

She tried to shake her head, to speak, but Liam whispered, "Shush, shush, don't try to talk. An ambulance is on its way."

Chloe flopped an arm over, trying to push herself up into a sitting position. Her limbs felt like jelly, almost spongy. It was the strangest feeling. "Where's—" she tried to ask, but her thoughts were incoherent. Her eyes finally focused on Liam. "How did you get here?"

"I've been here all the time," he said softly. "Where do you hurt?"

Chloe's eyes watered up again. "I feel—really awful."

She began to cough, and Liam helped her onto her side so she wouldn't choke. Her mother wiped her mouth and face with a clean cloth.

Sirens began to wail in the distance. "I don't need an ambulance."

"You're going to get checked out," Liam told her. "No arguing with me."

"Don't boss me around," she said weakly. "You're not even a true Italian—so there." It was one of those saucy taunts they used to fling at each other during their flirting days at Quantico when they were trying to outdo each other on the shooting range.

"What you're saying is that nothing has changed even though I saved you from certain death. Us Sicilians are still lower-class?" he asked with a grin.

"Don't you know your history?" she croaked like a toad.

Liam glanced up at Governor Romano. "I think she's coming back to us."

"Chloe was always my little spitfire," her dad said. He

squeezed her hand between his big warm ones while her mother lay a blanket over her.

Chloe's voice was hoarse. Breathing was hard, too. Her chest was on fire. She tried to sit up again, but her hands fell limply to her sides. The weakness alarmed her. Tentatively, she touched Liam's arm. He was drenched, too.

"A few of us jumped in after you," he said softly.

That made Chloe think of her dancing partner. The memory of twirling around the patio returned, and then the mansion power blackout and falling into the pool. "Brett?"

"I'm right here, Chloe," he said from somewhere behind her.

A second later, Brett came into view under the light of the flashlights that her mother and aunt were holding.

Liam said, "Brett jumped in and your brother, too."

"Carter won swimming medals in high school," Chloe said, even though it was completely irrelevant. Her brain wires were crossed. She wasn't making any sense.

With gentle fingers, Liam brushed a soft hand against her face. "Your temperature is a little low, but that may just be the cool night coupled with wet clothes. Boy, you're heavy when you're wet," he added impertinently.

Chloe wanted to punch him in the shoulder, but she had no strength.

"We were dancing," she said to Brett, trying to make sense of what had happened.

"The blackout was so sudden," he said. "Before I knew it, you had slipped out of my grasp. All I heard was a splash but I couldn't see where you were. Your uncle ran for flashlights, but it took a few minutes to get them here. We kept screaming your name, and that's when we realized you must be under the water, and the guys started jumping in after you."

Chloe squeezed her eyes shut, reliving the panic, her lungs closing in on her. Moments away from drowning. She wouldn't wish that desperate, horrible feeling on her worst enemy. "I was fighting so hard—somebody pushed me back down—"

"You were unconscious when we found you, Chloe," Liam said. "Limp on the bottom of the pool."

She shook her head. "No, I remember fighting so hard ..." Tears leaked from her eyes and Liam wiped them away with his fingers. Why was he being so attentive when she'd told him so often that she hated him?

Brett was the one she'd been brazenly flirting with all during dinner before going off to dance by themselves.

"You're going to be fine, but the doctors will want to make sure you don't have a concussion, that your lungs don't have water in them, and your temperature returns to normal."

"You sound like a doctor," she told Liam in her scratchy voice.

Worry flickered across his eyes. "You're shaking like a leaf. Maybe hypothermic."

"You're in shock," her brother spoke up, looming behind her father. "You scared the living daylights out of us. Don't ever do that again."

"Aye, aye," she said, trying to smile, but the whole experience was overwhelming her.

A moment later, the paramedics were there. Male and female voices taking her vitals, making sure she had no broken bones. They lifted her onto a stretcher and before Chloe knew it, she was being loaded into the ambulance, the red lights whirling bright and hard in the darkness.

"Where are the blasted lights?" she heard Uncle Max say to her father. "I've got Mr. Vincent and my head gardener in the garage with the breaker box. Already called the power company, and they say that it's just our house. The problem isn't from the local power pole, but they're sending a truck anyway to check it out."

The ambulance doors slammed shut, and Chloe closed her

eyes. For the first time since she was a kid, she wanted her mother.

CHAPTER 16

*T*he hospital was lit up like a Christmas tree. After the frightening darkness of the Romano property, it was a relief to feel part of civilization again, even as she was being zoomed straight to the Emergency Entrance.

"I'm taking this one straight back," her paramedic said, a woman wearing the name of Betsy on her name-tag. One of the hospital nurses asked for Chloe's status, and Betsy said, "Drowning. Family pool. She's conscious now, had a trained male in CPR in attendance. Temperature a little low, but rising."

"She's lucky," the nurse said. Chloe tried to catch her name-tag, but her eyes were blurry. "We'll need X-rays, perhaps a CT scan."

Chloe was transferred to a gurney and taken to a booth, where the nurse stripped off her evening gown and quickly dressed her in a cotton hospital gown, then piled heated blankets on top of her. "Chloe, I'm Serena, and I'm going to be your nurse tonight. Can you hear me?"

"Yes," she whispered, watching another nurse prepare an IV, opening sterile packages of needles and gauze, a frown of concentration on her face.

"How are you feeling?" Serena asked.

"Woozy. Cold. My throat hurts."

"That's to be expected, honey, but you're in great shape for being under the water for so long. The paramedic driver radioed in that you were coming in and said that you were under the water for nearly three minutes."

"I used to practice holding my breath."

"We're guessing you were unconscious for possibly up to a minute or so."

"I threw up a couple of times." For some reason, Chloe's responses sounded like she was a kid again.

"The water coming up naturally is a good sign. As long as you didn't choke."

"Liam made sure I didn't. Choke, that is. He turned me over. I think he gave me mouth-to mouth." Chloe felt herself blushing. "That sort of hurt, too."

Serena smiled. "That's what everybody says—if they remember it at all. You were probably coming back to consciousness at the time."

"I don't remember being unconscious."

Serena stuck three pillows under Chloe's head to raise her to a better sitting position in case she choked again on any water remaining in her stomach. Then she took her temperature. "Ninety-seven degrees, not too bad. A little low, perhaps. The blankets good? Are you warm enough?"

Chloe nodded. The warm blankets felt wonderful, like she was sitting by a toasty fire. The nurse on her right finished attaching the IV while Chloe looked away. She could never watch needles piercing her skin.

After hooking the IV bag on the drip stand, Serena put her stethoscope to Chloe's chest, listening with focused concentration. "Can you try to cough so I can hear if there's still water in your lungs?"

Chloe obliged, but it hurt. A second later terrible pain

wracked her lungs, and she coughed and coughed. Water dribbled out between her lips, and she grabbed for a wad of tissues. "Oh my gosh, that was awful."

"I'm glad it's coming up naturally, but I think we should do an X-ray to be on the safe side. I need to get a doctor's order. Dr. Abbott will be in shortly to check you out. He's in the next room. He just got done with his residency, so he looks like a baby." Serena winked and Chloe gave a weak smile.

At that moment, her mother and father parted the curtains. "Oh, darling, there you are," Diana Romano said. She gave Chloe a gentle hug and smoothed the damp hair off her forehead to gaze into her face. "You're looking better already."

Her father took her hand and kissed the back of it. "How are you feeling, sweetheart?"

"X-rays coming up, I think. But I'm better than I was. My sight and hearing are beginning to clear, but it's very strange."

"All that water," her mother said, biting at pale lips, her lipstick eaten off.

"What time is it?"

"Going on midnight now," Governor Romano said.

"I just want some aspirin and my pillow," Chloe said. "How's Mercedes? I'm letting her down." Most importantly, she wasn't there to keep watch over the diamonds in the safe. Uncle Max had probably already returned the earrings to the safe. At least he was there keeping watch. And Liam, too. If he hadn't already left for his hotel.

"Mercedes is perfectly fine now that Mark is with her. He has a calming influence, which is nice to see. Everybody is just worried about you and send their love and prayers for a speedy recovery. It was just a terrible accident."

"Did they ever figure out what was wrong with the power at the house?"

"Not yet, hopefully soon. Right now, there are candles and oil lamps all over the place so folks can get around the house."

A great weariness overtook her, and Chloe lay back against the pillows just as Dr. Abbott walked through the door.

"Hello, young lady. I hear you came straight from a wedding. Where's your groom?"

"I'm not getting married, I'm just the bridesmaid."

"We're going to wheel you down to X-ray to get more information on what's happening with your lungs so you don't get pneumonia."

"I hadn't even thought about that," Diana Romano said, a note of concern in her voice.

"How much does your chest hurt?" the doctor asked.

"A lot before I came in, but it's getting better."

"Good, good, that's what we want to see. Improvement every hour. Coughing very much?"

"Only a little now."

"I hear you had a certified person there who performed CPR, is that right?"

Chloe nodded, lifting a finger to run it across her lips when she remembered Liam's mouth on hers. At first, when she returned to consciousness, she had thought he was kissing her and pushed him away. How brazen of him. Had she really been unconscious? The idea of losing minutes of her life was so bizarre.

She tried to imagine the three of them, Liam, Carter, and Brett, all jumping into the pool to rescue her. Obviously, Liam got to her first. She had no clue as to where he'd been when she was dancing with Brett. She'd been so focused on the best man and their flirtatious banter.

Liam's instincts as an FBI agent must have automatically kicked in. The lights had gone out, he heard the splash, and acted instinctively. Now that she was more coherent and out of her wet clothes, she remembered that his tie had been torn off, his suit coat thrown to the ground. She pictured him diving in, lifting her into his arms, kicking back to the surface, and then laying her at the edge of the pool steps.

She must be the weirdest girl in the world to be thinking about Liam's mouth on hers while she nearly died. She had despised Liam Esposito for the misery he'd caused her the last year, and yet he'd immediately jumped into a dark pool to save her, risking his own safety.

He'd insisted there was more to the story of Jenna's death than she'd assumed, but she'd refused to listen to him. What other truths could there possibly be? He'd deserted Jenna when she was unconscious, leaving her to die in that horrible, evil house amid the debris of a bomb.

Once more Chloe cursed Agent Esposito and banished him from her thoughts. *She* wouldn't succumb to any Nightingale Effect toward Liam.

Dr. Abbott returned, clipboard in hand. "We're going to take your daughter to X-ray now, Mr. and Mrs. Romano. Then we're going to settle her into a room, take her vitals every two hours, and monitor the chest pain and cough. Then we'll discuss where she is in the morning and talk about when she can be released."

Worry creased her mother's face. "Should I stay with you tonight, darling?"

Chloe weakly shook her head. "Go home, Mom. I'm exhausted and I'll be fine. I'm going to bribe Dr. Abbott for some sleeping meds."

Her father bent down to kiss her cheek. "We'll see you tomorrow."

"We have a wedding and I'm a professional, you know," she said, cracking a smile. "Besides, my cousin deserves her bridesmaid."

"Only if you're well and can be released," Governor Romano said. "I'll be telephoning the doctor in the morning."

"Please ask for my colleague, Dr. Gaspar," Doctor Abbott

advised. "I'm off duty at six a.m., but I promise that Chloe will be in excellent hands."

Her parents hugged her once more before they departed, her mother blowing kisses from the doorway. Then Serena, her nurse, wheeled her down to the X-ray room. They took pictures from every angle, front and back, which seemed like overkill, but Chloe succumbed just so she could finally go to sleep.

Which she did after Dr. Abbott told her the test results. "Despite the residue of water, it looks like your lungs are clearing up. We're giving you an antibiotic for ten days and a prescription for lots of rest. See your primary care physician for a checkup when you get back to South Carolina. We'll be sending a report, too, so they'll have a record of everything we did tonight for you."

Chloe nodded and within a few minutes, she was taken to her own room, given a sleeping aid, and dropped into sleep—until her cell phone rang.

The caller ID read Liam Esposito. "What are you doing calling me at one-thirty in the morning, Esposito?" she demanded weakly.

"I couldn't sleep until I talked to you. What do the doctors say? How are you feeling?"

"X-rays show fluid is clearing. Antibiotic. Checkup with my doctor back home. That's my report, Agent. Anything else?"

"Come on, Chloe. You know I care about you. You scared the heck out of me tonight. I thought I was going to lose you."

"Liam, I'm not yours to lose," she said quietly. "I have no idea what gave you any idea that I was."

"Seeing you with that—Brett what's-his-name—drove me crazy. You drive me crazy. We argue, we fight. You're impossible; you won't let me talk to you—and all I want to do is be with you."

Chloe stared at the phone. What in the world was this man saying to her? "Have you been drinking?"

"Stone-cold sober, Chloe Romano."

"I hadn't seen you in ages until a week ago," Chloe told him. "I can't forgive you for Jenna."

"I know. But you owe me fifteen minutes to tell you the truth."

"I'll think about it, but I can't promise anything else. I have a wedding tomorrow. And some very important gemstones to worry about." She let out a cry of frustration when she thought about the diamonds. "Darn it, Liam, what's happening over there?"

"I had to take Max Romano aside and confide in him who I was. Showed him my badge. Your father also vouched for me. Your uncle brought the earrings down to the safe, and we locked them up together. As far as I could tell, nothing was out of place in the office or the safe."

Chloe shook her head, her brain spinning. "Are you thinking what I'm thinking?"

"Yup. Same thing you're thinking. The power outage."

"It wasn't an accidental outage," Chloe said quietly into the phone.

"Doesn't look like it. The power company said that the Romano house was the only home affected. The breaker box looked intact, no switches shorted out."

"What if there was someone in the house while we were all outside by the pool? Are you sure all the diamonds were in the safe when Uncle Max opened it?"

"All there and accounted for, although I need you back tomorrow to verify the authenticity. A crew from the power company will arrive at daylight to check into it more thoroughly. Meanwhile, the kitchen staff had boxes of candles for everyone, plus a few lamps placed strategically about the house. But hey, it'll be dawn in about five hours."

"Is Mercedes going out of her mind?"

Liam chuckled. "She had a bit of a meltdown after the ambulance carried you away. She's frantic about you and frantic that there may not be any electricity for the wedding tomorrow evening."

"Never had a power outage at one of my weddings before. This is a first."

"Right now," Liam said softly, "you need to focus on getting better and not having any lasting side effects that might weaken your lungs in the future."

"Call me the minute you hear from the power company in the morning. Can you check the diamonds once more? I know you weren't trained on them and you probably wouldn't understand my diagrams, but it would be nice to know that all the pieces are accounted for."

"They're accounted for, I promise. Besides," Liam joked, his tone teasing her, "I'm not married or engaged, so how would I know anything about diamonds?"

"Very funny, Agent Esposito. I'll bet you have a new girlfriend every month."

"Chloe," Liam said quietly. "I'm not a player and you know it."

"Actually, I don't really know you anymore. Where are you sleeping tonight?"

"Why? Do you want me to come to the hospital? I can be there in five minutes."

"Of course not." Chloe glared at the phone even though she knew Liam couldn't see her facial expression. "Ask Uncle Max if you can sleep on the floor in his office. You can deck anybody who tries to break in during the blackout."

"Already got my sleeping bag and air mattress set up. In fact, that's where I'm calling you from. Just lying here on my pillow, missing you."

"Knock it off, Agent," Chloe growled. "I'll be home first thing in the morning to do a thorough inspection."

"Not if the nurses tie you to your bed."

"Believe me, I'll break out of here. Besides ..." Chloe paused, her thoughts running away with her again. "I—Liam—something strange happened in that pool. I swear that at the moment I was trying to swim to the surface, somebody pushed me back down. I was panicking, about to pass out, but I *know* I felt someone's hand on top of my head pushing hard. Like how kids dunk each other horsing around. But it was so confusing, I couldn't tell which way was up or down."

"I think you answered your own question."

"What do you mean?"

"You were confused. You were panicking. It was dark. I'm sure your dress, your shoes, were dragging you under, hindering your ability to swim upward. Compound that with total darkness and vertigo and you have a perfect tragedy waiting to happen."

A rush of horror moved down Chloe's neck. Even now, she could feel the imprint of someone's hand pushing at her while she sucked in water. Could she really have just imagined it in her panic?

But who would want to hurt her? To *drown her*? Everyone there tonight was family. Unless the diamond thief had been among them tonight and knew that she had been placed there by the FBI—and was trying to get rid of her.

"Were you right all along, Liam? Is it Mark? Or his brother, Gary?"

"We've been investigating, but know nothing for certain. At this point, we can't do anything unless something happens to the diamonds. Then we get a search warrant for all the guests and their rooms."

"By then, the diamonds will be long gone."

"There's nothing you can do about it tonight," Liam finally said. "Put it out of your mind and sleep. I need you better. For me —for both our sakes."

Chloe let out another cough and then yawned loudly, her brain fuzzy with exhaustion.

"See? Those sleeping pills are working. Good night, Chloe."

CHAPTER 17

*C*lutching her X-ray results and a copy of her chart, Chloe dragged herself out of bed the next morning and rang for the nurse. She felt like she'd been hit by a Mack truck, she was so exhausted. Her body was like a rag doll, completely spent by the trauma of lying at the bottom of a swimming pool.

Chloe didn't have any regular clothes, either. Her sodden evening gown was hanging in the bathroom. It would probably begin to mold by tonight, so it needed to be taken to a dry cleaner as soon as possible for a rush job.

She texted Katey and asked her to bring her a set of clothes, then she forced herself to eat a little hospital breakfast so the nurses wouldn't try to detain her, citing no appetite. She willed herself to keep the food down, even though her stomach felt horrible.

Once Katey arrived, Chloe hurriedly dressed as best she could with an IV still stuck in her arm.

"Katey, please ring for the nurse," she called from the bathroom.

"I'm on it!" the young woman said, pressing the Call button.

"This is just like a movie. We're escaping from the hospital so we can see a woman in love get married before it's too late."

Chloe smiled at her. "They'll get married whether I'm there or not, but I appreciate the cloak-and-dagger aspect."

"How do you feel?" Katey asked, taking Chloe's hands in hers. "Your skin feels warm and normal."

"My last vitals were about two hours ago, and they were all perfectly normal. I'm back up to 98.3, my normal temperature. I haven't coughed since four a.m. I ate my breakfast, even though I feel a bit nauseous. But that's our little secret."

Katey crossed her fingers over her heart. "Mum's the word."

"How was everyone at the house last night? Anything unusual?"

"Most of us went to bed—or tried to—after you left in the ambulance. Mercedes was crying a little, but I gave her a Tylenol PM and she slept pretty good."

"I'm glad she was able to sleep. It's her wedding day, after all."

"I told her to stay in bed until at least ten while I picked you up. Since the wedding isn't until six o'clock, there's plenty of time to get ready."

Chloe nodded. "Perfect. Exactly what I would have told her."

"She said Brett is beside himself with guilt. He feels terrible, the poor man. He went over and over again what happened. It was *so freaking dark* out there. Since the neighborhood is a bit more rural, there weren't even any city lights."

"Without streetlights, I couldn't even see my own hand in front of my face."

"I was stumbling around and stubbed my toe on one of the patio bricks." Katey glanced down at her left foot, where her big toe was wrapped in a Band-Aid.

"That's how I fell when it went dark. I was twirling, so it didn't take much to trip and crash right into the pool."

"It's a good thing the water lilies weren't already floating on-site. You might have gotten caught in the roots and strangled."

Chloe grimaced. "That's a sobering thought."

The nurse arrived and frowned at Chloe already dressed and ready to leave. She was the new morning shift nurse, an older woman who obviously thought her patient should still be in bed. "I don't have your discharge paperwork ready, young lady."

"I have a wedding to go to. I'm the bridesmaid."

The nurse pursed her lips. "Not sure that's more important than the bride."

"Well, I really do need to go, and I'm feeling much better now. I even ate—a little."

She studied her chart and marked a couple of things with a pencil. "Doctor's ordered another chest X-ray before you leave."

"Okay, let's do it," Chloe said, heading for the door.

"Not so fast. I'll be taking you there in a wheelchair."

"Can I get the IV out before we go to the lab?"

"Nope. Just in case we need to give you anything, it stays in until we officially discharge you. Who will be picking you up?"

Chloe lifted an arm toward Katey. "My ride is already here."

"Let's boogey down to X-ray," Katey said, putting both thumbs up.

"Let's not overdo it, girls," the nurse said drily. "I'll get you out of here as soon as I can. It's only eight right now. I'll get you in for an X-ray no later than nine. Will that work for you?"

Chloe smiled, wanting to stay in her good graces, but antsy to get back to the Romano mansion. "We'll sit tight," she finally said, sliding back onto the hospital bed.

Katey sat across from her in an armchair. "Mercedes was upset last night when that man, Stan Crowley, showed up as your date. She had you all lined up with Brett. You two looked great together last night dancing to Frank Sinatra. At least, I think that's his name. Your grandmother loved it when the DJ played his stuff."

"Frank Sinatra is an oldie, but goodie."

"It's got to be hard to choose between Brett or Stan, but you and Brett were pretty tight during dinner. I could tell Stan was so jealous."

"Really? I hadn't noticed," Chloe said vaguely.

"He was shooting daggers at you two while you danced. Every time Brett pulled you in close or whispered in your ear, he was ready to punch the guy's lights out."

"Now that's interesting." Seriously? Or was Katey just having fun talking boys like they were still in high school?

"By the way, Katey, do you have a boyfriend?" she asked to change the subject.

"I did, but he went away to school this fall." Katey sighed. "We FaceTime and talk every night, but it's not so fun to stay stuck at home without a date on Saturday night. The wedding has been a wonderful distraction."

"Yes, it has," Chloe agreed. "A grand distraction."

"Chloe Romano," a nurse spoke from the doorway, holding a wheelchair for transport. "We're ready for you in X-ray."

An hour later, Chloe and the doctor were discussing the results. Doctor Gaspar said, "Your X-ray shows improvement from last night. Excellent news. Very little to no sign of lung damage. But you need to rest the next week. Take it easy, Chloe. No marathons or swimming. Tell your boss that you need some medical leave for a week or so."

Chloe gave him a tentative smile. "What if I'm my own boss and I have a very important job to finish tonight?"

"I'm serious. I don't want to see you back here tomorrow. Go home and take a nap. Watch television. Eat your favorite foods."

"Katey, can you pack my things?" Chloe asked, sitting up higher on the bed.

"Chloe," Doctor Gaspar said sternly. "Your body has gone through trauma. If your friends and family weren't on-site to help you, they'd be planning a funeral today. Take care of yourself."

She nodded, sobered by his words. "I will, doctor, I promise."

He signed the release papers, and Katey went to round up the car while Chloe gathered the bag of toiletries the hospital had given her, plus her damp evening gown. Katey was at the curb of the exit when the nurse wheeled her out and helped her into the car.

"If you have any more coughing or chest pain, come back and get it checked out," the nurse told her before shutting the car door.

Twenty minutes later, Katey pulled up to the Romano mansion. Chloe breathed a sigh of relief while at the same time her stomach was in knots. She had to get into the safe and verify that the stones were still the genuine diamonds.

Twisting her neck, she gazed at a white work truck pulled onto the access road between the Romano residence and the adjoining neighbor. The local power company logo was on the side of the vehicle. What had they discovered about the power going off—accidental, or part of a plot to incapacitate her last night?

When she got through the front door, the house was insanely crazy. The catering company was already on the premises in full force, chefs in white jackets cooking in the large restaurant-style kitchen.

The smells wafting through the closed doors were heavenly. Chloe's stomach growled. That must be a good sign.

Even so, she had moments when her head was fuzzy and heavy, as if she needed to hold it up with her hands.

Memories of the plunge into the swimming pool remained elusive. She was forgetting something, but what? She'd been dancing with a romantic and excellent partner in Brett Sorenson, the blackout happened, and she twirled straight into the pool, sinking to the bottom before she could comprehend what had happened.

Through the rear french doors, Chloe spotted Suze Perry in full wedding planner mode, ordering tables and chairs moved, decorating the wedding bower and trellis where the nuptials would be officially performed.

A grizzled, bearded man was cleaning the swimming pool to get it ready to place the floating water lilies. The final touches on the dance floor were also in progress. Two men were on their hands and knees, polishing the wood to a bright sheen.

Suze Perry's employees were currently laying dramatic centerpieces on the dinner tables. Three vases of varying heights were filled with white and burgundy roses, adorned by a floating candle just above the flowers. When the sun went down, the candles would glow with a soft radiance.

Several others were hanging white fairy lights in all the trees. Mercedes's dream wedding was definitely going to be magical.

"Isn't it going to be gorgeous?" Mercedes said, coming down the patio steps. She embraced Chloe hard and wouldn't let her go for several long moments. "How *are* you? My gosh, you gave everyone a scare. I'm so sorry, Chloe. I feel horrible that such a terrible accident happened at my wedding."

"It's not your fault, and I'm much better, just a little tired."

"I order you to take a nap. I slept until almost eleven, had brunch, and feel terrific."

"That's good! It's an exciting day, Mercedes, and I'm so happy for you. In case I don't get a chance to tell you this, I hope you and Mark have a wonderful life together."

"Thank you, Chloe; that means a lot to me. Did they feed you at the hospital? I assume they gave you a clean bill of health if they sent you home."

"X-rays are better, but the doc told me to spend a week in bed watching Netflix." Chloe moved toward the house, scouting out the location of family members and wedding workers to see if she could slip into Uncle Max's office without being interrupted or questioned.

"Did the doctor really say that?"

Chloe laughed. "Not in so many words, but it's a good thing I don't have another wedding for two weeks. My muscles are so sore, I swear I just worked out with twenty-pound weights for ten hours."

"I'll get you some Aleve. Why don't you go up and see Granny?" Mercedes suggested. "I know she was worried sick when she heard the news."

Chloe smiled tightly, on the verge of telling Mercedes to go take a hike so she could do her job.

Katey rushed through, hunting for scissors and tape on orders from Suze. "Katey," Chloe asked, "when you get a chance, do you mind dropping my dress at a dry cleaner?"

"No problem. Guess we should have done that on the way home, but I wanted to get you back here so you could lie down. Which you are not doing," Katey pointed out.

"You've both turned into mother hens," Chloe said. "I'm fine, go scoot and get back to wedding prep. I promise that I'll stay far, far away from the pool today."

"Don't forget the hairdresser later this afternoon," Mercedes reminded Chloe. "Now go to your room and get under the covers!"

Chloe had every intention of disobeying her, of course, quickly changing her clothes and then checking her phone. There were several text messages and two voicemails from Liam, so she called him back.

"Chloe! Where are you? Did the hospital knock you out with a triple dose of sleeping pills?"

"Got here about thirty minutes ago."

"You're back in the land of the living, then. Good." Liam sounded so relieved, it surprised her.

"What did you find out about the power outage? I haven't seen Uncle Max or my parents yet. Where are you right now?"

"Staying a few blocks away at a safe house. Even though I slept in Max Romano's office last night, I thought it would be strange if I was hanging around the house when everybody got up this morning. Too many questions to be answered that are not fully answerable. I intercepted the repair crew on my way out though."

Liam *was* close by, not at a hotel ten miles away. The news both comforted her and alarmed her. After all, she was still capable of handling this job. And Liam was, well, Liam. The man she couldn't stand the sight of. "What did they say?"

"They checked the breaker box and the power lines, including the transformer at the power pole at the back of the property. The verdict was that the lines coming from the pole to the house were purposely cut."

Chloe sank to the bed, a sick feeling rising in her stomach. "Are you telling me—?"

"Yes. Someone *purposely* plunged the house and yard into darkness. The power company guys suggested the possibility of a prankster in the neighborhood who knew there was a wedding going on and thought it would be funny to cause mayhem. He's putting in a report to the local police, but the police already know that the FBI is handling this case."

"Did you give an opinion on the prankster possibility?"

"I didn't dissuade him from thinking that. Not when there's over half a million bucks in diamonds sitting in the house."

"Now we know for certain that the power outage was done on purpose." Cold shivers ran from her neck all the way to her toes. "The timing of my fall wasn't coincidental. Somebody is *watching* me, Liam. Call me officially spooked."

"Don't jump to conclusions yet. Try to stay calm."

"Hey, you didn't almost die last night. This confirms our worst fears. Someone on the premises last night is part of a diamond heist. I kept assuming the FBI had their info wrong."

"Appears that we were correct. I'm sorry, Chloe."

A weak sensation came over her. "If this is Mark Westerfield—"

"I know I said he's our primary suspect, but there was a

147

catering crew there last night, as well as a DJ and a lot of the wedding planner's people, too."

"True enough." Chloe blew out a breath, her pulse rising. "When will you be here?"

"You're on your own for the afternoon, agent," Liam told her, his voice softening. "I'll get to the wedding as soon as it's not odd for me to show up early. Even so, I'm not leaving your side tonight."

There was a moment of silence, and then Chloe said, "Thank you for saving me last night. I never told you that. But I'm grateful."

"You know I'd do anything for you, Chloe," Liam said, his voice gently and meaningful.

She ignored that, adding, "Don't you dare give me mouth-to-mouth ever again without my permission."

Liam gave a low chuckle. "Hard to get permission when you're unconscious."

"That's an order."

"If you think I was going to allow some strange paramedic guy to put his lips on yours, then you don't know me very well. Besides, you weren't breathing and I was terrified that I'd already lost you."

A rush of sensations came over Chloe. The old familiar longing for this man nearly overpowered her before she came to her senses once more.

"This conversation is over now," Chloe said firmly. "I'm going down for inspection. I'll text you my results."

"Don't let anybody see you go in and out of the office. It's safer if nobody knows what you're doing. We have no idea who's watching you."

"You don't have to tell me the obvious."

Chloe hung up and sighed. Why couldn't she be doing this job with someone other than Liam Esposito? He gave her way too much stress and angst. Still, a secret part of her wished she had been conscious last night when he was trying to revive her. All the time they had hung out together and worked together while trying to tamp down their attraction, she had dreamed of what Liam's lips on hers might be like. And now she would probably never know.

CHAPTER 18

There was an intercom system in the house, and Aunt Aurelia made use of it. Just as Chloe was about to saunter downstairs, she heard a beep from the box near the bedroom door.

"Happy wedding day, everyone!" Aurelia said gaily. "The back-yard has been taken over by our illustrious wedding planner, so we're serving a light lunch on the front porch if you'd like to partake. Don't want our guests to faint from hunger before the wedding dinner is served."

Before the Westerfield's or the Romano's could depart from their bedrooms, Chloe dashed down the curving staircase and darted into the drawing room before the first bedroom door opened and closed.

She could hear voices moving downstairs to the foyer when she slipped into Uncle Max's office and locked the solid wood door.

The office appeared untouched from last night. Not a single thing out of place. Not even a stray sock under the desk forgotten by Liam.

He was actually an excellent FBI agent, advancing quickly

after his training. He'd come to the FBI with a degree in political science and a background with guns and law enforcement from growing up in Alabama with a police detective as a father.

Moving quickly so nobody would begin looking for her, Chloe turned the combination until the tumblers opened the latch. Opening the lids to the jewelry boxes, she sucked in her breath at the three pieces of wedding jewelry in all their glory. Goodness, they were gorgeous.

After inspecting the stones and poring over her diagram of each gem one by one, Chloe finally leaned back and removed the headlamp.

These were the original, authentic diamonds. No swap had been made during the last twelve hours. Of course, that would have been difficult with Liam sleeping a mere two feet away. Even so, she could finally breathe normally again after worrying all night.

She made a quick call to Liam. "They're genuine."

"Good. After last night's cut power lines, I thought we'd have to call in the forces."

"You don't have to attend the wedding," Chloe told him. "Everything's under control, and I'm sure after last night you're bored stiff by all of us Romano's."

"Hey, I wouldn't miss the chance to see you in your professional bridesmaid role if you gave me tickets to the Yankees. Besides, I'm still on duty. Not until the diamonds are safely back in Davis Jewelry's armored vehicle will we both rest easy."

"I wish it was over with already. I just want to go home."

"I'm sure you're exhausted and done with all of this, including me. After tonight, you won't have to see me ever again."

The phone clicked off as Liam hung up.

A heavy melancholy came over Chloe as she tossed her cell phone onto the desk and buried her head in her hands. Liam's words were so final. For all her animosity toward the man, the thought of never seeing him again bothered her more than she thought.

On one hand, she wanted to tell him off and throw him into a pit of fire and brimstone with the devil. On the other, she wanted to know what it would be like wrapped up in his arms.

Closing up the boxes and her notebook of diagrams, Chloe stowed them in the safe with her tool bag and locked everything up.

Tiptoeing out the door, she heard voices crossing the marbled foyer. Chloe plopped down on one of the sitting room sofas and picked up a fashion magazine lying in a stack on one of the end tables. She was flipping through it when her mother entered a moment later.

"There you are, Chloe," Diana Romano said, embracing her tightly. "I wish you had called me to bring you home from the hospital."

"I didn't want to disturb you after such a horrendous night. Today is another long day, too."

Her mother pressed a hand to Chloe's cheek. "You're so pale, sweetheart. Are you sure you should have been released so soon?"

"I'm fine, Mom. Just tired."

"Come and eat and then go lie down. I'm sure Mercedes will need you later."

"Yes, hair and dressing will take time." Chloe rose to link her arm with her mother's and went out to grab a sandwich and some lemonade.

She sat next to Granny Zaida, who fussed over her and wanted to know all the details since she had already gone upstairs to bed when Chloe had fallen into the swimming pool.

"Be careful, my darling Chloe. The entire episode sounds fishy."

"At least the pool wasn't filled with those big fat koi fish that look like radiated goldfish after a nuclear war," Chloe joked. "I see them in the pond at the zoo, and they can stay right there."

Frowning, her grandmother tsked her tongue. "My instincts are telling me that something isn't right. And my instincts never steer me wrong."

"The doctor gave me a clean bill of health," Chloe promised. "When I get back to my little apartment in South Carolina, I'm going to sleep for three days straight. No evil is afoot," she fibbed.

"If you say so," Granny Zaida said, but she didn't look convinced.

A few minutes later, Chloe skedaddled from the family lunch, pulled the blinds, and flopped into bed, falling asleep within seconds. An hour later, she woke, certain that somebody was in her bedroom. "Who's there?" she called out.

"It's only me," Mercedes whispered, standing just inside the closed door. "I didn't want to wake you."

"Too late." Chloe yawned and groaned, wondering if somebody spiked her lemonade with a sleeping agent, she was so groggy. Getting up, she splashed cold water on her face.

"The hairdresser has arrived, and the makeup girl will be here in two hours, so it's party time! As soon as we're dressed, we head to the bottom of the hill to do the wedding march. I can't believe we're less than four hours away from showtime."

Chloe smiled. "You've been engaged for a year."

"I know," Mercedes laughed. "You wait and wait, and then suddenly it's happening. I'll be Mrs. Mark Westerfield very, very soon!"

Grabbing her own makeup bag, Chloe scurried over to Mercedes's suite, where Katey was absorbed in wedding hairstyle magazines.

There were two hairdressers, one for each of them, which surprised Chloe. "I thought I'd be watching you get your hair done," she told Mercedes.

"I only have one amazing bridesmaid. Besides, after falling into the pool, you probably have chlorine stuck in your strands."

"That's true. All I did today was run a brush through it at the hospital. It's pretty nasty."

"You just got out of the hospital and you're the bridesmaid?" the hairdresser said, whose name was Margo.

"Long story, but yes. I'm fine now."

"An ambulance whisked her away with an oxygen mask," Mercedes told Margo's partner, Lisa.

Her cousin launched into the wedding rehearsal's events, complete with dramatics. Mercedes kept them all entertained while they got their hair washed, conditioned, blow-dried, and styled.

Margo snapped the curling iron around strands of Chloe's hair, creating soft ringlets and waves. By the time she was finished, her hair had never looked so good. It was like getting ready for glamour shots with a professional photographer.

"You girls are going to look stunning," Katey said while she painted her toenails a hot pink.

"Now we need to discuss Brett Sorenson," Mercedes said.

Chloe let out a choked laugh. "No, we don't."

"He was smitten with you last night. No doubt about it."

"He's very nice," Chloe admitted.

"What did you two talk about? It looked like you were hitting it off."

Had she and Brett taken to each other immediately? Chloe wondered. Or was it because she had been trying to make Liam jealous? She wondered about her own motivations, despite the lovely idea of a romantic weekend in Savannah.

"We talked about all kinds of things. Savannah, mostly."

"Are you going to visit him?"

Chloe gave her cousin a wide-eyed gaze. "He has to officially invite me first."

"Well, that's not going to be a problem," Mercedes said knowingly.

"You two looked adorable together when you were dancing," Katey added.

Mercedes grinned. "I overheard Mark and Gary and Brett talking about you this morning in the breakfast room."

"Oh, great. In what capacity? How klutzy I am falling into a swimming pool while dancing?"

"Not at all. Brett's interested and would like to get to know you better."

"Hmm," Chloe said. "I think I'd like that, too."

"And I think you're done," Margo said. She sprayed Chloe's hair with a ton of super holding mist. "Gotta make sure your hair doesn't fall if we get humidity tonight. You're going to be partying for hours, I hear."

"Not me," Chloe laughed. "At midnight, I turn into a pumpkin."

"I'll forgive you," Mercedes said. "I know you're not completely well yet." She reached over and squeezed Chloe's hand. "Thank you for being here with me. Now that today is here, I knew I couldn't have had any other bridesmaid."

Forty-five minutes later, their makeup was finished, too. It was after four and the wedding party had to dress no later than five-thirty.

Chloe's phone buzzed with a text message from Brett Sorenson.

Since there's still a couple hours before the ceremony, would you care to take a drive with me for half an hour? I'm downstairs, and I'll wait.

Chloe gulped, turning to Mercedes. "It's Brett. Did you put him up to something?"

Her cousin assumed an innocent look. "Who, me? No, silly. He likes you, Chloe. Go enjoy some time with him before the wedding starts. Mark told me that Brett has to take the red-eye flight out tonight, so this is your only chance to get to know him without a hundred people around."

"Well, when you put it that way." Chloe typed out her response. **Sure. I'll meet you in the driveway in ten minutes.**

"Just don't drive with the windows down," Margo warned. "You'll ruin your hair."

"Duly noted," Chloe assured her.

She was downstairs in one minute flat. The main floor was quiet. Everyone was either resting in their rooms or showering. This was her last chance to examine the diamonds before Mercedes put them on.

In ten seconds, the safe was open. Holding up the necklace in both hands, she zeroed the UV light and the microscopic loupe on each stone, glancing down at her list of angles and imperfections. Every single one checked out perfectly. As did the tiara and the earrings.

"Genuine as can be," Chloe whispered. "The real deal."

Except for last night, the weekend of the diamonds had gone smoothly. Not a single stone has been pried loose or swapped out.

She locked everything up tight again, checked the quiet, empty sitting room, and moved swiftly through the foyer without bumping into anyone—except for Uncle Max.

"Hi, Chloe," he said. "You look ready for the ceremony. Have you girls been doing your hair?"

"I'll bet my teased hair was a dead giveaway," she said with a grin.

"Everything good down here?" her uncle asked, subtly referring to the safe in his office.

"All good. We'll put them on Mercedes when I return in thirty minutes."

"I'll slink about the halls and keep watch," he assured her.

A smile lit up Brett's face when Chloe walked out to the driveway. He gave a low, admiring whistle. "You look beautiful."

"Amazing what a professional can do to transform an ordinary girl, huh?"

"You're not ordinary. Anything but," Brett said, taking her hand in his as they walked to his rental car, a midnight blue Mustang. He opened the door for her and Chloe slid inside, running a hand along the pristine leather seat. She had never expected to meet a man this weekend. It was proving to be full of surprises.

After putting the car in gear, Brett pulled out of the circular drive and glanced both directions, his gaze landing on Chloe's face and pausing. "You really are a beautiful woman. I wanted to come to the hospital, but didn't want to disturb you or the doctors while they were getting you back to perfect health."

"I think I'm almost there. Perfect health, that is."

Turning in his seat, Brett brushed a hand against Chloe's cheek, and her face flamed. "Last night was pretty frightening."

"Let's not talk about it or I'll get the heebie-jeebies. Buy me a drink, Savannah boy."

"Deal." He pulled onto the narrow road and reached over to take Chloe's hand again, enclosing it tightly in his. "Got any druthers?"

"Actually, just a Coke will do. Is there a Sonic drive-in close by?"

He laughed. "I have no idea, but I think I can afford something better than sitting in a car at Sonic."

"We only have thirty minutes before I have to get dressed and walk down the aisle. With you, as a matter of fact, Best Man."

In a few minutes, Brett pulled into a small, upscale sandwich shop. "It's probably quiet right now."

Once inside, a waitress showed them to a booth and Brett seated himself next to Chloe, placing an arm along the seat's high back cushion in an intimate gesture.

"Since we don't have much time, is Cokes and fries okay?" When Chloe nodded, he added, "I don't normally take a girl out for plain old fries on a first date."

"Is that what this is—a date?" she teased.

Brett's expression was apologetic. "I hope so, because I have to catch my plane tonight."

"That's what Mercedes said."

"It's too bad, but I hadn't planned to meet a gorgeous woman this weekend," Brett agreed. They chatted about jobs and hobbies and favorite vacations for about twenty minutes, and then he said, "Will you consider coming to Savannah so I can wine and dine you?"

"Perhaps," Chloe flirted in return, speaking vaguely.

He leaned in closer. "I'd love to get to know you better."

"Are you always this fast and flirtatious with someone you've recently met?"

"Only when I'm captivated. Which doesn't happen very often."

"You are a flirt."

"Hey, don't call me a liar. I mean every single word."

Late afternoon dusk was descending and the restaurant was quiet, especially in their corner booth. Brett Sorenson leaned in closer and brushed his lips softly against Chloe's lips. Her breath caught, and he pressed more firmly, putting a hand behind her head. When he tried to part her lips, Chloe pulled back slightly, but not enough to put him off.

"That's enough for a first kiss the day after meeting you, Best Man."

He lifted his shoulders boyishly. "What can I say? You're irresistible."

"I have to get back," she said softly. "Bridesmaid duties call."

"Of course." He scooted out of the booth and helped Chloe to her feet. Holding her hand, he walked her back to the car and opened the door. "Thanks for a quick getaway this afternoon. Now it's showtime, huh?"

"I've got to run inside to dress, and so do you. Did they give you a closet somewhere in the house to change?"

"Mrs. Romano—your aunt—gave me a room for my suitcase and tux since I already checked out of my hotel."

"They're a great family. Mark is lucky."

"He is." Brett gave her a meaningful smile. "I hope I'm just as lucky one day."

Chloe shook her head at the innuendo in his words, but took his arm as they walked up to the front door. "See you at the opening notes of the Wedding March, Mr. Sorenson."

He gave a quick salute when they parted ways at the upstairs hallway junction.

Chloe glanced at her cell phone. Forty-five minutes to dress and get down to their starting positions. She checked herself in the mirror. Her hair had hardly moved, and her makeup was mostly intact, even after Brett's kisses.

She reapplied the lip color the makeup girl had given her for touch-ups during the evening. Then she pulled the bridesmaid dress off its hanger and slipped into it.

The dress was a smooth sheen of burgundy satin chiffon with a neckline in a sweetheart cut that was flattering on her. Not too much cleavage, more like a hint that was romantic without being too sexy.

She finally got herself zipped and arranged and stared into the full-length mirror. The dressmaker had done a great job, fitting it to her figure perfectly. It was flattering and snug without being too tight, so she could move around during the evening without fear of ripping out a seam.

Tonight was going to be the perfect wedding. Exactly as Mercedes had always hoped and dreamed.

CHAPTER 19

*C*hloe poked her head into her cousin's room. "What can I help you with?" She broke off at the sight of her cousin. "Oh my, you look stunning! That dress! I need the name of your dressmaker if I ever get married."

"You're going to get married. There's no question of that. I'll bet within the year. How did it go with Brett?"

"Good, good," she said with a smile.

"I can tell from the look on your face that he kissed you. He did, didn't he?"

"I'll never kiss and tell," Chloe said mysteriously.

Mercedes twirled around the three-way mirrors in her suite, admiring herself from every angle.

"That dress—and you in it—are simply incredible," Chloe told her. "Once the diamonds are around your neck, you're going to dazzle like no other bride ever dazzled."

Mercedes put her hands to her face, jumping up and down on her toes to let off the nerves. "I'm so excited I can't stand it. Am I doing the right thing, Chloe? Promise me that I am. Mark's wonderful, isn't he?"

"He is. I also love his professorial glasses."

"Oh, he's brilliant," Mercedes said with a laugh. "I love his glasses, too. But he's also funny and sweet and kind. I've never swooned with any other man like I do when he kisses me. That's when I knew he was the one."

"Okay, Ms. soon-to-be Mrs. Westerfield, let me do a quick check of you."

Chloe examined the zipper and hem and then helped Mercedes into her white shoes. She fixed a stray hair and helped her reapply lip liner and lip color.

Finally, she opened the bedroom door and helped her cousin with the train of her wedding dress as they descended the curving staircase. Mercedes was chattering nervously about various wedding details while Chloe's own thoughts ran wild.

Kissing and swooning went together, huh? She had never thought about it like that before. Sure, she liked kissing a nice-looking man, but she wouldn't have described it as swooning or melting into someone's arms.

As sweet as Brett's kiss was this afternoon—was it only an hour ago?—Chloe hadn't felt any sort of special jump in her stomach. Maybe she just didn't know him well enough. It had only been two days since they'd met. Perhaps after a trip to his own turf in Savannah she could better assess her feelings for him.

The downstairs foyer was empty, thank goodness. Uncle Max and Aunt Aurelia had already escorted the house guests and relatives out to find their seats.

Faint music from the musicians drifted through the rear patio doors. The string quartet was playing romantic classical music as arriving friends, neighbors, and coworkers took their seats.

After locking Uncle Max's office door, Chloe smiled at her cousin. "It's time to be a princess."

Mercedes's smile was as wide as the Potomac while Chloe fastened the diamond-encrusted jewelry around her neck and ears. Then she clipped the tiara on her head just in front of the lace veil, fastening them together.

Chloe held up a mirror she'd brought down from her room. "You, my dear, are wearing more than five hundred thousand dollars worth of diamonds."

The gemstones sparkled like a million bucks under the hanging lights of the office. Chloe could only imagine how they would shimmer and glitter under the fairy lights in the backyard.

Mercedes's jaw dropped, and she put a hand to her chest. "Seeing the entire set all at once is stunning. I can't even describe it."

"Let's go dazzle your guests. And Mark Westerfield, that lucky dog."

"Oh, Chloe, you have such a way with words," her cousin laughed.

Chloe shrugged, her lips twitching with humor. "I had a minor in English."

The joking helped calm the bride. It usually worked every time. Chloe had discovered that getting the bride to laugh just before walking down the aisle created a genuinely happy and relaxed bride. Nerves and stiffness disappeared.

Tugging Mercedes's hand in hers, she walked her cousin out the door and around the house, skirting the guests whose backs were to them while they met Brett, the twin girls, and Uncle Max down below the pool. The sky was dusky enough that nobody could have spotted them unless they knew just where to look.

Suze Perry appeared and thrust the bride's bouquet into Mercedes's hand and another, smaller bouquet into Chloe's fist.

Uncle Max took his daughter's hand. "Are you ready, sweetheart?"

Nodding her head tightly, Mercedes managed to gulp out a whispered "Yes."

Brett had been gazing at Chloe with a soft smile, and now he stepped forward to take her hand in his while the wedding party walked closer to the starting point.

"You ready, too?" he asked in a low voice.

Chloe nodded, squeezing his hand in the excitement of the moment while they listened to the opening notes of Pachelbel's Canon. Out of all the wedding marches she'd ever heard over the many weekend weddings she had participated in, this was her favorite, especially when it was played by an on-site string quartet.

While she walked up the grassy aisle, her hand tucked into Brett's elbow, Chloe smiled at her beaming family eagerly turning in their seats to watch the procession.

Once she was standing at the front with the minister and Mark and Brett opposite, the flower girls were next, tossing handfuls of red petals up into the air like a rain shower of roses. The audience loved it, while the young girls' laughter charmed the guests.

Finally, Mercedes appeared at the end of the aisle on the arm of Uncle Max. The guests literally gasped when they rose to stand and watch.

She was a vision of loveliness, sparkling like the glittering diamonds she was wearing. Chloe knew the sight of her cousin would be imprinted on her eyes forever.

Soft murmurs rose at the sight of Mercedes in her sleek white satin dress with a bodice that molded her hourglass figure. The lace train was exquisite, and the blindingly beautiful diamonds sparkled under the fairy lights.

Chloe could tell Mercedes was loving every gasp and murmur, even as she had eyes only for her groom, who was mesmerized by the sight of her, too.

When she and her father reached the dais, Uncle Max kissed his daughter's cheek before releasing her to Mark, who looked like he wanted to sweep Mercedes up into his arms and ride off into the sunset.

They held hands, unable to stop smiling at each other while the minister greeted the audience. "We are gathered here today in this beautiful spot on God's earth, to unite these two hearts in the bonds of holy matrimony. Into this sacred bond, these two now come to be joined together."

He spent a few moments talking about the power of love and the eternal nature of marriage that God ordained in the beginning of time.

"Before Mark and Mercedes speak their vows, they would like to say a few words to each other," the minister finally said. "Mark, you're first up."

When Chloe sneaked a peek at her family on the front row, Aunt Aurelia was wiping tears away with a handkerchief while Granny Zaida's face split with a wide grin of joy and pride.

Mark lifted Mercedes's hand to his lips and kissed the back of it. "When you walked into my life, Mercedes, love walked in. It was a magical moment that I will treasure forever. I promise to walk side by side with you for the rest of our lives. To always cherish and honor you, my beautiful wife."

Mercedes clenched her groom's hands with both of hers, her eyes fixed to his face. "I enter into this life with you without reservation, without fear or confusion, but with a clear and trusting heart. I love you with all my heart, Mark Westerfield."

The minister cleared his throat and led Mark and Mercedes through the traditional wedding vows. For a moment, Chloe began daydreaming about her own wedding. Wondering how long it would take to find Mr. Right and if she'd be pushing forty before he showed up with unconditional love and a ring.

All at once, Mercedes hissed from the corner of her mouth, "Chloe, the ring."

"Oh, sorry." Chloe took the wide gold band off her finger and passed it to her cousin. Then she watched the two of them exchange rings.

The minister then concluded the ceremony. "Mark Westerfield and Mercedes Romano, by the authority vested in me, I announce with great joy that you are now husband and wife. You may seal your vows of love and fidelity with a kiss!"

Mercedes raised her arms around Mark's neck, her bouquet of white lilies high in the air, while her husband gathered her close and kissed her passionately. The audience burst into enthusiastic applause.

Behind the groom where he'd been standing, Brett gave Chloe a wink. It took her off guard, and she gave him a faint smile in return, not sure what the wink meant, exactly, but it was all in good fun, right? Everybody loved it when the bride and groom kissed each other with more passion than just a peck on the lips.

The minister instructed Mark and Mercedes to face the audience. "I'm happy to introduce Mr. and Mrs. Mark Westerfield."

With broad smiles, the newly wedded couple walked down the grassy aisle hand in hand while the guests applauded and rose from their seats, bombarding them with congratulations and hugs while Suze, the wedding planner, went into high gear.

She radioed her chef in the house with her walkie-talkie. "Dinner should be served in fifteen minutes. We're on target, right?"

The chef from Sergio's replied in the affirmative. Stepping closer to the patio, Chloe could see the waitstaff ready to begin placing the first course.

About ten minutes later, the guests began to take their seats at the tables, which practically covered the entire yard since there were well over a hundred people in attendance.

The gift table was loaded with packages in white satin ribbons and bows, and Chloe gave a happy sigh. Everything was going off without a hitch.

The bridal party had a special table at the front, and Chloe worked her way through the crowd, skirting the glistening swimming pool, which was now evil in her mind. She gave it the stink eye as she passed.

When she neared the table where salads had just been placed at each silver and china setting, Liam appeared from the crowd.

Chloe hadn't seen him yet. Hadn't spoken since she'd called to tell him the diamonds were fine.

It appeared that the FBI's sources were wrong on this one. The knowledge gave Chloe a sigh of relief.

"Hey, you," Liam said softly when he stood in front of her. "You look gorgeous, Chloe. I couldn't take my eyes off you during the ceremony."

Chloe bit her lips, not sure how to take his compliment. "Where were you seated?"

He shrugged. "In the back. I always give the best seats to those who actually know the bride and groom." His eyes looked into hers curiously, but he wasn't smiling. "What's up with you and Sorenson?"

Chloe started. "What are you talking about?"

"He was staring at you the entire ceremony. He also seemed a little extra friendly while you did the two-step together up the aisle."

"You're being ridiculous."

"Maybe, but I have a good sense about people. Especially when males are in your sphere."

"Is that right?" Chloe arched an eyebrow. "You know body language now?"

That was a dumb question. Of course he did. There were classes at Quantico in body language, including identifying emotions when interrogating a witness. How to know when someone was lying. How to get someone to confess.

"Don't answer that, Mr. Es—Crowley."

"I want to sit next to you at dinner."

"I think I'm promised to the best man. You know—best man, best bridesmaid, that kind of thing."

Liam eyed her. "Tell the best man to go take a hike. I'm your date. Besides, it might look suspicious if you completely ignore me."

Chloe lowered her voice. "Do you think anyone suspects who you really are?"

"Nope, not a clue. I'm just your jealous date. Most people ignore me, or else I turn invisible. They're too busy having fun or worrying about themselves. I like that when I'm on a job."

"What's your job?" a deep male voice asked, interrupting them. It was Brett, a smile on his face as he came around to Chloe's side, slipping a hand around her waist to pull her closer.

She deftly stepped out of his possessive stance. One quick kiss in a restaurant booth didn't give him the right to assume she was exclusively his.

"I'm an insurance agent," Liam replied, watching Brett's body language with a strange contempt. Chloe rolled her eyes at the macho preening. "Just checking out the possible clients."

"That's pretty crass, man," Brett said.

Liam smiled pleasantly, completely unruffled. He didn't care if he came across as tactless or ridiculous when he knew he'd never see the person again.

Dinner was a little uncomfortable with all the male posturing going on between Brett and Liam. The food was supreme, and Chloe hadn't realized how hungry she was. Her appetite was returning, and she only coughed once in a while, pretending to be clearing her throat while she dabbed at her lips with the linen napkin.

There were toasts to the newlyweds from the best man and the bridesmaid. Chloe gave a small speech to the happy couple with her water goblet raised in salute. "May you have joy and abundance during your life together," she ended, and everyone clinked glasses.

By the time dessert was served—a fluffy chocolate mousse with whipped cream and dark chocolate shavings—the guests were relaxed, enjoying the night. That always made Chloe happy.

The wedding cake would be cut soon. A three-tiered extravaganza near one of the backyard waterfalls.

The dance floor was unveiled on the far side of the yard while the DJ changed the soft background dinner music to a more upbeat dance style.

"Time to throw the bridal bouquet," Suze called out.

Chloe had hoped this wouldn't happen since Mercedes didn't have more than one attendant. "All the single girls come forward," she called out, and the DJ repeated the request by microphone.

There were laughs and groans as Mercedes's still-single friends or daughters of her parents' friends were urged forward.

Chloe found herself next to Katey when Mercedes turned with her back to the small group of young women.

"I'm single," Granny Zaida declared, hustling over. "Think I can still catch a man, girls?"

Chloe said, "Granny, you're the best catch of all. The rest of us should sit this one out."

"Not sure my leaping skills are in good shape, though," her grandmother shot back.

Chloe gave her two thumbs-up while Mercedes did a count-down from five—and then the bouquet came soaring through the air into the midst of women, ribbons flying.

Chloe glanced up just in time to see the flowers heading straight for her face. She put up her hands at the same moment Katey did and they caught it together, laughing as they bumped into each other. "You have it, Katey."

Shaking her head, Katey thrust the bouquet into Chloe's arms and stepped back, relinquishing all claims with her hands up. "Hey, I'm only twenty-two, I'm not getting married for years, but you—you're already way older—" The young woman stopped, suddenly aware of what she was saying. Putting both palms to her face, she stammered, "I'm sorry—I didn't mean—awkward moment."

Chloe waved the apology away. "No problem. Hey, maybe the bouquet will bring me luck. I certainly need it."

"I'm not so sure about that, Chloe," Katey told her. "You and Brett Sorenson are really hitting it off. Despite your plus-one in that Stan Crowley guy."

"Maybe we are," she answered vaguely.

She held the bouquet, the smell of the lilies rising up to her nose. She'd never caught a bridal bouquet before. Maybe tonight *was* lucky. She was still alive, and she'd like to get to know Brett Sorenson better.

A trip to Savannah sounded fun, especially when it was only two hours from where she lived, but Chloe wasn't sure if what she was feeling were sparks. Perhaps she was the kind of girl that needed to know someone better, rather than instant fireworks.

Fireworks were pretty fun, though. She glanced surreptitiously at Liam. When they had first met, there had been sparks—lots of them. Flirting and small touches, but purposely keeping their distance at Quantico.

Her face turned warm when a memory washed over her. Chloe had never forgotten the evening she and Liam had sneaked away from their quarters at Quantico to one of the city parks.

Spreading a blanket on the lawn, they stayed up until midnight talking about their lives and dreams while gazing at the stars, including making a contest out of naming the constellations. It had been so easy to be with Liam.

When the nonstop conversation and laughter had died down, Liam had rolled onto his side to gaze at her, his eyes and masculine scent overwhelming her. Waves of attraction and longing had engulfed her—and she felt the same desire coming from him as well.

That magical night, Liam had come perilously close to kissing her, but Chloe sat up instead, brushed the grass off her palms, and got to her feet, saving them both from embarrassment—or the possibility of not being able to keep their hands off each other.

From then on, they had been careful to keep their distance,

since they didn't want to jeopardize their careers—but Liam's arms, holding her with such warmth and comfort on that summer night, had been more perfect than any other man she'd ever dated.

Why did she hold such a strong attraction to a man that had hurt her so deeply?

A few months later came the horrible raid, and the bomb detonation before the team could evacuate. The accident had shaken everyone involved, and condolences poured in from all of the agents they'd trained with at Quantico.

But Jenna had died. And the love that had been blossoming for Liam Esposito had turned to hate.

CHAPTER 20

*C*hloe gave a small shake of her head. She had a strange premonition to check the diamonds Mercedes was wearing, but there was no reason to believe anything was wrong with them.

She had inspected them two hours before the wedding and then again right before she placed the jewels on Mercedes.

Neither she or Liam had spotted a smidgen of suspicious behavior around the house or amongst the wedding guests. Once in a while, she spotted Liam walking about the reception, his eyes steely and watchful. Just like the Secret Service. Plus, her father had installed his security detail here the entire weekend, although they stayed in the background on the perimeter of the property.

When Chloe caught Liam's eye, he spread his hands to indicate nothing was out of the ordinary. A moment later, he smiled, shrugging his shoulders, and she bit her lips to keep from smiling back. Liam Esposito's smile had always been infectious. Even when she was furious with him.

When the song "A Thousand Years" by Christina Perri came on, Mark and Mercedes danced the bride and groom number, swirling around the dance floor while everybody gazed on in delight.

On the next number, Brett was at Chloe's side and taking her in his arms. "Hey, our first dance of the evening. Where have you been?"

"Here, there, and everywhere," she said vaguely.

They moved around the floor to "First Day of My Life," avoiding the sudden onslaught of dancing couples now that the floor was open to everyone. "So how long have you been hiring yourself out as a professional bridesmaid?" Brett asked with an amused grin.

"How do you know that, Mr. Sorenson?" she asked primly.

"I confess that I looked you up on Facebook. And then I found your website. Pretty slick. It's an unusual profession, but it sounds like fun, too."

"If you like drama queen brides who have frequent melt-downs. There are only a handful of us in the country, but I've discovered that I have a talent for it. Or maybe I'm a sucker for mental torture."

Brett gave a low whistle, shaking his head. "Count me out of melting down brides. I'll elope when the time is right. All this fuss and expense is over the top."

"I agree on eloping. So much easier and more romantic. Plus, it doesn't consume a year of one's life to just run away."

"We think alike, Chloe Romano." Brett tightened his arm around her waist and brushed his cheek against her hair. The music enveloped them, and Chloe thought about how nice it was to just dance under the fairy lights and not worry about anything for a little while.

"Uh-oh," she said a minute later. "I'm getting summoned. By my boss."

"What?" Brett pulled back, glancing to where Chloe was gazing.

"Mercedes is flagging me down. I'll be right back. I hope."

"We still need to choose a weekend to rendezvous."

"You are an impossible flirt," Chloe told him flippantly. "And just so you know up front, I require my own hotel room."

Brett raised a hand in salute. "Your wish is my command, but we'll have to bid farewell now, actually. I'm leaving for the airport to catch my red-eye back home."

"So soon? I was hoping for another dance and someone to eat wedding cake with." Now that would have to be Liam, although Chloe couldn't handle dancing with him. It would bring back too many memories of their dance on the lawn on that stargazing night—when Liam had played music on his iPod and they swayed in perfect rhythm to a stream of romantic love songs.

Granny Zaida could be her cake-eating partner.

"It's almost ten," Brett said now. "At least there won't be commute traffic to contend with to get to the airport, but I have a rental car to return, too."

"The joys of flying," she said sympathetically.

He embraced her, whispering, "I look forward to seeing you very soon."

Chloe nodded, giving him a little wave. Brett said goodbye to the bride and groom, hugged Aunt Aurelia, shook hands with the rest of the adults, and bent over to kiss Granny Zaida on the hand.

After exiting through the side gate, the Mustang's headlights came on a moment later while the engine revved. Putting the car into reverse, Brett drove down the street while Chloe gave him a brief wave.

Brett was charming and funny and successful, and she'd probably have a good time with him in Savannah. There was potential there. She'd know more when this wedding was over and she could focus on something other than diamonds and Liam Esposito.

When she strode back across the lawn, Liam watched her, arms folded, expression severe. Could he read lips now? Did he know that she and Brett were talking about a weekend together? The idea of Liam knowing that she'd be spending significant time with Brett bothered her. But it shouldn't bother her, he meant nothing to her—but even that annoyed her.

"Chloe, will you please help me take off the earrings?" Mercedes asked. "Mark and I have had two dances, and they're getting heavy on my ears. Besides, my hair covers them up most of the time anyway."

"Too many diamonds, my queen?" Chloe teased.

Her cousin made a face, and Chloe guided her over to one of the hanging lamps so she could see better. After unhooking the jewels, she folded the earrings lightly in her fist.

"Go have fun. I'll return them to the safe. Be sure I'm with you when you get out of your wedding dress later so I can put the necklace and tiara away. Davis Jewelry is coming at eight a.m. sharp tomorrow."

"Oh, ugh. Nobody is going to be awake by then. We'll probably dance until long after midnight. Of course, I guess I don't have to worry," she added with a laugh. "I'll be with Mark in our honeymoon suite by then."

"That's what I'm here for. To take care of everything, including your audacious diamonds."

"Come right back. We're about to cut the cake and smear frosting all over our faces."

When Chloe entered the quiet house, she scouted out the first floor for any wandering guests. Even the kitchen was cleaned up and empty, with only a nightlight lit over the stove. The catering restaurant was fast and thorough.

Walking barefoot since she'd ditched her heels at the door, Chloe slipped into the office. She opened the safe and got out her testing equipment to examine the earrings. The suspects the FBI were surveilling had obviously changed their minds about trying to hit the Romano house to steal the Davis jewelry.

Sitting at her uncle's desk, her notes on the diamonds in front of her, Chloe snapped on the lamp and put the magnifying loupe to her eye. She didn't really need to study them since she'd done two thorough exams that afternoon before Mercedes put them on, but it was her task, of course. She had to add the time of every inspection to her final report.

After five minutes, Chloe's stomach began to sink lower and lower. The differences were very slight, but the stones were wrong. Or was she just tired?

She turned each earring around and started over again. The angles weren't as sharp as they used to be. She couldn't see a single natural flaw, and the gemstones had almost no blue color to them under the UV light.

Panic rose in her throat and Chloe straightened, her ears buzzing. The earrings were a fake. She'd bet her tiny bank account on it. How in the world could someone have switched the jewelry—right before she'd put them on Mercedes?

Was Liam correct in suspecting Mark? Had the groom given some excuse to his bride about the earrings and swapped it with fakes hidden in the pockets of his tux?

Chloe locked everything up as fast as she could and returned to the party. "Mercedes," she said, coming up behind her. "I'm sorry, but I need to do a test on your necklace."

Her cousin's eyebrows lifted in surprise. "But I haven't taken it off all night."

"Blame it on protocol," Chloe fibbed. "Test times."

"Well, if you insist. It's actually getting heavy after six hours, too."

"Go back to your party," Chloe told her, suppressing the urge to race across the lawns and back inside the house.

She forced herself to remain casual so she didn't draw unwanted attention. But once she hit the sitting room, she darted inside the office and spun the safe's combination dial with trembling fingers.

She spent a full twenty minutes on the necklace she'd come to know intimately, going over it twice, but these diamonds didn't match her diagram notes either. Not one single bit. The necklace was a fake, too.

With fumbling fingers, she sent a text to Liam. **Just examined the diamonds. They're fake! I'm positive. Do we call the police? What are your orders?**

Liam: **I'll be right there. Sit tight.**

Chloe put her head in her hands. She'd failed. Someone had been able to get into this locked office *and* the safe and swap out the jewelry. All before the wedding began. Or had she been cross-eyed the last time she'd examined the diamonds? Her brain was muddled, trying to sort out that last busy hour before the wedding.

She'd been with Brett Sorenson, and then come home to dress. So that ruled him out. He'd also been staying at a hotel the previous two nights, so he'd had little access to the house—and no time to figure out how to break the combination of the safe.

The only people who were in the house were the immediate family. No stranger could have crept past without somebody noticing.

"The kitchen staff!" Chloe whispered out loud. It had to be one of them. Someone who had purposely hired on to be at the Romano mansion the same weekend the diamonds were. "Oh, hurry, Liam!"

She got up to pace the floor and was suddenly jerked backward when a black bag was thrown over her head like a noose, blinding her in utter darkness.

CHAPTER 21

*H*er scream was cut off when Chloe's mouth was suddenly crammed with a thick gag. She tried to suck down a breath, but her air supply was severely cut.

When she breathed in, she only managed to slurp some of the gag into her mouth. It was made from some sort of satin material that sucked straight down her throat. Were they trying to make her pass out?

Desperate not to fall unconscious, Chloe's FBI training kicked in. Jerking her feet and flailing her elbows to sucker punch her assailant, she only managed to bang her hip against the corner of Uncle Max's desk.

Remembering that she'd left her tool kit on top of the desk's surface, she quickly fumbled to retrieve it—just before her attacker hauled her across the office floor.

Despite her attempt to fight back, whoever had her was strong, holding her in a backward lock, one arm around her neck. Her attacker was taller than she was, too, and much bulkier, so she knew one fact—he was male. The man breathed heavily, but had yet to speak a single word. Which was a little strange.

But only strange if he was afraid she'd recognize his voice.

Chloe tried to breathe through her nose when the office door was kicked open and her kidnapper dragged her through the sitting room. She felt the softness of Aunt Aurelia's carpet under her bare feet.

At the opening to the foyer, the attacker paused as if assessing who might be close by. Satisfied that the house was empty, he turned right and headed to the back of the house, walking with purpose, as if he knew where he was going.

Through the black bag, Chloe could hear the faint sound of laughter while Mercedes and Mark cut the cake. Which meant that her attacker wasn't Mark Westerfield. Even while she was grateful that her cousin's new husband wasn't a criminal, Chloe was terrified for herself.

Could the man who was dragging her through the house be Mark's brother, Gary? That didn't seem possible, because Gary was such a quiet, unassuming man—and he had twin girls, for heaven's sake! But appearances could be deceiving.

Brett was long gone to the airport, and her own brother seemed impossible. Who did that leave? Her father, Uncle Max? The idea made her nauseous.

Her uncle certainly had access to his own safe.

"Please don't hurt me," she whimpered, but the words were garbled with the cloth stuffed into her mouth. Her throat was scratchy, her eyes leaking tears. When her assailant turned into another room, her foot caught on the door and she twisted her ankle, but he held on tight, pulling her roughly through, despite her effort to grab onto the doorjamb.

The faint smell of chocolate alerted Chloe to where they were. The kitchen. Would somebody hear her if she tried to scream again? Chloe attempted it, but she sounded like a weak kitten, unable to get any sound past the gag that was choking off the little oxygen she could gulp down.

The kitchen was locked up tight on the opposite side of the

house from where the reception was taking place. Nobody would hear her even if she didn't have a gag in her mouth.

Once more she tried yanking on the man's arm, but he had her in a headlock and all she could do was try to avoid banging into doors and counters while he dragged her across the tile floor, one arm around her neck, the other holding her wrists behind her.

His strength and ability to keep her from using her self-defense tactics raised the hair on the back of her neck.

Dear Lord, her kidnapper wasn't Liam, was it? Had he been playing her all along? Had the man turned from a good agent into a dirty one? After all, he was the one who had set her up with this assignment. He was the only one who knew the details.

She tried to choke out his name to get some kind of reaction, but all she could do was gasp for breath. A sudden grunt sounded when the guy halted. A door banged against the wall.

Had they left the kitchen? She tried to remember what other rooms were on this side of the house? The dining room that adjoined the kitchen? The breakfast nook? A hall closet?

Not a speck of light came through the black bag. She was getting more disoriented with every passing moment.

After nearly drowning last night, it was hard not to panic at the lack of air. All at once, she began to cough, but before she could beg for air, the attacker shoved her forward and Chloe felt herself falling into empty space.

She crashed to the floor, banging her knees and elbows. It didn't take long to figure it out that he'd thrown her into the broom closet. The smell of a moldy mop and the dust from a bristly broom assailed her nose.

"Don't leave me," she choked out, certain he was going to lock her in the closet.

All of a sudden, someone was breathing next to her and chills raced down her neck at the sheer creepiness of his close, silent presence.

Before she could kick out at him, the man was sitting on top of her and tying her wrists together.

"No!" she shrieked, but the word was garbled and only wasted air.

In response, he grunted again and she grabbed at his arm, touching the material of his sleeve, the softness of the hair on his arm along his wrists.

"Please," she pleaded. Despite her choked words, she knew he understood her, but he gave no response at all. Merely shoved her legs inside the cramped closet and locked the door. His footsteps retreated and then disappeared. The man was in a hurry.

Chloe's head fell against her knees. *Think*, she told herself. What was her FBI training for escaping bonds and a locked door? The door wasn't so much an issue, she could take it off its hinges, but getting out of the knots was harder.

Closing her eyes and taking a few slow, shallow breaths so she could focus, Chloe flexed her fingers and began to work at the knots. Her attacker had tied her up so quickly they weren't complicated knots, and she'd been trained in how to undo a variety of knots.

It shouldn't take more than half an hour of painstaking work, although by that time he'd be long gone. All he'd needed was to get rid of her so he could get the rest of the diamonds and escape.

Shaking out her hands so her fingers would loosen up, Chloe let her mind relax so she could think more clearly. Something kept nagging at her.

Her fall into the swimming pool still bothered her. Thinking about it made her cough again. If she vomited, she'd choke with this gag in her mouth. Now that she wasn't being dragged around the house, Chloe tried to spit it out, but it was so tight her mouth and jaw were aching.

Last night, she and Brett had been dancing and spinning. Twirling and laughing like goofy teenagers. When he'd spun her out that last time, the lights were cut at the exact same moment—

literally—and she'd slipped and fallen *directly into the very deepest end of the swimming pool.*

Brett should have been the first one to dive in and save her. Not Liam, who was across the patio. Or her brother, who had been talking with their parents at a distant table. Obviously, being so close, Brett would have heard the loud splash despite the DJ's music. He would have felt her fingers slip from his.

Chloe shivered, playing back those moments, almost erased from her memory when she went unconscious at the bottom of the pool. Followed by the trauma of being revived and rushed to the hospital.

After tests and sleeping pills, her mind had become muddled. Now it was confirmed that the lights to the house had been purposely cut. Cut at a precise moment. Timed to the second.

"Oh, dear God in heaven," she whispered, her body turning cold.

Her fingers hadn't slipped from Brett's hand—Brett had purposely opened his hand and let go of her the very moment the lights were slashed.

She hadn't stood a chance of maintaining her balance, especially on those stiletto heels.

Chloe had also told Liam that she was certain that somebody *was* in the pool with her that first minute before Carter and Liam found her at the bottom of the pool. Somebody had pushed her back down just as she was trying to swim to the surface.

Under cover of darkness, Brett must have slipped down the side of the pool, the sound of his movements covered by the confusion of the blackout and her own loud splash.

Later, after she was being given CPR, Brett had said that he'd also jumped in to save her. Which explained why he was soaking wet.

"Instead, he tried to make sure I drowned," Chloe said hoarsely. "So that nobody would know the diamonds were ever swapped."

She was the only one who'd been given training to detect the fake stones. Only she had the key to the office door and the combination.

At the very least, he'd put her out of commission for twelve hours so he'd have time to figure out how to get into the safe. But it wasn't long enough to make the swap when Liam ended up sleeping inside the office.

How Brett had managed to get into the safe late this afternoon was another question altogether. He had to have had an accomplice. Someone who could take the combination code he'd figured out and do the swap in two minutes or less.

Or his co-conspirator had gotten into the safe while she was out on her date with Brett.

Perhaps Mercedes had never worn the real diamonds at all.

Chloe's head ached with it all while she continued working at the knots around her wrists. Her skin was rubbed raw, growing more tender as the rope slowly loosened, her fingers doing calisthenics to get under the crisscrossed knots.

Holding the one end of the rope that was now free, Chloe tucked it under her chin the best she could to keep it from tightening up again while she worked at the last knot.

Two minutes later, she let out a burst of relief, tears of emotion close to the surface. Scrabbling out of the rope, she tossed it aside and tugged at the knot holding the black sack over her head.

Panting, Chloe finally managed to loosen the bag and yank it off. Fresh air never tasted so good. Yanking the silk scarf out of her mouth, she breathed in big gulps of blessed air.

Slits of faint light came through the cracks around the perimeter of the pantry door. And with it, the acrid smell of smoke.

"What in the world—" Chloe spit out.

That particular burnt smell was much too familiar. And terrifying. There was a fire in the kitchen just beyond the door she was locked behind.

Whipping out her tool kit, she shook the bag's contents into the lap of her bridesmaid dress, *seeing* each tool by only the touch of her hands, including the various screwdrivers and pliers included by Jim Greene. Just in case she needed to delicately take out one of the diamond stones to look at it more carefully.

Taking off a door wasn't something she'd originally learned in her FBI training, although they'd practiced doing it. As a kid, she'd helped her father change out a few doors in the house when he was on a painting kick, long before his success as a politician.

She knelt at the bottom of the door and rammed the screwdriver up along the bolt that held the door on its hinges.

The air inside the pantry grew thick with bitter smoke.

Chloe let out a cry of frustration. The entire wedding party was blissfully unaware that the house was on fire. She prayed it wouldn't spread beyond the kitchen to the rest of the house.

"Come on, door!" she choked out, wiping her sweating face with the back of her hand. Her eyes were burning now, painful tears leaking out.

Finally, the first bolt was out and she rose to her feet, banging her head on a shelf that was invisible in the dark. The top bolt was easier, looser, but the last few minutes in a smoke-filled room could be deadly. She was coughing in earnest now.

One hand on the doorknob and the other grasping the bottom of the door, she jiggled it loose from the hinges. "Come on, come on," she urged. "Blast you, door!"

All at once, the door fell off the hinges and crashed forward, taking Chloe down with it. She landed straight on the kitchen tile, dazed and wondering if she'd broken anything when she slammed down so hard. Every bone in her body ached.

A moment later, footsteps approached.

The outer door to the hallway banged open. "Chloe!" a male voice shouted. "Chloe, are you in here?"

It was Liam.

"Here," she croaked out, trying to see past the billowing smoke.

"Chloe, what the—" Liam spewed out a few curse words as he raced forward to kneel beside her. "Are you alive? Chloe, talk to me."

"I—I can't breathe."

"Someone started a grease fire on the stove and in the oven both," Liam grunted. "And it's getting worse."

He jumped up, grabbing the fire extinguisher from the wall. He pulled the pin and began foaming the room. But the small extinguisher wasn't enough to stop all the flames. He tossed the empty can to the floor and was at Chloe's side again.

"Do you have the strength to put your arms around my neck?" he asked, placing his arms underneath her. "Don't pass out. So help me, Chloe Romano, I refuse to allow you to die for a second time in two days."

Tears were streaming down her face from the bitter smoke, and Chloe swore she'd swallowed most of it.

"One more burst of strength, and we're out of here," Liam said close to her ear.

Pushing with her feet, Chloe rose halfway up, her legs trembling like a newborn kitten. Orange flames were now licking the ceiling. Gripping her, Liam staggered out of the kitchen, slamming the door behind him to contain the smoke.

"Fire!" he yelled. "Anybody in the house?"

There was no answer, but a haze of sharp, acerbic black smoke was climbing up the stairs and filling the twenty-foot ceiling of the foyer.

Liam carried Chloe out to the porch, but despite the clean fresh night air, she wanted to claw her throat out from her mouth, it hurt so badly.

Setting her down on the steps of the porch, Liam said, "I'm

going back inside to make sure nobody is upstairs in the bedrooms."

"No—you'll get hurt—" Chloe said, clenching at his shirt.

"What if Granny Zaida went to bed already? I have to make sure. I want *you* to get down to the bottom of the yard. Down by the trees and the river. I called the police when you texted me that the diamonds were fake."

"Oh no!" Chloe whimpered. The thought of her grandmother passed out in her room from the smoke that was filling the house was enough to rip her heart out from her chest.

When she turned to tell Liam to be careful, he was already gone. Long, slow seconds passed while Chloe's chest heaved. Somewhere in all the commotion of the last hour, she'd misplaced her cell phone. It must have been left in Uncle Max's office when she was attacked.

Staggering to her feet, she clung to the porch railing. "Liam Esposito, you are an idiot!"

The sound of sirens pierced the air. The police. Hopefully a fire truck, too.

Chloe was sure she was going to vomit or pass out any minute, but she kept walking down the porch and back toward the reception, staggering on her feet, every single inch of her body in pain.

It had to be after midnight by now. Many guests had departed because the road and driveway were emptying of vehicles, but a group of dancers were still going, and her family was milling about under the tree lights.

Carter spotted her first, coming over to stare into her face. "Chloe, what happened to you? Your dress is torn. You have black smudges all over you."

"Fire," she choked out. "In the house."

"What!" Carter stared up at the house, then back at her. "Don't pass out or I'll never forgive you," he said bluntly, and then he turned to cup his hands around his mouth and shout above the noise of the dance music. "Fire!"

Carter must have run off and grabbed the band's microphone, because his voice got louder as he shouted, instructing everyone to get away from the house.

The sound of sirens grew closer, and when Chloe glanced up, three police cars and two fire trucks roared down the road and pulled through the mansion gates.

There was nothing more she could do except put one foot in front of the other. The grass was cool under her bare feet. Had her high heels come off during her struggle with her attacker?

She couldn't even remember now. No, she'd taken them off before going into the house. But she was more convinced than ever that the diamond culprit was Brett Sorenson.

He'd flirted with her. Pretended to woo her, to distract her so she wouldn't suspect him. That's why he took the red-eye flight. To be long gone when all heck broke loose.

He must have started the fire, too. To keep her from escaping the pantry closet when she went unconscious from the smoke. Once again, he'd tried to kill her, or at least gravely incapacitate her.

Walking with slow but steady steps around the driveway back to the front of the house, Chloe glanced over her shoulder. Only a few guests were following her while several others had gone down toward the Potomac.

The rest of her family had hurried around the other side of the house and were standing on the front lawns, out of the way of the fire trucks.

Firefighters were already in action, moving quickly with hoses and gear.

Poor Uncle Max and Aunt Aurelia. The diamonds were gone and possibly their house, too. And poor Mercedes's wedding reception was ruined.

The more pressing question was her grandmother. Had Liam

186

gotten to her in time? She strained her burning eyes to see across the yard, but couldn't see Granny Zaida.

Carter appeared out of the blue, touching her shoulder. "Are you okay, Chloe? You're walking like you're drunk."

"Do you know where Granny Zaida is? Did Li—Stan get her out of the house?"

"Haven't seen your date in quite a while, but Granny is with Mom and Dad and Julia."

"Are you positive?"

"I swear." Her brother pointed past the wedding lights to the cluster of people near the fence line by the road. "There she is, right there."

"I think I've gone a little blind," Chloe said, wiping at her face. "I hope you guys are far enough from the house. Don't want a gas line explosion."

"The fireman said we were fine as long as we didn't try to move any closer. This is unbelievable. I wonder if one of the cooks left the stove lit."

Chloe didn't have the strength to explain the story at the moment.

"Come back with me, Chloe. You look terrible."

"I feel terrible. But have you *seen*—Stan at all? I know he went back into the house to look for Granny."

Concern crossed Carter's face. "I'll tell the fire chief to check the house for anyone who might be inside. I'm going to check on Julia. Are you okay if I leave you for a few minutes?"

"Yes, yes," Chloe whispered, choking down a fresh onslaught of tears. "It's happening all over again," she groaned hoarsely. "A fire killed Jenna. Now Liam—" She broke off when her legs gave out and she collapsed onto the cool, green grass.

Where was Liam? Why hadn't he come out of the house yet?

CHAPTER 22

"I'm not going to watch you die when that house bursts into flames, Liam Esposito," Chloe said to the cold, hard stars overhead, summoning every last ounce of strength and mental willpower left inside of her.

One leg at a time, she crawled to her knees, and then rose to her feet, lurching drunkly toward the front porch. She was the only one who had seen Liam re-enter the house.

Police officers were speaking with her family down by the road. Firemen were going in and out of the rear of the house where the blaze had started. Black smoke billowed through the french doors, forming a haze over the canopy of wedding lights.

The smoke grew stronger and uglier as Chloe staggered closer. She faltered over the wet, slippery grass from the dew that was already rising in the chilly night air.

Keeping her eyes on the porch, Chloe finally stumbled up the steps. She was winded and coughing badly. Her lungs would eventually heal, but if Liam didn't come out of that house, he was going to die, just like Jenna.

"Good grief," Chloe spit out. "You'd think I cared about the man." She had tried to hang on to her animosity, but Liam had gone inside to find her grandmother and hadn't been seen since. "Why didn't you try to save Jenna?"

She had never given him a chance to explain what happened that night. She'd brushed him aside. Told herself she hated him when deep down it wasn't actually true at all.

She had to see Liam again. She had to talk to him. She had to feel his strong arms around her one more time before it was too late.

"Miss, don't go in there," an officer shouted behind her.

She ignored him, even as smoke was curling out the front door. Chloe slammed the door open and heat assaulted her.

Picking up the hem of her ankle-length dress, she held the material over her nose and mouth, lunging across the slippery marble to take the stairs two at a time.

The house was hot and dank, but thankfully the twenty-foot-high ceilings were capturing the majority of the smoke far above her, hovering like an angry storm cloud.

Chloe reeled forward, heading straight for her grandmother's bedroom. When she reached it, she shoved the door open and ran around the bed and into the adjoining bathroom, but Liam was not here.

She raced back to the hallway, screaming past the pain in her throat. "Liam, where are you? Answer me, Agent Esposito!"

The noise of the firemen dragging hoses and yelling instructions at each other drowned out everything else.

One by one, she ran into each of the bedrooms, finding them all empty, except for the very last guest bedroom—hers. She almost fell over Liam, who was lying so very still on the floor near the canopy bed.

"Liam!" she screamed, shaking him by the shoulders. "Wake up! Get up, get up, you idiot!"

He moaned, and Chloe used her knees to push against his back to get him into a sitting position, where he slumped over onto the hardwood floor again. His face was gray and his pulse weak.

Fear stabbed her in the chest so she did what had come naturally during her career with the FBI.

"On your feet, Agent Esposito!" Chloe growled sharply. "That's an order!"

His eyes finally split open, and he opened his mouth in an effort to speak. "Chloe—what happened?"

"I have no idea other than you passed out."

"Granny Zaida," he whispered hoarsely. "Can't find her."

"She's out of the house. She's safe. We all are, except for you. So help me, if you die, I'm going to personally kill you. I won't attend your funeral, either."

His lips cracked a smile. "Oh, Chloe. My girl."

"Come on, you have to help me. I'm about to pass out from lack of oxygen myself."

From somewhere inside her, Chloe gathered strength she didn't know she had to help this big, hulking man to his feet. Wrapping her arms around his waist, they lurched through the door, leaning on each other until they reached the banister.

One step at a time, they maneuvered the stairs, Chloe hanging on to Liam by her fingernails. He was so tall and unwieldy, Chloe feared they'd tumble down the stairs and break their necks.

An instant later, the front door was ripped off its hinges, and three firemen raced forward holding a hose. They stopped when they saw Chloe and Liam clinging to each other on the stairs, ready to collapse.

Before Chloe could open her mouth, two firemen were up the stairs, grabbing Liam from her while the second firefighter slung her over his shoulder. Seconds later, they were pounding down the front porch and running forward to the ambulances—and her family.

When the fireman laid Chloe on the soft, damp grass, he said, "We're taking you to the hospital."

Chloe shook her head, desperation making her heart slam against her ribs. "I have to see Liam. Is he okay, is he alive?"

The firefighter nodded reassuringly. "You're both going to be fine, but it was insane to go back into the house to rescue him," he scolded her.

"I know, but wouldn't you go back inside to find your missing partner?"

The fireman gave her a crooked smile, pressing his lips together with a nod, gazing at her with admiration.

The whirling lights from so many emergency vehicles were hurting Chloe's eyes more than the smoke was now.

She reached out a hand when a figure came out of the darkness. Liam sank onto the lawn next to her, throwing out his arms and legs in an exhausted spread-eagle position.

"Are you a ghost?" she asked, crawling over to stare down at him. Before she could check his pulse, Chloe groaned with a blinding headache, and she sank down next to him, her eyes so heavy they closed from the pain and fatigue.

Liam's arms went around her as he helped her lie down next to him on the pillowy lawn. "I am *not* a ghost, my beautiful, brave, amazing Chloe," he said, pulling her close and pressing her face against his chest.

She caught the front of his shirt with her fist. "You disappeared inside and didn't come back out. Don't ever do that to me again!"

"I couldn't find your grandmother. I had to keep going, but then I was overcome and passed out. You saved my life, Chloe Romano. I'll love you forever."

"Don't joke around, Agent."

He stroked the back of her head, his hand smoothing down her long hair. "I'm dead serious. You think the paramedics have any water? I need a drink, and so do you, Agent Romano."

A moment later, Chloe was surrounded by her family, faces

worried, everyone talking at once, her parents holding her tight while they laughed and cried with relief.

A water bottle appeared out of nowhere, and Chloe was forced to take a sip.

"Drink slowly," a voice commanded. "Small sips." The voice belonged to a paramedic who was taking her vitals. "Going to give you a ride to the hospital, too."

"I was at the hospital last night. I don't want to go back."

The medic said, "You don't have a fever, which is good, but smoke inhalation is nothing to mess with. You should have a doctor look at you."

"I have a raging headache and a very sore throat."

"I'm not surprised," the paramedic said. "I can't force you to go because you're not unconscious, but I'm going to continue to pester you before this night is over."

Chloe gave her a weak smile.

"Come on, Chloe," Liam said. "I'll go with you and hold your hand."

"I couldn't possibly get to my feet, let alone walk. I'll just lie here all night."

"I'll carry you then."

"No, you won't," she told him fiercely.

"Ah, there's the Chloe I know and love."

"Don't—" she choked out, hot, burning tears slipping down her face. "Don't say something you don't mean."

Liam's eyes locked with hers, and Chloe's stomach shot past her heart. She couldn't speak for a moment. He was much too close, his face only inches from hers, the warmth of his body radiating toward her in waves of comfort and longing.

"I always tell the truth, Chloe Romano," he whispered softly, brushing a lock of hair from her face while he gazed fiercely into her eyes. "Especially when it comes to you."

A thousand emotions ran through her, and Chloe could only bury her face in his chest, unable to say another word.

They were both alive, and Chloe's nerve endings were on fire along with her throat. Why did this man do this to her when she wanted so badly to hate him?

The two of them hadn't been this physically close since that long-ago night on the lawn under the stars. Now here they were again, lying on a lawn, Chloe held tightly in his arms while desire overpowered her. This man was so alluring and so confusing all at the same time.

On one hand, Chloe wanted to push him away and then she wanted to hold him with every inch of her being, but she didn't have the strength to do either. She also didn't have the strength to get up and walk away. Or to roll over and tell him to get lost, which made her lift her lips in a tiny smile.

Liam's white teeth sparkled in the darkness as he held her face in his large palms. The look in his eyes rocked her world and her soul, while the world of the Romano mansion could have been a million miles away.

The silhouettes of Chloe's family huddled together in small groups with somber faces and shocked eyes. Uncle Max had his arms around a stunned Aunt Aurelia, and Mercedes was crying into the jacket of Mark's tux. Granny Zaida was sitting in a folding chair Carter had carried over from the garden area, but her fancy wedding dress was smudged with dirt and soot.

The air continued to buzz with the sound of the fire engines and the blast of hoses while the firemen worked to prevent the blaze from spreading.

Surrounded by blankets, Chloe was finally getting warm, the trembling in her body beginning to subside. She lifted her chin at Liam. "What's that supposed to mean, anyway—the Chloe you know and love?" She poked a finger into his chest. Darn him, his muscles were hard as rock.

She was having a hard time breathing , and her heart pounded against her ribs. Whether it was the smoke that had seeped into her pores from being locked in the kitchen closet or

Liam's closeness, she didn't know, and it was too hard to figure out.

"I'm trying to square up your unexpected heroics when you ran into a burning house to find my grandmother," she added. "But you ran *away* when Jenna was trapped inside an exploded house."

"I know that's what you think, Chloe. But you're mistaken . . ." Liam's voice lowered. "A lot of things went horribly wrong that night. We weren't anticipating the drug cartel planting a bomb to take out our team."

"The nightmares of that night never go away," Chloe said with a ragged breath.

"While you were pulling Agent Holmes out the front door, I ran around to the back of the house and lifted Jenna out through a rear window that had exploded."

Chloe shook her head. "That's not how I remember it."

"You didn't read the final report that included our team interviews during debriefing. I knew the reports were too painful, so I don't blame you, but you have to know that I would never have left one of our own behind. Least of all, Jenna."

Chloe folded her knees to her chest, her shoulders shaking with silent sobs while she tried to gain control of her emotions. Liam gathered her close while he gently stroked her back.

"You need to cry, Chloe. You were amazing that night, carrying Agent Holmes out on your shoulders. I was so proud of you. We all thought Jenna would make it. Her death rattled our entire team—and still does."

"I wanted to run back inside and get her," Chloe said in a muffled voice. "But the heat—the smoke—the flames, it was too much. I choked. I lost my nerve. Then the house collapsed. All this time, I've been guilty, too. But you were the one I blamed. It was easier to hate you."

"Oh, Chloe." Liam put a finger under her chin so that their

eyes met. "You have no guilt at all. I already had Jenna out, but the burns she suffered were too great for her to overcome."

"I never saw you at the hospital after the accident. You didn't visit Jenna, or pay your respects at her funeral."

Liam let out a breath and didn't speak for a moment. "That's because I couldn't go. I was in the hospital recovering from my own injuries."

She reared back in shock. "What are you talking about?"

"While you were keeping vigil at Jenna's bedside, I was being treated for burns."

"Where were you burned? Show me."

Liam gave a self-deprecating laugh. "There's a reason I never wear short-sleeved shirts. And suit jackets are a favorite part of my ensemble even in the heat of summer. I don't want to scare people. Although I could probably be convinced to go skinny-dipping at midnight by myself," he added with a quirk of his mouth.

"You are impossible. And I'm serious. Where were you hurt? Show me."

The idea of Liam being hurt that same, tragic night was overwhelming. He had never breathed a word. Just kept it quiet so nobody fussed over him.

"In order to show you, I have to take off my shirt, and I'm not sure you really want to see the scars."

"But I do. So take off your shirt. That's an order, Agent."

Slowly, Liam loosened his tie and tossed it onto the grass. Then he unbuttoned his white shirt and opened the front of it. There was enough moonlight to see that along the right side of his stomach lay a swath of wrinkled skin caused from second-degree burns.

Next, he rolled up the sleeve of his left arm. More burn scars stretched along his forearm to his elbow.

Tears swam in Chloe's eyes all over again, and she bit at her trembling lips.

"Oh, Chloe," Liam said, brushing a finger along her cheek. "Don't cry for me. It's just part of my job. I was proud to be part of that mission, despite its tragic outcomes."

Bending down, Chloe traced a finger along the scars of his abdomen and arm. Then she took Liam's hand and pressed it against her face, gazing at him, love spilling out of her heart just like the tears in her eyes.

"It's okay, Chloe," he said again. Liam placed a kiss in her palm and then grasped her fingers with his, tightly lacing their hands together.

Chloe's skin sizzled with the fireworks of his touch. Her heart raced, and her throat filled with an emotion so strong she was overwhelmed.

Liam smiled at her, his eyes grazing her face hungrily. He reached out to brush his other hand across her cheek and then skimmed his thumb along her lips.

"That feels much better, Agent Romano." Liam's words were teasing, but his eyes were dead serious. "You have no idea how much I have longed to touch you again."

"Don't tease me, Esposito," she said with a shake of her tangled hair. "Besides, I'm dirty, and I lost my shoes and my cell phone."

"Well, I don't want to kiss your dirty cheeks or make a phone call, so we're all good."

Time paused, hanging suspended in the night air, while Chloe gazed at Liam, overwhelmed by the truth of his heroics, his burn scars, and the feelings of his heart. She rose to her knees and crawled into Liam's arms, holding him tight for several long breathless moments.

"Hey, you need to lie down now and rest, you adorable woman," he finally said, laying her back against the blankets. "You've had a busy night."

When he cradled Chloe's face with both of his big, gentle hands, a rush of warmth spread through her. Agent Liam

Esposito was too handsome by half. Those shoulders, that jawline. His lips coming closer, making her lightheaded, dizzy.

Chloe's stomach jumped to the moon when Liam gently pressed his lips against hers in a soft, warm, and delicious kiss.

"You are crazy, Agent Esposito," she murmured. "Kissing me for the first time while my entire family is watching."

"Why hide? Why wait?" he said, and then planted another one straight on her lips while he smiled broadly.

Chloe thought her brain would explode, along with her heart and her soul. "You are impossible."

"It's been a long two years waiting for this very moment," he said quietly. "I've loved you all this time, Chloe. I hated that we had to put aside our feelings."

She traced a finger along the length of his jaw and then touched his lips. "When we couldn't be together, I decided that hating you was easier."

"I wanted to punch Brett Sorenson all weekend. I almost put a fist through your uncle's wall when I watched you flirting and dancing with him. Making plans to go to Savannah for a weekend. I also heard Mercedes talking about your little pre-wedding date."

"Oh, did you? I guess I can't choose men very well, can I?"

"The fact that he tried to kill you—twice—is a pretty good indication you should have thrown him off a cliff. Or you could let the authorities toss him into prison and throw away the key."

"Guess I'll take the latter," she joked, and then sighed. "How do you know when you can trust someone?"

"You're looking at him right now, and in case you need more convincing, I'm also an Eagle Scout. It's part of my motto, including the one I took with the FBI."

"Very funny," Chloe said. "I always wondered how you could keep working for the FBI after the accident. After Jenna's death, I lost my nerve so I resigned. I knew I couldn't be a good agent.

Instead, I feared I'd become a liability to other agents and hurt someone, even accidentally."

"Perhaps you're much more suited to weddings," Liam said with a grin. "But I don't see the role of bridesmaid as your only future."

"Oh, you don't, huh?"

"I see you as the main attraction one day. All in white. With a boatload of diamonds around your neck."

"No thank you! Diamonds are not necessarily a girl's best friend!"

"Will you finally be my best friend?" Liam asked quietly, kissing her again. "And possibly my future bride?"

Chloe's eyes widened, staring into his face. "Are you proposing, Agent Esposito? It's quite sudden, isn't it?"

"Nope. It's been almost two years in the making, but at the moment, I'm proposing something else."

"What's that?"

"I'm taking you to the hospital for smoke inhalation. You need another chest X-ray."

EPILOGUE

*C*hloe cracked open her eyes to find Liam gazing at her while she slept. She tried to speak, but her voice came out parched and husky, despite the medicine and liquids they were giving her.

"See, I'm much better," she croaked, noticing the doctor standing on the opposite side of the bed railing.

"This time around, we're keeping you an extra day," Doctor Abbott said. "We want your vocal cords to heal some more, so please try to limit talking to what's absolutely necessary. Hand signals are good," he added with a smile.

"Listen to the good doctor," Liam told her, pressing Chloe's fingers to his lips.

"Your chest X-ray hasn't changed, and I want that to improve as well," Doctor Abbott went on. "You just *had* to leave here yesterday to be in a wedding."

"It was a really important wedding," Chloe whispered.

"The wedding of the decade—in more ways than one," the doctor said, raising both eyebrows, and Chloe let out a hoarse laugh.

After the doctor left, Liam scooted next to Chloe on the bed, taking her in his arms. He kissed her long and slow and so passionately, Chloe swore she went cross-eyed. She would have collapsed into a swoon if she hadn't been lying down already.

Liam murmured, "Doctor's orders say that kissing is good for healing."

"Doctor Abbott said that, did he?" She laughed, but the giggle turned into a cough.

Liam grabbed the water bottle and straw from the side of the table, and Chloe sipped at it slowly.

"You need to keep drinking, too," she told him. "You're just lucky you got discharged this morning. I think the doctor likes you better."

"You are not to be trusted, Chloe Romano. If we turn our backs, you'll make a getaway."

She made a face, knowing he was right. They sank against the bed pillows, arms wrapped tightly around each other, not speaking for several long moments.

Chloe breathed him in and held him close, amazed that they were actually alive and together, yet wholly comforted by this amazing man that now belonged to her.

"Hey, I have something to tell you," Liam said suddenly. "We found Brett Sorenson."

Chloe sat up. "Give me the details!"

"They arrested him when he landed in Georgia early this morning."

"Where were the diamonds? How did he get away with them in his suitcase?"

"Ssh, sh, no talking now."

"Ergh," Chloe growled under her breath.

"First you might want to know that the Romano mansion has been saved. Water and smoke damage, but carpets and furniture and paint can all be replaced. The kitchen will need a major overhaul. Your aunt is pleased that she can redo the cabinets now."

Liam grinned, and Chloe tried to punch him in the shoulder, but he caught her hand and kissed it instead.

"They searched Brett's hotel room and nothing turned up, but after the fire was extinguished at your uncle's house, the real diamonds were found hidden in one of the guest rooms. Intact and perfectly fine."

Chloe's eyes widened in shock. "*What?*"

"You'll never guess who the guest room belonged to. Katey Higgins, Mercedes's assistant."

Chloe's jaw dropped. "*No!* That's the last place we would have searched."

Liam nodded. "The one and only innocent Katey. Except not so innocent. She comes off as young and silly, but she's actually much older than she appears. Trained in a family organization of jewel thieves to crack safes and enter locked offices—by her own father, who is also Brett's boss. Diamonds are an obsession with them. Katey had full access to everything in the house, of course."

"She watched me open the safe when the diamonds first arrived in the armored vehicle and Mercedes tried them on," Chloe whispered, trying not to strain her raw throat. "If she was trained in cracking combination locks, she listened as I first put in the numbers. She knew from the start how many numbers she had to figure out."

"Exactly. And ..." Liam paused, reaching out to hold Chloe's hand. "Brett purposely gained your confidence for all the reasons we talked about last night. If he got close to you, it would be easier to both incapacitate you and earn your trust—and then Sorenson gave himself an alibi with your date an hour before the wedding while Katey was up to her shenanigans in Max Romano's office."

"I figured that was the reason Brett didn't speak in the kitchen when he was tying me up. He knew I'd recognize his voice. But you know what else I recognized, although I wasn't cognizant of it at the time with all the fear rushing through me?"

Liam frowned. "What's that?"

"When I felt my assailant's wrist, and the texture of his suit coat, it came to me later that I had been dancing with that very same man."

"Davis Jewelry has their diamonds back. Two crooks—maybe more—are locked away awaiting trial. And," Liam added, his voice turning low and sexy, "I have you. I'd say it's a job well done, Agent Romano."

Chloe placed her hands on either side of Liam's face. "Thank you for going into the house for my grandmother. Thank you for searching the kitchen when I was locked up. You knew the house was already on fire and you came for me, too."

"I always come back for my partner," he told her, tucking a lock of her hair behind her ear. "I only have one question left to ask you, Chloe Romano."

"Hmm?" She snuggled back into the pillows once more.

"How does Savannah sound for our honeymoon?"

Chloe growled. "That is not funny, Esposito."

Before she could say another word, Liam was kissing her deeply and passionately, and Chloe knew she was truly swooning for the first time in her life. This man made her feel things she'd never felt before. He always had.

Perhaps Mercedes was correct. When you met the right man, you just knew deep inside. You didn't have to convince yourself.

When Liam finally broke from Chloe's lips, he said, "I'm going to make you laugh for the rest of your life. And you're going to be the most beautiful bride South Carolina has ever seen."

"I'm going to make you sign a contract that you won't rent any diamonds for the ceremony."

He chuckled. "You don't need diamonds to dazzle me, my love."

"There's only one thing I need to know before this goes any further. If you don't like old movies and southern plantations, we're just not compatible, Agent Esposito."

"Those are deal breakers, huh?" He nuzzled her neck, sending shock waves of desire through Chloe in spite of the antiseptic smell of the hospital surrounding them.

Being with Liam was inexplicable happiness, even lying in a hospital bed with a raspy voice and weak lungs. Despite suppressing their feelings for each other during their time at Quantico, the passion and budding love had never disappeared. In fact, it was more intense than ever.

"I can't visit Savannah until the bad taste of Brett Sorenson is gone," she said now. "But there's this gorgeous plantation on the Mississippi in Louisiana called White Castle. They have a honeymoon suite, and we can watch *Gone with the Wind* on DVD all night long. I have the Blu-ray edition," she added with a saucy grin.

"I have an even better idea for our honeymoon nights," Liam said huskily. "I can give you a preview if you'd like."

"You need to be a good boy until we're married. But you can kiss me like Rhett Butler kissed Scarlett when he left her stranded on the road to Tara."

"I'll do you one better," Liam said, gathering Chloe up in his arms. "I'll kiss you like a man in love with the woman of his dreams."

"Honestly, I never thought I'd be someone's dream," she said, her voice catching.

"Believe me, that's all I could do for the last two years—dream about you while you held me at arm's length."

"Rules are rules," Chloe said flippantly. She was enjoying teasing him, but emotion welled up in her chest when she gazed at this incredible man. "I do love you, Liam Esposito," she added in a soft voice. "I've always loved you."

"And I love you, Chloe Romano—I mean, Scarlett O'Hara."

She laughed, swatting at Liam's arm while his lips came down on hers, and the walls of the hospital melted away while their future became a reality at last.

~

THREE WEEKS LATER . . .

~

Hi Chloe!

Enclosed please find a check for services rendered on October 7th. Quoted price is doubled for bravery in the call of duty—and almost losing your life. Use it for your own beautiful wedding.

Hugs and Kisses!

Your favorite cousin,

Mercedes

P.S. Our honeymoon in Italy was divine!

P.P.S. Didn't I tell you that I'd match you up with the love of your life during my wedding weekend? And Liam Esposito is the perfect catch, girl! You have very good taste.

Maybe I should go into the matchmaking business alongside my estate sale enterprise. . .

DEAR ROMANCE LOVER

~

I hope you enjoyed reading *The Undercover Bridesmaid!* I love writing sweet romance that sweeps me into new and wonderful worlds. The diamond research for the story was particularly fun.

Thank you for reading, and please check out my other romance novels on Amazon, including my *Secret Billionaire Romances.* They're all FREE on Kindle Unlimited, too.

If you'd like to be the first to hear about new releases subscribe to my Reader's Club Newsletter and never miss a thing. When you sign up, you'll receive two Free books! Just go here: http://eepurl.com/NBXon

xo,

~Kimberley Montpetit

P.S. I will be eternally grateful if you have a moment to write a quick review of THE UNDERCOVER BRIDESMAID on Amazon. Reviews help other readers find enjoyable sweet romance, plus it helps me to be able to keep writing new books! A thousand thanks!

ABOUT THE AUTHOR

Kimberley Montpetit once spent all her souvenir money at the *La Patisserie* shops when she was in Paris—on the arm of her adorable husband. The author grew up in San Francisco, but currently lives in a small town along the Rio Grande with her big, messy family.

Kimberley reads a book a day and loves to travel. She's stayed in the haunted tower room at Borthwick Castle in Scotland, sailed the Seine in Paris, ridden a camel among the glorious cliffs of Petra, shopped the maze of the Grand Bazaar in Istanbul, and spent the night in an old Communist hotel in Bulgaria.

Find all of Kimberley's Novels on Amazon

Get FREE Books when you subscribe to Kimberley's Newsletter: http://eepurl.com/NBXon

Keep reading for a sneak peek at the first chapter of *The Neighbor's Secret* and *The Executive's Secret,* part of Kimberley's Secret Billionaire Romance series!

THE NEIGHBOR'S SECRET: A SECRET BILLIONAIRE ROMANCE

BY KIMBERLEY MONTPETIT

It was the perfect day for a wedding. After months of trying on wedding gowns, ordering invitations, and searching every bridal boutique in Toronto for the perfect shoes, Allie Strickland was ready to walk—maybe even run—down the aisle of the church and into Sean Carter's waiting arms.

She'd licked stamps to post the more than one hundred announcements until her tongue was dry. She'd suffered through at least that many long-distance phone calls with her mother that sometimes ended in arguments and tears.

If she didn't stop weeping, Allie's mother joked, their tiny town of Heartland Cove was going to flood over. The calls and planning were finally over, and Allie's wedding day was here.

That morning she'd taken her big fat red marker and made an X on the calendar.

"Mrs. Sean Carter, here I come," she whispered as she capped the pen and tossed it inside a packing box.

During their five years of dating, she and Sean had gone through grad school together, first jobs, and now Sean was climbing the ladder to become a partner with Learner & Associates Law Firm.

Tonight she'd be with the man of her dreams forever. No more work interruptions. No more hurried lunches. No more agonizingly long street car rides to get to one another's apartments. Lately, they'd just meet somewhere for a late dinner.

Tomorrow, new renters were moving into her apartment on Bloor Street. When she and Sean returned from their honeymoon to the Bahamas, Allie would unpack the boxes sitting inside Sean's apartment and officially move in.

Allie's stomach jumped as she checked the time on her phone. Her wedding began in ninety minutes and it would take at least half of that just to get through Toronto traffic.

She sent a text to Sean and then tried to take deep breaths in an effort to settle her nerves while staring at tightly packed buildings and Roger's Stadium glinting in the late afternoon sun.

With her brother Jake at the wheel and the car full of her mother, sister, and best friend Marla on their way to the Episcopal Church, Allie's brain went over her luggage packed for fun, sun, and the beach.

Three bikinis; red, black, and purple.

Slinky dresses for candlelit dinners.

Five pairs of shoes, including a pair of running shoes.

Lingerie and toiletries.

She couldn't *wait* to get on that plane tomorrow morning and leave work and stress and family behind.

Seven perfect days with Sean. Finally, finally, finally.

"I don't think Toronto has ever looked lovelier," Allie sighed happily, pressing her nose against the window glass like a kid.

She was excited, anxious, and terrified all at once—and missing Sean. She hadn't seen him in three days due to his working overtime so he'd have a few days off for their honeymoon.

"I promise we'll have a longer honeymoon when I'm finished with this current trial," he'd said last week. "A cruise of the Greek Islands in autumn."

"You know all my dreams," she'd told him, throwing her arms around his neck and feeling the beat of his heart against hers.

Pulling her arms down, Sean had given her a peck goodbye. "You know I have to be in the courtroom at seven a.m., Allie."

She'd frowned, turning away to stare out the window of her apartment. It was a spectacular view of downtown and the lake. She'd been lucky to get this flat a year ago and hated to let it go, but Sean had a bigger place so she'd reluctantly given up her dream apartment.

"That case has taken over your life. *Our* lives," she said, trying not to whine. "We haven't been out in ages. We've hardly kissed in months."

"But we're getting married in a few days, Allie. Be a grown-up and get used to the hectic life of a criminal defense lawyer."

She despised those moments when he treated her like a child. But all she could say was, "But I *miss* you. Don't you miss me?"

As soon as she spoke the words, Allie chomped down on her tongue. Sentiments like those merely underscored his assessment of her as a petulant child.

"Your dress!" Mrs. Strickland suddenly shrieked from the front passenger seat, motioning to Jake that there was a red light before throwing a glare at her daughter in her wedding finery.

"These darn no left turn streets," Jake muttered, braking so hard they all lunged forward. "Traffic is horrible. They've got the next two streets blocked off for a 10K run."

Quickly, Allie hitched up the beaded satin wedding gown around her to prevent wrinkles on the back end.

"You simply *can't* have wrinkles when you walk down the aisle," her sister Erin said with a dose of sarcasm. "It would be, like, a crime or something."

Mrs. Strickland gave her youngest daughter a second glare and then silently held out her palm when Erin snapped her gum.

Erin stuck her wad of chewing gum in her mother's hand,

smashing it down vehemently in revenge, and leaned back with a sulk.

"Thanks for the gum sacrifice," Allie told her, nudging at her sister's shoulder.

"Huh," Erin grunted, sliding another pack of spearmint contraband from her handbag.

"Look at the blue sky and enjoy the fact that there isn't ten feet of snow on the ground."

"You mean smog and obnoxiously tall concrete they call architecture."

"You only think that because you're sixteen."

"Girls!" their mother cried, craning her neck to check the name of the cross street. "Don't fight on your wedding day."

Jake remained stoic, his mobile giving out directions in an English accent.

"It's not *my* wedding day," Erin said, making one of her famous faces, eyes wide, nostrils flaring.

"Obviously. But today is Allie's most special day in her entire life. Be nice. Mind your manners. And *please* don't put your chewed gum on the dinner plate at the reception this evening."

"I'm not eight!" Erin crossed her arms over the deep maroon bridesmaid dress. Lower cut in the bust line than Mrs. Strickland had suggested, but nobody had listened to her protests when the wedding planning rose to extreme levels of tension.

Marla Perry, Allie's best friend since Kindergarten, reached over with a tissue. "You've got a smudge of frosting on your face, Allie."

"Where?" Allie scrabbled inside her white lace-covered wedding bag for a mirror, which, of course, only held two tissues and a lipstick for refreshing. Allie had a tendency to bite off her lip color. "How could you let me leave the house like that?"

"It's just a tiny smidge," Marla assured her. "Probably cream cheese from the cinnamon roll."

"You just *had* to go and make cinnamon rolls for breakfast on the day I wanted to be my skinniest best self," Allie teased.

"I knew you'd go all day without food if I didn't give you something. And then we'd be picking you up off the floor in front of the minister when you fainted from starvation."

"Not starvation. Sugar overload. I should have had a granola bar."

"Granola bars are for birds, not real people," Marla said. "Fainting can be a means to an end. Sean could scoop you up from the cold floor and kiss you passionately."

Marla had snagged the lead role in *Romeo and Juliet* in their high school drama production class and swore she'd leave the tiny town of Heartland Cove and run away to New York City. She'd gotten as far as Toronto—which, for a Heartland Cove resident, that boasted a population of 899 was, nevertheless, a major feat. But her Fine Arts degree in photography was proving difficult to find a decent paying job.

She'd finally taken a position shooting kids school photos all over town with Life Touch, but was determined to open her own business.

The thought of having your own business was exciting. Despite using her MBA to snag a good paying position, Allie was bored to tears with financial reports and office politics as the manager at a small branch of The Royal Bank.

"Mom. Chill," Jake said at last. Miss British GPS voice told him to turn right, but when he did he hit another red light and jerked to a stop. All the women braced a hand on their seats, then adjusted dresses and jewelry.

"Warn us next time, Jake," Mrs. Strickland said, the frown deepening between her eyes.

Allie did not miss the family dynamics living in Toronto, although she sometimes got nostalgic for Heartland Cove, the town where she'd been born, worked her teen summers at the Strickland Family Fry Truck, and had her first kiss on the Bridge of Heartland Cove with a boy who told her he'd love her forever —and then promptly moved to Newfoundland three weeks later. It might as well have been Timbuktu.

After a few sexy Facebook messages, he'd posted a picture of himself with a suntanned blond girl—and disappeared from her life forever.

In Heartland Cove he'd been her only possibility for a boyfriend until she'd met Sean her senior year as an undergrad in Business School.

Sean Carter was the complete opposite of the boy from tiny Heartland Cove High. Tall, slim and dark-haired with smoldering eyes and a crooked grin that melted her heart.

"I think butterflies have set up permanent housekeeping in my stomach," Allie said, while the clock ticked down to the moment they both said, "I do".

Sean was now on the verge of being offered the position of junior partner at Learner & Associates. He'd worked hard and received top marks in law school. Now the man lived and breathed law, briefs, and depositions. He had a sharp mind and was quickly becoming a talented and incisive criminal lawyer. Being in the courtroom gave him a thrill like riding the most daring roller coaster at Six Flags.

Sometimes, Allie worried that *she* wasn't thrilling enough. The only time Sean got truly passionate was after he'd argued a heated and feisty trial.

Mrs. Strickland patted her hand. A little bit comforting. A little bit impatiently. And a little bit sadly.

"You alright Mom?" Allie asked.

Her mother gave a wan smile, and a tug of empathy rose in Allie's chest. She'd never seen her mother wearing red lipstick. Any makeup really. Frying burgers and fries for the tourists that swarmed the town every day wasn't exactly conducive to glamour.

Heartland Cove's main industries were potato farms and

lavender fields—and buses that disgorged tourists three times a day to gawk at the Heartland Cove bridge—the world's longest covered bridge.

Mrs. Strickland brushed off any discomfort she was feeling. "I'm a fish out of water in the glamour of Toronto."

"You look lovely, Mom."

Her mother was wearing a maroon sheath trimmed in lace, black pumps, pantyhose, and a ton of hairspray in a traditional middle-aged pouf. A far cry from jeans and a splattered, greasy apron.

Her cell phone began to buzz, and she recognized the familiar ring of her fiancé. "It's Sean!" she shrieked, patting at her dress and then peering along the floorboard of the car. "I can't find my phone! Why's he calling? I talked to him just before we left the apartment. What if he got in an accident?"

"Calm down," Jake said, speeding through a light. He turned to give Allie a grin. "Knowing him, he's calling about the cop giving him a speeding ticket right about now."

"Be useful and help me find my phone, Erin!"

Her sister pressed her lips together and folded her arms across her chest, tapping one toe on the floor mat.

"Okay, sorry," Allie quickly corrected. "I'm sorry. I don't know why I'm panicking."

"Wedding day jitters," Marla said soothingly, searching under the car seats.

Allie lifted wads of satin as delicately as possible. She shook out the folds of her gown, but there was no sign of the phone. It was as if it had disappeared into another dimension.

"I wish you'd gotten married in Heartland Cove, sweetheart," Mrs. Strickland said wistfully.

The ringing had stopped by now and Allie's stomach clenched. Sean had trained her to never miss a phone call from anyone.

He always said that if they were going to excel at their careers and strive for every possible promotion, they could open their own law firm one day, Allie as office manager and head of PR. "Let no opportunity go to waste," Sean said. "Grab them all."

"My phone couldn't couldn't have vanished into thin air."

"It's probably on the floor," Erin said with a yawn.

"Can you help me reach down and get it?"

Erin heaved a second deep sigh and dug around the floor, swishing yards of satin and tulle out of her way.

"Careful of my dress!"

"I'm being careful. And . . . it's not here."

"Marla!" Allie said, panic bringing tears to her eyes.

"Don't you dare cry and mess up that makeup job. Here, grab the seat back and lift your bum." Marla ran her fingers along the leather seat under Allie's wedding gown. "Aha!" She held up the cell phone between two fingers and plopped it into Allie's lap.

"You're a lifesaver." Allie quickly checked her voicemail. Sean's deep voice spoke into her ear. "Hey, Allie, I had to run by the office to pick up a new report for this case. Mr. Thompson said I have to read it tonight. The defendant was caught—well, never mind what he was doing. I can't tell you that. But I *will* be at the church. Hitting green lights now, almost to the office."

His voice abruptly stopped and Allie stared at the lifeless phone. It would have been nice to hear an "I love you", but perhaps he'd found a parking space and run inside the office building.

"What's up?" Marla asked.

"Nothing," she lied. "Everything is fine." Inside, she couldn't help fuming. "He might be five minutes late," she added, just to prepare her family.

She hated when they complained about Sean and his awful work schedule. She didn't want to give them any more ammunition than necessary. Sean was there for all the important occasions. Right now was a critical time in his career and when they were able to be together in the same house it would be so much easier to support each other.

"At least your flight isn't until the morning," Erin said, kicking off her tight dress shoes and studying her tanned legs. No doubt, Allie's sister wanted to be at the lake water skiing.

"Sean will be there waiting for Allie with the minister," Marla said reassuringly.

Despite her words, the sick feeling grew in Allie's stomach.

When Marla nudged her, Allie thoughts scattered. In a low voice her friend said, "I know what you're thinking."

"What?" she hissed under her breath, not wanting the rest of the inhabitants of the car to overhear them; namely her diary-reading younger sister.

"You don't want to be embarrassed if Sean is late because you know Courtney Willis is going to be in the front row of the church, watching you marry her old boyfriend."

"The front row is reserved for family."

"That was supposed to be rhetorical."

Sadly, Allie knew what she meant. "In what universe is it fair that Sean's old girlfriend gets paired up with *my* fiancé on this new high profile case?"

"In the universe of Ally Strickland," Marla said prophetically.

"That is *not* funny."

"I'm trying to get you to crack a smile. You should be glowing. You're marrying the man of your dreams—not Courtney's dreams. She lost him. Bask in the triumph. Hold your head high."

"Why did Sean invite her in the first place? We had two arguments about Courtney over the past month."

"I stamped all your wedding invitations myself. Sean sent one to every employee at the firm. He couldn't leave her out, especially when they're paired up on this case."

"Why did she RSVP? Doesn't she realize that she wasn't actually expected to attend?"

Before Marla could answer, Jake turned off the ignition and jumped out to open the doors all around. "We're here!"

Allie's stomach lurched. The journey to the beautiful little church was over. The moment had arrived.

In forty-five minutes she would be Mrs. Sean Carter.

∾

Grab the rest of THE NEIGHBOR'S SECRET HERE!

FREE on Kindle Unlimited!

THE EXECUTIVE'S SECRET: A SECRET BILLIONAIRE ROMANCE

BY KIMBERLEY MONTPETIT

Caleb Davenport gripped his briefcase, sliding out of the hired car paid for by the company account. After a transatlantic flight it was a relief not having to worry about throwing a few twenty dollar bills at the driver, or digging out his credit card. He strode toward the double glass doors of the high-rise club in downtown Denver.

Breathing in the crisp fall air, Caleb finally relaxed, even though he was jet-lagged after making the transfer from Hong Kong via Los Angeles.

He was home, and the Rocky Mountains exuded their own sweet, familiar scent. The high altitude was bracing, clean and fresh. No more stifling hot, crowded streets with a hundred different scents of food vendors, perfumes, and body odor.

Eager to meet up with the rest of the partners of DREAMS, Caleb punched the elevator button for the ninth floor. His stomach grumbled demanding food. Maybe he and the rest of the guys should have met up over dinner. It was later than he'd thought and the small sandwich on the plane hours ago hadn't exactly been filling.

Waiting for his luggage had taken longer than expected, too, and on this particular Friday night Denver's downtown streets were packed with taxis, rental cars, the 16th Street mall shuttle, as well as the Light Rail commuter train coming in and out of the convention center tracks. A couple of buses rumbled past, filled with name tag wearing folks. Must be some big conventions going on this weekend.

Personally, Caleb was convention-ed out. Three of them back-to-back overseas with more than a dozen companies signing onto the hot new app. His baby, DREAMS; the computer site and app he'd spent years working on.

All in all, the past week had been a resounding success. His little company had grown by leaps and bounds over the past few years, serving thousands of consumers with insanely inexpensive products around the world.

It was mind-blowing to think he was going to bank close to a billion dollars by the end of the year—and it all started with his group of high school computer geek friends.

Caleb's pace turned brisk when he pushed through the glass doors into the posh vestibule of the bar. The five of them; Troy, Brandon, Ryan, Adam, and himself, sent each other a deluge of text messages while overseas—but they often didn't convey many details. Even more often were missing text messages. As if they disappeared traveling through long distance phone lines in third world countries.

The one message that had managed to get through to everyone was his invitation to celebrate at their favorite bar.

"**Meet me at *The 54*,**" he'd texted and, like a ten-thousand-mile miracle from across the Pacific Ocean, he'd received four thumbs up from his partners.

At the end of the plush carpeted vestibule, Caleb opened the second glass door that spelled out *The 54* in swirly gold letters. He was greeted by the hostess, a woman of about twenty-five dressed in a black dress that shimmered from a luminescent fabric. Sleeveless, plunging neckline, the woman had a terrific figure, and toned arms as if she had an exercise trainer.

"Good evening, sir. Welcome to *The 54*," she purred in a cultured voice with a slight accent. Italian? English? He couldn't quite detect her country of origin, although he should, he'd been to London and Rome often enough the past few years on business. "Do you have a reservation with us tonight?"

"Reservation's under Caleb Davenport."

The hostess placed a red manicured finger on her wait list. A small lamp on the tall desk illuminating the ledger with a golden glow.

"I have you right here, Mr. Davenport," she said. "Please follow me."

When she sashayed Caleb to his reserved table in the back, he noted the shapely legs in five-inch high stilettos. With the heels, she was still much shorter than Caleb, who, at six feet four often came across as a big, lumbering bear, even while keeping in shape by running five miles every day. She couldn't be more than five feet two. Despite the attractive women he ran into making business deals and traveling, most women were too short for his taste. He'd love a girl who was closer to five foot ten or taller, actually. Someone he could dance cheek-to-cheek with. A woman he could kiss without breaking his back.

Of course, Caleb wasn't planning to hit on *The 54's* hostess, despite her beauty and lovely accent. But once again, whenever he saw a woman he admired, Caleb instantly found himself thinking about the woman he did want. The woman he wanted for his wife and the mother of his children. Someone to share all this—this crazy life—the money—the travel. And yes, the burden.

Having DREAMS thrive so quickly was often disorienting. When he returned home, Caleb had to purposely ground himself by spending time with his best friends. He'd eat at his favorite restaurants, kick-back at home with a Jason Bourne flick, sit outdoors at the Red Rocks Amphitheater for a concert, or take a hike in the pine forests.

And, of course, make a visit to his parents. Despite the pain that visit brought. Tonight he was feeling guilty, knowing he hadn't visited them in nearly a year. It was too difficult, emotionally distracting, and exhausting, but his mother's birthday was coming up and she'd never forgive him if he didn't bring himself bearing a gift.

It might be crazy to make a list of what he wanted in a woman, but when the hostess showed him their table for five and laid out their menus, Caleb realized he could practically reach down and pat her on the head like she was twelve-years-old. Girls who could wear heels and look him in the eye were hard to find, but a definite priority for his "list". Harder to find in the Asian countries he was currently visiting setting up accounts for DREAMS. Idly, Caleb wondered if women were taller in London where Troy usually traveled. He'd have to ask, he thought, and then grinned to himself.

Pushing thirty, Caleb was ready to find *the* woman. A woman he could spend the rest of his life with. His business and travel didn't leave much time for dating. Let alone women he could talk to without an interpreter. Even if they spoke English and he loved their accent, it wasn't the same. Whether it was books or music or movies or favorite foods, they had little in common.

Caleb gave a sigh and dropped his briefcase to the floor by the table, glancing about for any sign of his team.

The 54 was quieter than most upscale Denver club for the rich citizens of this city. And for him, having a membership here was a reality that was hard to calibrate with his old life.

When Caleb stared at the art deco on the walls, the polished 1920s furnishings, and the painted ceilings, he felt like an outsider.

Heck, he'd grown up in a poor neighborhood, attended a passable elementary school, but fortunate that it fed into a better high school. His father had been a drunken mechanic working odd jobs at home, his mother a part-time school aide who kept her husband company at night with the bottle.

At ten years old, he used to dream of buying them a new house one day. A house that wasn't hanging together with duct tape. Mostly because *he* was the one who wanted to escape his depressing life. He never had friends over. Never told anyone where he lived.

Sitting here now in a posh bar was so diametrically opposite to how he'd grown up that his life felt surreal. As if he could blink his eyes and it would all disappear like a dream.

"Hey, buddy, what are you doing here?" a voice came from behind, echoing his thoughts uncannily.

He whipped around to see Troy Thurlow, his best friend since high school, barreling toward him. "Hey yourself."

"They let riffraff in these places now?" Troy teased.

"Nope, I sneaked in. Like usual."

"That's what I figured." Troy plopped into a seat and grabbed the drink menu.

Caleb still had moments where Troy's friendship and their partnership in DREAMS felt bizarre. But the two of them discovered they had a talent for calculus and computers so they'd end up at the Thurlow home doing math homework while watching *Breaking Bad,* and surreptitiously studied the cheerleaders during lunch in the quad.

Caleb was the greasy geek of the school. A loner who purposely stayed under the radar in the computer lab, except for moments with Troy—when he was virtually invisible next to the vastly more popular football player. There were times during high school that Caleb had wondered if he was Troy's pity project, or a dare. Now he didn't know what he was. Still a geek? Finally grown up when he turned twenty-nine in January?

"Looks like you're overthinking things as usual," Troy said, slapping him on the shoulder.

Caleb gave a snort. "What makes you say that?"

"Your expression was very studious. Bad flight home?"

"Nope, completely uneventful. Just . . . thinking, like you always say."

"It's a woman, isn't it?" Troy gave a grin, waggling his eyebrows. "Who'd you meet in Hong Kong?"

"Nobody," Caleb burst out with a laugh.

"The airline attendant must have been hot then."

Without warning, Brandon appeared and slid into a chair. "You met a babe flight attendant? Tell us more."

Caleb let out a longer laugh. "I couldn't even tell you what the flight attendants looked like. Short? Dark hair? Polite? Served food and drinks. End of story."

Brandon flipped open a menu. "Here I was all ready for a juicy story."

"You mean you didn't meet the woman of your dreams in Brazil, Brandon?" Troy kicked back in his seat and placed his hands behind his head after signaling to the waitress.

"Next time please send me to Rio during Mardi Gras," Brandon told Caleb.

"Nothin' doin'. You'd never come home again."

"There are perks to this job, right?" Troy went on. "But, no, our boss is all work, work, work. I spend the other half of my life sitting on planes."

"Welcome to the real world," Ryan Argyle said, coming up to the table and bumping fists with the rest of the men. Right on his heels was the last member of the DREAMS team, Adam Caldwell, pulling off his tie and unbuttoning the top button of a crisp blue shirt.

"Good, we're finally all here," Caleb said. "Now we can order."

"Hey, I came as soon as I shut down the office," Adam said. "I work longer hours than all of you put together, flying around the world, dancing with luscious foreign women at night."

"Hardly," Troy said with a glance upward at the waitress, a

thin woman of about thirty-five wearing black slacks, a black blouse and thick black eyeliner. "I'll have a ginger ale."

The other guys laughed and Caleb held up his hands to ward off their teasing. "A Coke with vanilla," he said. "And keep the nachos coming, please. Mini sliders, too."

"What's with all the fizzy drinks, guys?" Ryan said. "I know Caleb doesn't touch anything hard, but what about the rest of you guys?"

"Headache," Troy said. "Jet lag is getting to me. I can't even remember what time zone I'm in."

"Mountain Time, poor baby," Adam interjected. "Try sitting at a desk logging orders and shipments until your eyes go numb. I'll have a cold beer, please."

"Didn't know eyes could turn numb," Caleb laughed, giving the youngest member of their crew a teasing grin. Adam Caldwell had been in the class a year behind them in high school. But his computer skills were ferocious so Caleb had hired him two years ago. "That's a new one."

He'd known these guys for so long, but what most of them forgot—except for Troy—was the fact that Caleb never drank. He'd grown up with alcoholic parents and after binge-drinking at a party his senior year, he'd passed out and wouldn't wake up. Terrified, Troy had called an ambulance, afraid Caleb was going to die from alcohol poisoning.

Caleb would never forget his mother speaking at his hospital bedside in a soft voice. "Isn't it bad enough that your father does this?"

She'd been so hurt, her tired face so full of despair, that Caleb hadn't touched a drink since. Despite the teasing during college, the parties going on at his dorm, he just *didn't*. It wasn't worth it. Besides, he wanted to live rather than get a buzz. And avoid liver damage like his father was now suffering with.

Troy ran his hands through his thick dark hair, slouching back in his chair. He was a big man, wide shouldered, with a chest as broad as a football field. Played wide receiver during high school at their alma mater, Southfield High School, but loved the intricacies of computer hardware. He was the guy that could trouble-shoot anything. "Man, it's good to be home."

"Homesick, buddy?" Adam teased.

Troy gave a half smile, shrugging. "There's something about the fall mountain air of Denver that clears your head. South America is just hot and sticky, no matter what time of year you visit."

"Speaking of autumn, what month are we in?" Ryan said, scrolling a thumb across his phone screen. "I've been in too many time zones to remember."

"Months—times zones—it's all the same, oh brainy one," Caleb said, and then added, "Just turned October. We have to hit the office tomorrow, guys. It's only Tuesday and we've got a boatload of data to enter and organize and get on the app."

"Yeah, yeah, we know boss," Troy said, stuffing a burger slider into his mouth now. "You don't have to remind us."

September had proven to be a grueling month and the guys were just doing their usual complaining when they put in an eighty-hour work week during travel but some days he hated being the CEO. They'd known each since their teens, and it often was uncomfortable to be their boss, having to crack the whip with his high school friends.

Ryan dipped a tortilla chip into the nacho cheese dip. "Only asking because I just remembered that we have our ten-year high school reunion later this month."

"We couldn't possibly be that old," Troy quipped, picking up his second slider in under sixty seconds. "Wasn't it only last June that we graduated?"

Ryan gave Troy an eye roll. "Oh, wise one, thank you for that. Did your invitations arrive in the mail? I think it's being held at the Hotel Monaco on Champa Street. Dinner and a DJ, of course. No host bar."

"Ooh, fancy," Adam said. "They must think we're rich."

Low chuckles erupted around the table while Troy said, "Hopefully they don't make us play any stupid games. I'll never forget our senior picnic. Getting dragged in the mud during the tug of war."

"You should have hung on," Caleb teased him.

"If I recall the food was good," Brandon added. "Never-ending barbecue and pie."

"To you, the food is always good," Troy told him. "You have a bottomless pit for a stomach. Your travel reimbursement for restaurants is astronomical."

"Have we made a pact to go—or not?" Ryan asked. "Don't want to show up alone and make small talk with people I don't recognize."

Caleb had forgotten about the reunion, actually. It wasn't in his planner. He shook the hair out of his eyes and stared around the table. All the guys were gazing at him. Like he was the boss of the high school reunion, too. "We could draw straws," he said with a half smile.

"Better than tossing a coin," Adam said, pulling out his calculator to figure out the odds.

An odd shiver ran through Caleb. Recalling the insane stuff that had happened with his parents during high school still felt surreal. He'd basically been on his own since seventeen, but instead of a fierce independence without having to care about anybody but himself, the opposite had happened.

Traveling the world, making bigger bucks than he could ever have dreamed, had produced a lonely, untethered life. Sure, he could do whatever he wanted, but running a company on which hundreds of employees relied on you in twenty different countries, including a team of accountants and lawyers watching your every move created stress that was also far greater than he could have imagined.

He relied on the men sitting around the dinner table very

much. Not just for business, but for friendship and support, saving him from total loneliness. They'd certainly become his surrogate family, and having the support of his friends meant that he avoided obsessing about the past and his derelict parents —except for one person that had never left his memory.

The girl he'd had a crush on since he was a freshman. English class. Staring at the back of her head like a dunce. Caleb sat two desks behind her, fantasizing about running his hands through the silky strands of her shiny hair that swayed along her shoulders and down her back like a waterfall. Yeah, typical teenage boy stuff.

But that girl was untouchable. Far above his low class life. She was soft-spoken and gentle with a laugh that used to make him smile. She wasn't annoying or loud like most girls in high school, vying for attention or queen bee status. She was perfect. The kind of girl you could fall in love with and live happily ever after —if there was such a thing. Unfortunately, he didn't know many happily ever after's. None of his friends were married. A few of his international clients were happily divorced or living up the bachelor life.

He must be the most peculiar man out there to crave a traditional marriage and family. A house that smelled of fresh baked cookies and filled with people who loved each other and didn't have yelling matches or drunken stupors.

There were a lot of reasons Caleb used to hide out in the computer lab, learning C++. When he created computer games it was like submerging himself under water. He could be immune from the world until the janitor kicked him out.

But *that girl* topped the list of reasons. Seeing her every day made him drown with a desire like a vice squeezing at his heart. Caleb just made sure he didn't drool on his desk.

The most bizarre thing was the fact that he still thought about her. More than ten years later. Images would flash through his mind of her standing at her locker spinning the combination lock. In the cafeteria thoughtfully eating French fries. Bent over a class assignment, scribbling furiously while her satin hair draped her arm.

He'd get up to sharpen a pencil just so he could sneak a peek at her touching the tip of her tongue on her top lip in concentration, erasing a line, rummaging in her purse, or drumming her slender fingers on the desk as if practicing piano scales. Everything about her mesmerized him.

So, the question was, would *she* be at the class reunion?

Caleb gulped down his drink, inwardly shaking his head at his idiocy.

She was probably married and had three kids. Plus, a mortgage and an accountant for a husband in the ritzy suburb of Greenwood Village.

Of course, maybe she'd moved far away, like California, South Dakota, or Florida.

For all he knew, she could be serving as a Red Cross nurse in Africa.

When Caleb discovered the high school reunion notice in his mail a couple of months ago, fresh hope had lodged firmly in his throat.

"Hey, earth to Caleb, earth to Caleb," Troy said punching him on the arm.

Startled, Caleb knocked over his glass, soda drizzling across the white tablecloth. He grabbed napkins and blotted it out. "Hey, watch it," he joked in an attempt to hide his daydreaming.

"You alright, Mr. Boss?" Ryan said, motioning to the waitress for more napkins and a fresh drink for Caleb.

"I'm fine," Caleb said, glancing around the table at his co-workers. "Never better."

"Jet lag, I tell you," Brandon said. "Especially when you've been in Hong Kong. It's the worst. You lose a day, you gain a day. Over and over again."

Deftly, their waitress served a fresh glass of soda and ice, mopped up the spill, and then scooped up handfuls of soggy napkins.

Adam stared after her retreating figure, obviously wishing he could flirt with her. The guy flirted with every female within ten feet.

"So," Caleb said, glancing around the table. Most of the food was gone, but he dipped a tortilla chip into the last of the salsa with a nonchalant air. "Everybody going to the reunion, then?"

Adam snorted and Ryan cocked an eyebrow. "Yeah, Mr. Boss. Five minutes ago, we decided we were all going together. Stag. It'll give us a chance to check out the girls who broke our hearts ten years ago. Fourteen years for old Troy here since he's been dopey about some girl since his freshman year. Now I call that pathetic."

Caleb gave a forced laugh, hoping the guys hadn't noticed that he'd missed the last thread of the conversation. He reached for the menu, still hungry. "Where's our waitress?"

"You just zoned out," Troy said, staring at him. "We're leaving *The 54* and just waiting for the check. We decided we need real food so we're going to *Rossi's* for dinner. This was just appetizers."

"Okay." Caleb wondered if he could stay awake. "Haven't been to *Rossi's* in ages."

The check came and he stuck his American Express on the plastic plate. The waitress whisked it away and was back again in moments. Caleb scribbled his signature and rose, suddenly needing fresh air.

The other guys filed out noisily, talking, catching up, while Caleb followed, tucking his wallet into his back pocket.

It was only eight o'clock. He'd look like a wimp if he went home without treating the guys to a nice dinner after their ten days of travel. It was a tradition, actually. But man, he was dead tired. What was wrong with him?

A stupid question. It was the class reunion. The thought of it depressed him. He could imagine getting dressed up, making the effort, only to find out *she* was living in a village in Bulgaria teaching English to eight-year-olds.

The October air was brisk, smacking him in the face while they congregated around the taxi circle in front of *The 54*. The bar's sign blared a bright neon blue behind them while they waited for a taxi to come around the block.

Standing just outside the circle of light spilling from the lobby, Caleb surreptitiously reached into his wallet and flipped open the billfold. Tonight's talk had made him nostalgic.

Inside the leather billfold was a small compartment. For years, he'd kept a secret within the small pouch—a dainty chain of silver with a red ruby dangling from the bottom.

He'd kept the necklace with him for almost eleven years. Ever since she'd accidentally dropped it the middle of their senior year and he'd snatched it up.

Caleb didn't take it out very often. The necklace was one part guilty pleasure, the other part pure guilt that he'd never returned it.

While clenching the necklace in his fist, a taxi pulled up and the other four guys piled in, leaving the shot-gun spot free for their CEO.

"Let's hit the road," he heard them call while the vehicle's doors slammed shut and the engine idled, waiting for him.

Caleb slipped the ruby necklace with its two small diamonds back into the tiny pouch of the billfold, jammed it into his rear pocket, and clenched the handle of his briefcase.

Enough was enough. He had to return it. It was wrong to have kept it. But first he had to find the girl who used to wear it, the red gemstone dangling in the air when she hovered over her math homework in the corner of Algebra class. Far away from him.

Over the years, he'd run into old classmates at the movies, or at restaurants. But never her.

Not that he hadn't made an attempt. He'd looked all right. Her parents were still in the phone book but on a different street than where she had grown up.

But she wasn't listed.

And she wasn't on Facebook.

He was too embarrassed to reach out to her old friends. Or to call her parents.

Even though they'd been in classes together, off and on, she had never given him a second glance. Heck, he would have died and gone to heaven for a first glance, but he'd been a geek in every sense of the word. Frizzy hair. Dorky glasses. Nerdy jeans that never fit properly, bought at second-hand shops, and perpetually hiding his family's secrets from the world.

Years had become a decade.

Caleb gave a snort of self derision. Wow, his lack of confidence when it came to women had become a numbing force that froze him into limbo.

"Where to?" the cab driver asked, pulling into traffic.

"*Rossi's*," Caleb said, noticing how the other guys let him answer. Deferring to him as the boss. It was still odd, even after five years.

Her necklace had become a memento of his stupid high school years, but she was lost to time and distance.

How did you get over a girl you never had in the first place?

A small surge of hope rose up his throat. Would she be at the high school reunion? It might be his only—and last—chance.

Grab the rest of *The Executive's Secret* right here!
FREE on Kindle Unlimited!

Many thanks for reading my novels!
www.KimberleyMontpetit.com